THE *way* THAT YOU *play* IT

BJ THORNTON

OMNIFIC PUBLISHING
DALLAS

Omnific Publishing
P.O. Box 793871, Dallas, TX 75379
www.omnificpublishing.com

First Omnific eBook edition, June 2011
First Omnific trade paperback edition, June 2011

The characters and events in this book are fictitious.
Any similarity to real persons, living or dead,
is coincidental and not intended by the author.

Library of Congress Cataloguing-in-Publication Data

Thornton, BJ.
    The Way That You Play It / BJ Thornton – 1st ed.
    ISBN 978-1-936305-77-3
    1. Romance — Fiction. 2. Music — Fiction.
    3. Atonement — Fiction. 4. Atlanta — Fiction.
    I. Title

10 9 8 7 6 5 4 3 2 1

Cover Design by Micha Stone and Stephanie Swartz
Interior Book Design by Coreen Montagna

Printed in the United States of America

Chapter One

Trent Buckney was pretty damn sure that he did much more than his fair share of drinking, until he walked into his favorite bar and saw how many folks were drunk as skunks at four on a Sunday afternoon.

Windowless and painted ceiling-to-floor in cheap black paint, the slightly dank recesses of the Hold-Up Saloon teemed with the out-of-work, underpaid, and generally disgruntled residents of Bibb City, Georgia, or rather what used to be Bibb City before the Bibb cotton mill shut down and nearby Columbus absorbed their little community. The way he reckoned, no place with five hundred people in its peak census year had any right calling itself a city, but at least they'd been something nine years ago besides the place where the Georgia state line caved in to Alabama the Beautiful. At least he'd been something besides a man who ought to be on the run from justice but had nowhere to go.

Sunlight illuminated his long, lanky frame when yet another acquaintance came in the front door. Trent crowded even closer into the corner behind the bar's office door and knocked again. He tried to shrink his six-foot and white-as-a-sheet body into the general dimness of the Hold-Up. Probably he should have known better than to think he could go unnoticed anywhere amongst the remaining residents of Bibb City, most of whom had known Trent his entire twenty-nine years. That was exactly why he knew that when his sister showed up to high school in a new wheelchair, they'd all suspected he'd stolen it. He actually *had* bought it with stolen money, and a secret couldn't be kept in a small town; it could only be concealed for a while. It certainly wasn't a secret that he'd been working three jobs to support his mother and baby sister. Both of them were broken in ways that months' worth of uninsured medical treatments had only halfway fixed. It wouldn't be a secret much longer that he'd walked out of one job, showed up to the next with bloody knuckles, and then had gotten fired from them both. He just needed to keep that concealed for as long as it would take to talk Chris, the bar owner, into giving him an advance on a few hours of work, any kind of work.

The curtains flickered across the window where Chris collected cover charges on the odd nights he could get a band. A smug son of a bitch, Chris kept Trent waiting a good while before he wrenched open the window's sliding glass. "What?"

"You got a minute?"

Chris's salt-and-pepper eyebrows receded toward his close-cropped and all-gray hairline. "For what?"

"I need to talk to you."

"Uh-huh. How's your Mama and Ginny?"

Trent pursed his lips. Acting sorrowful wasn't going to get him anything, whereas acting desperate might; Chris loved putting himself above the little people. "Ginny's still a gimp. Mama's getting around pretty good, just slow as molasses. Whatever happened inside her head ain't healed yet." He shrugged and waited for his eyes to drift off to that red place where they went when he felt pissed, but they didn't. "I reckon it ain't gonna."

"I'm sorry to hear that."

"I'm sorry to have to say it," Trent automatically replied, even though feeling sorry, like feeling pissed, had worn out for him. "Be a lot easier to do inside your office." He glanced toward the pool tables nearest the door. Sam Tatum had already noticed Trent standing in front of what looked like a closed window and seemed to think that Trent was talking to himself. "C'mon, Chris."

"I'm only hesitating because I know you want something, and I hope it ain't money because I ain't got none." Still, he buzzed Trent through the metal office door.

Trent tried not to flinch while Chris disdainfully took in the more tattered than usual uniform that Trent had been wearing since he'd lost track of who he was besides a provider. He lived in four sets of Dickies work shirts and pants, all the same shade of beige and splattered in tar from the one on-and-off job he had left with a Columbus roofing company. The uniform included living with bags under his aqua eyes, a mess of thick brown hair that always looked greasy and never looked cut, and scruff all over his jaw. It had been a good while since he'd had the time or money to look clean-cut the way his mother would have liked when he took his ladies to church on Sundays. It had been exactly four days since he'd been grateful he had the scruff to cover a developing scar dead center of his chin.

"You're losing weight, boy." Chris averted his eyes from what was surely a man up to his eyeballs in distress, despite the bland expression Trent affected. "You want a burger? Kim's making my dinner in the back as we speak."

"Thought you decided against turning this place into a bar and grill." Trent couldn't imagine the Hold-Up smelling like anything other than stale beer and cigarettes.

"I changed my mind, now that Mae's is going out of business," Chris said of Bibb City's one eat-in diner. "If things keep closing like this, pretty soon I'm gonna have to go to Columbus every time I want so much as a bar of soap to wash my ass. And on that note, how much do you want?" Chris scowled when Trent didn't answer right away. "I don't got time for you to play coy, boy. Still gotta set up the stage for the band tonight."

"It's Sunday, though."

"Yeah, a little thing called a calendar alerted me to that fact this morning. How much do you want, Trent?"

Trent's hesitation came from honestly not knowing; he didn't have it in him anymore to feel shame at being so obviously needy. He had to go home with enough to pick up his ladies' prescriptions, but Chris's open-ended offer had him also thinking about Ginny's lunch money and next week's light bill that he'd already planned to pay two days late. Trent didn't want to take advantage of Chris's generous spirit and treat his bar like a savings and loan. "As much as I can get in exchange for working here the rest of the month?"

"I'm not giving you a job; I'm giving you a loan." Chris put up his hand against Trent's mouth, which had opened to protest. "I know you're handy, but I pretty much got all the fixing covered."

"I could work nights."

"I already got a hostess too."

"Security?"

"You barely rate a grown man, as skinny as you've gotten, and don't think that hit-and-miss beard is hiding the baby face your Mama gave you. Lord knows Margie always had the prettiest strawberries-and-cream complexion." Chris shook his head at Trent for having inherited the same. "You don't look like you could stop a strong breeze, much less a fight."

It figured that keeping his shirt buttoned up and his ravaged knuckles in his pockets would give Trent no credit for the fight he'd recently been in. "I know how to throw a punch." He laughed a little after Chris quirked a brow.

"What's so funny?"

"Nothing." Trent sputtered a laugh and wondered if he were going loony. Of the dark and obvious truth, he repeated, "Nothing's funny at all."

Chris studied him before swiveling in his seat and bending toward a small safe under the desk. "Security ain't about fighting; it's about preventing fights." Despite his two hundred and fifty or so pounds obscuring everything, Chris motioned for Trent to turn around before he punched in the safe's code. A bank bag zipped open, and there was the wheeze of Chris straightening up. "Here's two hundred. Take it," he spat when Trent didn't put out his hand, "then go sit your ass down at the bar, have a beer, and wait on that burger. I mean it. Don't scowl at me."

Trent blinked. His lips hadn't moved; his face hadn't so much as twitched after that inappropriate laugh. "Can I work nights?"

"You can work tonight, dragging the speaker stuff out of storage and up on stage. Need a sound check too. You still sing, don't you?" He didn't wait for Trent to answer. "I'm only making you eat so you don't pass out on me." Chris averted his eyes again and thrust the money forward at Trent, who hesitated for a moment before taking it. "Tell Margie I'm still waiting to take her out on that date."

"You asked her to the prom. You were ten, and she was sixteen," Trent said in the just-the-facts way he'd been talking lately.

"It's never too late for love. Now get your scowling mug out of my office."

Out in the small foyer and on his way to do whatever would earn him the money shoved deep in his pocket, Trent caught his reflection in Chris's sliding window. He paused to check for a scowl and found his features cast in plaster. Nothing was written on his face, but the blue hues in his chameleon eyes deepened to match his sunken feelings. Soon his eyes were so blue that they seemed like vacant pools in the darkness of the bar.

Nine o'clock came before the band, scheduled to play at eight thirty, actually took the stage, and Trent was two beers into ten o'clock before he found the urge to go home. He didn't really want to retire to the tiny rental house his family had on what was Bibb City's wrong side of the tracks. Mostly, he was eager to avoid the too-loud and definitely tipsy sound of his friend Shane's laughter pouring through the front door, but as had been the case before, it was hard to hide.

"Hey, boy! Whatcha know good?" Shane beat a bruise into Trent's shoulder, and hitched up the legs of his white painter's coveralls before perching on the adjacent bar stool.

"Nothing." Though he didn't want to talk, he knew it didn't pay not to answer Shane who, like a puppy or a whore, would do destructive things to hold onto attention.

"Nothing? You look worried." Shane raked a hand over his sandy crew cut and shifted his wide brown eyes around the Hold-Up. He hushed his booming voice to a whisper that still cut halfway across the bar. "Last I heard, the fucker ain't even regained consciousness. You ain't got nothing to worry about."

Trent shot him a look. *We* had turned into *you* even faster than it had taken for them to hear the word *manslaughter* in conversation. Since the fucker in question hadn't actually died yet, *assault* was probably the more appropriate term, and Trent wondered with dull interest whether Ginny's wheels had earned him a misdemeanor or felony.

"Keep your voice down."

"I'm just saying, if he's in a coma, you're free and clear. Hell, you cleaned his clock so fast maybe he didn't even see who did it. Maybe he's blind." Shane slapped the back of his hand against Trent's chest.

"And I'm just saying shut your fucking trap, Shane. You're drunk."

Shane laughed. "I'm always drunk."

They lapsed into a loose silence that was quickly broken by the band's lead singer. The singer was dressed in black from his dyed hair to his leather bracelet, T-shirt, pants, and combat boots, a fact that had not given any edge at all to the series of Nickelback covers he'd performed for the crowd. Hell, Trent had sounded more raw begging the Lord for "Amazing Grace" at Shiloh Baptist that morning.

"We're gonna take a break," the singer shouted over a smattering of applause, mostly from the girls in front of the stage at whom he'd winked all during the first set. "Ya'll head to the bar and join us for a round. We're headed to Atlanta tomorrow! Woo hoo!" He rolled his hips, seemingly for the girls' benefit. "Got an appointment with Island Records. Yeah!"

Trent noticed that the band didn't look as excited about that as they should have.

The singer continued, "C'mon and clap, somebody!"

No one in the bar but the girls responded to his plea, probably because the singer had a high-class Savannah accent to match the shiny RV that he'd pulled up outside. Twenty minutes into downing the shots the girls had bought him at the bar, Savannah told Trent that he did indeed have a rich daddy who was bankrolling his artistic endeavors. Even his Atlanta appointment was the gift of a friend-of-a-friend-of-Daddy's, which explained the rest of the band's lack of enthusiasm.

"They're really after me. I got a couple of numbers I've been working on, in private," Savannah slurred, long past the time when the second set should have begun. No one seemed to notice, not even Chris, which led Trent to believe that setting up the stage on a Sunday was all the bar had paid for the gig. Every word that Savannah spoke was sloppy and soaked in Jägermeister. He was sprawled all wrong across the bar, more like a junkie than a drunk. "Matter of fact, I'm gonna play a couple right now. Yeah! I'm going out and getting my 1959 Les Paul, and I'm taking you with me."

Both Trent and Shane snapped away from Savannah's finger and toward each other; it took several perplexed looks for them to realize he was curling his finger at the one groupie who'd perched at the end of the bar behind them.

"Island Records?" Shane spat literally onto the floor after Savannah left with his trophy in tow and apparently gave up on the second set completely. "You could sing circles around him on your worst day. Maybe you ought to go to Atlanta with him."

"You betcha," Trent twanged sarcastically and watched the other three band members fail to respond to the loss of their leader.

"You ought to at least take the guitar."

That was for damn sure. If Savannah really did have that '59 Gibson, he didn't even deserve the right to drop it into conversation, but there didn't seem much point in stealing something that Trent knew he wouldn't have the heart to sell. He wouldn't mind taking a look at it, though — just because — so it was with an impish smile that Trent left Shane at the bar thinking that he was about to rob yet another loose-lipped fucker. Instead, he made it all the way to his '99 Chevy Silverado without so much as glancing at the RV. Impish caved into the impassive expression that had earlier made his gaze seem vacant. Trent hadn't been able to hold onto a warm thought for weeks; he constantly saw blue instead of red behind his eyes, an oozing licorice-blue that reminded him of day-old bruises.

Bothering Savannah didn't even occur to him until after the groupie tore out of the RV's side door cussing long and loud. She was back in the bar before Trent found Savannah face down on the floor, clutching that beautiful '59. Later on, Trent would tell himself that he'd been rescuing the Gibson, that Daddy's Boy wouldn't have made it to the audition anyway. Even *later* on, he'd realize that a man in his right mind would have rescued the boy from drowning in his own vomit.

As it was, Trent didn't see anything wrong with walking calmly back to his truck with a guitar and a business card that would open a door he'd never thought to see in his lifetime. He saw blue instead of right and wrong and felt nothing at all but an obligation to drop a hundred dollars by the house on his way up the road to Atlanta.

Chapter Two

Extortion was a lot more nerve-wracking in practice than it was in theory. When Caroline Curran had hatched the plan to get her overdue songwriting royalties from her ex-boyfriend, Nez Peterson, she'd imagined slinking into his office in a badass black suit, snatching off a big pair of sunglasses, and shouting at him.

Theoretically, Nez would have shaken in the Prada boots that his new girlfriend, a child bride who Caroline hatefully called Bratney, had bought him from the massive proceeds of her pop-starlet career. In reality, after Googling the legal definition of *extortion*, Caroline had settled on paying cash for a courier to deliver her demands to Nez's office instead, with instructions for him to messenger the money back by the end of the day. She wasn't mercenary so much as determined, mostly because she was not actually in possession of anything badass or any ability to slink.

She hadn't even asked for everything that he owed her. She'd started with a five-thousand-dollar show of good faith in exchange for the most recent of the sex tapes she'd found in their apartment before leaving his cheating behind. The oldest tapes, specifically one of Nez singing over a pink-frosted cake he'd made the day before Bratney's eighteenth birthday, would stay locked in a safe deposit box until Caroline got every last penny of her $72,453.22. Eventually, though, she was going to give all the tapes back without showing them to anyone beforehand.

The message was supposed to have been delivered to St. Peter Music Publishing at seven, in time to mix inconspicuously with the morning mail, and the four hours that Caroline spent staring at her cell phone since then had made her nuttier than usual. Knowing Nez, she figured he'd called Bratney first to ask if the note was a practical joke, and then he'd rushed in a panic to the enormous Buckhead apartment they'd shared to look high and low for the tapes. He was probably being short with his secretary, Tasha, right at that moment, refusing all calls while he sorted out any way his career would survive a statutory rape charge. Being a secretary herself, Caroline pulled out her day-planner and made a note to send Tasha some flowers when it was all over.

She was just looking up the right arrangement for remorse when an incoming call hammered her eardrums. Nutty as she'd become, it took Caroline three rings to figure out whether to answer the office headset in her left ear or the personal headset in her right.

"Jacqueline Goode's office…No, she isn't in. May I take a message?" Caroline's gaze cut to the smoked glass doors right behind her desk, which was located in the front room of a small commercial suite. "She won't be in until, uh, after lunch. May I take a message?"

Jackie was in, but there was no telling when she would make that known to her clients. Despite being a bona fide entertainment lawyer, Jackie got by in the music world mostly on her former fashion model looks, her connections, and her amazing ability to remain aloof even when she was staring someone in the face. Typing the message in an electronic slip that would email straight to Jackie, Caroline sighed, feeling bad for lying (even on behalf of her boss and best friend since high school), then funny for being so provincial. She was, after all, an extortionist.

Seconds after the caller disconnected, her eardrum jumped again, but Caroline didn't pick up or even glance at her cell phone display. The ring tone of Rod Stewart's "Da Ya Think I'm Sexy?" belonged only to her and Jackie's mutual friend, Reyes. She couldn't help but groan when the office phone shrilled as soon as her cell phone stopped. The only thing Reyes did better than smolder was hound her.

"Jacqueline Goode's office."

"Caroline, *mi corazon,*" Reyes sang with his smooth Texas twang.

Her straight, black shoulder-length hair shaking as she cleared the ringing from her ears, Caroline mumbled, "What's up, Rey-Rey?"

"Of all the nicknames you picked up from Jacks, it had to be the one that I despise." He drew out a silence that seemed filled with disdain. "I called to see if you've received the gift that I sent you."

Caroline's eyebrows shot up. Reyes's gifts usually were expensive and overwhelming, as befitted a senior executive at Island Records whose job description was granting dreams or crushing lives. His signature was as deadly a weapon as a smiting finger. "I know for a fact that I said no more gifts, Rey."

His smug smile carried over the line. "You said not to buy any gifts, a request to which I've adhered despite not actually signing off on it."

Whenever he put his perfect Princeton diction on her, Reyes was angling for a date.

"Please, Rey. Don't. I'm fine. It's been weeks," she said of the time that had passed since Reyes, of all of Nez's important acquaintances, had taken her side in the aftermath of Bratney-gate. "I'm fine. You don't have to keep being nice to me."

He chuckled. "Nice is a basket of muffins. What I'm sending you screams ulterior motive, *querida*, but which one is the question."

"I'll just send it back."

"I think you'll find that difficult to do. Call me back when you get it. *Hasta.*" Reyes hung up before Caroline could complain again. His timing, like the rest of him, was impeccable.

Once again, the disconnection was immediately followed by another buzz from Jackie's office, and Caroline's lips pursed against the question that was coming. "Yes?"

"Was that Reyes? What did he want?" Since Jackie and Reyes had met as teenage catalogue models, Jackie had been waiting for Reyes and his Texas charm to put her in the spotlight.

"Uh, the usual. You know. Teasing me about Nez," Caroline said after Jackie patiently waited for elaboration.

"Teasing you how? What did he say?"

"The usual, Jacks. 'You want me to bankrupt him? You want me to drop him off in the middle of a Civil War reenactment and see what happens?' He always calls to mess with me when he's bored," Caroline downplayed.

Evidently pleased that friends still came before men, Jackie changed the subject. "Is Kit back with my sushi yet?"

Caroline glanced at her watch. "No. You want me to call her?"

"Nah, that's all right. She's still mad that I make her go for the lunch run when she's the paralegal and you're the secretary."

"You know you ought to quit that, Jacks."

"I'll quit when she quits running up my phone bill. Make me an appointment for a manicure, please, ma'am, and call me when my food gets here."

The rest of the lunch hour counted down like a dripping faucet while Caroline waited for the two men in her life to come through. Nez's hesitation was torture and kept her mind on whatever Reyes was sending, a much more pleasant thought than the possibility that the police might turn up instead of her money. When noon rolled around and brought with it a scruffy-faced boy who clearly wasn't a cop, Caroline stifled a squeal of joy. Cooperation was a nice side dish to coercion.

"Hi. Come in." She watched him drag his feet through the office door in threadbare jeans and a tar-spattered shirt rolled up to his elbows. Caroline eyed the envelope he had in one hand and frowned slightly; she'd specified cash, and the package looked a little thin for five grand. Inclining her head just so, Caroline pointedly asked just above a whisper, "Can I help you with that?"

"I'm Trent. Are you Caroline Curran?"

He'd pronounced it "Kay-ruh-line," like the Carolinas, but five times as country.

"Carol. Lynn. Caroline." She emphasized every consonant since being from Atlanta was only a step away from the stigma of being a Southerner. "Is that for me?"

She regretted asking as soon as he stepped up to her desk and thrust the envelope forward between the busted fingers of a scabbed hand. Her breath caught, and her imagination went wild with the thought of Nez sending a redneck to assassinate her; the nutty part of Caroline's heart regretted having had only kettle-cooked chips and Diet Coke for a last meal. Wariness widened her eyes, and noticeable revulsion swept across her pecan complexion.

"Hey." He put up one not-at-all-innocent-looking hand while the other dug in his pants pocket. "I came from Ray, uh…Reyes A. Bardem's office, at Island Records," he said as he read from the business card that he'd retrieved. "He told me to give this to you." He eased the white envelope across her desk and backed up a couple steps.

The mention of Reyes's name didn't do much to reduce the air of threat that lingered around the messenger; he stood too still and blank-faced, like a sociopath. Watching him for some tiny sign of what he was thinking, Caroline opened the envelope and found a birthday card, even though it was January and her birthday was in July. "Like a fine wine," it said on the front. Inside, "You age gracefully with each passing year. Happy Birthday" was scratched out and replaced with "Here's a little something to get you started on your new career," penned in Reyes's bold script. "Dinner Friday, seven o'clock? We'll discuss that label you mentioned."

He had to be kidding. She'd mentioned having her own record label exactly once in a drunken rant on Jackie's back porch at New Year's. Caroline scanned the front and back of the card, then the envelope, but there was nothing else. She glanced at the messenger. "This is it?"

"That's what I'm wondering," the man muttered as he glanced around the sparse office. His fingers moved to scratch the thick hair at the back of his neck. "You're just a secretary?"

She took umbrage at his tone. "Part-time, temporary secretary. And who are you?"

"Nobody. I'm just here for the audition. I suppose I could get on with it, if you have a spare lying around."

Caroline's lips pursed. "A spare what?"

"Guitar? For the audition?" He licked his lips while she gaped at him. "I left mine behind in Reyes A. Bardem's fancy-ass office."

"Can you just…one second," Caroline mumbled as she held up one finger. Chunky-heeled boots clacking across the tile, she rushed to Kit's office door only to find it locked. "Damn!" There was nowhere else to go but Jackie's office or the hall, and she wasn't quite comfortable with the idea of passing closely by Mr. Still Waters Run Deranged. Caroline speed-dialed Reyes as she knocked on Jackie's door and went in.

"Sushi time?" Jackie asked, while in Caroline's cell phone headset Reyes brightly chimed, *Mi querida?*"

Caroline shut the office door and spun around to squint through the ash wood blinds. "You sent me a man?"

"I sent you a singer," Reyes coolly corrected. "And I apologize for the crap ninety-nine-cent birthday card; it was all that my assistant could scrounge up. You don't age at all, Caroline."

He knew how to worm into her heart, now that birthdays carried a dreaded new weight since thirty-three-year-old Nez had taken the last of Caroline's twenties and publicly dumped her at thirty-one the second Bratney turned legal.

The scent of Dior perfume wafted off Jackie's navy blue Jil Sander suit and onto Caroline's shoulder. Bending to compensate for her seven-inch height advantage over her friend, Jackie squinted through the blinds and pressed her ear to the outside of Caroline's headset. "Who is that?" she asked.

"I don't know."

"His name is…" Reyes continued, "Travis? Trucker? Something. But he has the voice that you've been looking for, Caroline, for your new songs."

"He looks like Hugh Jackman," Jackie taunted.

"No, he doesn't," Caroline said quickly, but not quickly enough to stop Reyes's silent disapproval from filling the line.

"Jacks," Reyes said.

Jackie declined to greet him. "Hugh Jackman. Seriously, he's as hot as Wolverine."

That was difficult to dispute given the stubble and the electrified hair, but Caroline still tried to diffuse the flattering comparison. "Maybe if Wolverine had a younger brother who went to English prep school. Wolfy. He looks like Oliver Twist to me," Caroline insisted, certain that she could hear Reyes grinding his perfect teeth.

"Oliver Swirl, you mean, and I wouldn't mind a scoop of that. How about it, C.C.? You, me, and the Wolverine make a banana split sundae with a cherry twist?"

"Jackie," Caroline reprimanded, knowing that her friend only wore her bisexuality on her sleeve when provoked.

Reyes took the bait as usual; he cleared his throat, and it was like a pistol cocking. "Give him a try-out, *querida*. He's perfect for your new pieces, and if you can get something polished to me, your label might be much closer than you think. We'll discuss it at length over dinner Friday. Seven o'clock. I'll send a car for you at six, since you insist on living way out in the sprawl. *Un beso.*" He hung up.

Eyes shut, Caroline lamented the way that he and Jackie went to war when it would have been easier, for all of their sakes, if the two of them would just fall into bed to one-up each other's perfection.

"Oh, yeah! He asked me out for a pity dinner," Caroline explained without turning to face her friend. She could already feel Jackie's eyes boring into the side of her head.

"Financing your record label doesn't sound like pity to me," Jackie replied.

"Of course it is. I'm not starting a label." Caroline choked back the hurt that accompanied fabulous Jacqueline not believing in her. "I can barely pay for my rental house, and you know I'd be living in an apartment if you hadn't given me this part-time position." She sometimes felt that appeasing Jackie was her full-time job.

Thinking of Nez, she excused herself to the front office to check her cell phone, easily done with Jackie eager to distance herself from jealousy. Following the awkward trend of the morning, Nez of course had called while she'd been on the phone with Reyes.

"Just a second," she said to the stranger, who was now seated in the waiting area. She dialed Nez on her cell, and then thought better of it by the second ring, but it was too late to hang up and call from an anonymous line. She was going to have to work on her extortion skills.

"C.C., have you lost your damn mind, trying to blackmail me?"

Her throat inflamed to hear her nickname from his lips. "It's Caroline. And the only thing I've lost is my royalties, which I want back."

"You ain't getting nothing from me."

"Oh, I think I will, unless you want to play a game of Jeopardy with 'Phrases That Start with *Statutory.*'" She heard him choke. "That was real cute, what you and Milan"—which absurdly was Bratney's real name—"did with the cake frosting. If I'd known you were that nasty, I would've—" But she wouldn't have and didn't need to start back down the road of wondering what she'd done wrong to lose Nez Peterson's trifling behind to a child. "I would've been more careful with my copyright assignments. I wouldn't have let you shortchange me, Nez."

"You're still on that? C.C., I let you clean out my place when you left, and did I say a word? Had to be at least twenty-five grand worth of guitars and shit, then—"

"I know—"

"—took the damn piano? I let you tear the frame out of my sliding glass doors to move that piano out of here. Between that and clothes alone—"

"I know, Nez! I know I'm not a megabucks marketing franchise like Milan Taylor!" Admitting as much hurt worse than everything else. Hands shaking and teeth tight, Caroline primly continued, "Which is why I tallied up the value of everything you did for me for two years, less depreciation, and"—she said over his bellow of protest—"credited your account. You still owe me."

"Not seventy thousand dollars, C.C."

"Caroline!" She had to bite her lip to quell the bitter and barking tone that time. "I'll expect that messenger by the end of the day."

"Oh, you can expect something, all right."

"You'll be sorry if you come anywhere near me, Nez," Caroline threatened, though there really wasn't much that she could do in that event except to call Reyes. She'd put herself outside of police protection, and suddenly the idea of Nez's wrath sweeping the office like a squall dried out her mouth. Extortion was a stomach-turning business.

Across the desk and in the corner of the suite where the chairs were, Trent sat silent and watched Caroline Curran's round, brown eyes pitch toward some invisible horizon and widen to the size of half-dollars. She'd apparently forgotten he was there; there was no way she would have meant for him to hear that bout between her and whomever, not when she'd almost doubled over under the desk trying to keep the lady in the office from hearing. He'd seen them sizing him up from behind the blinds moments earlier and had almost walked out right then. Caroline Curran clearly wasn't a big-time melody maker, and Trent was losing money just sitting there dreaming about all the things that a record deal would fix. He didn't want much really, just to pay off the hospital bills, start a loan on a new house to replace the one his Mama had given up, and maybe get his Chevy a paint job. Unfortunately, that little list didn't explain why in the back of his mind, during the hour that he'd spent trying to make himself drive back to Bibb City, he'd day-dreamed of strumming his fingers across that Les Paul just one more time.

"Oh my God!"

Knowing that exclamation was meant for him, Trent stood up from the chair and crossed the room to Caroline. "Listen—"

"I'm so sorry," she said from behind her hands covering her face. She pulled them away from the deep raspberry stains in her cheeks that matched her sweater dress. "I totally forgot about you. Sorry."

Trent blinked. Her courtesy was a long way from the terror she'd shown him earlier. "Well, I'm sorry about your, uh, situation. It sounds real nasty." His lips moved toward what he hoped was a sympathetic grin. "But I gotta know if there's any paying gigs in me being here, or if this is just something your boyfriend Bardem cooked up to entertain you."

"He's not my boyfriend."

Trent quirked a brow. "You betcha." His disbelieving tone seemed to irritate her.

Caroline lifted her chin. "What did you do?"

"What?"

"Reyes is a good judge of talent. If you were any good, he would have kept you for himself, unless you did something to piss him off."

"I sing circles around good." He didn't address how he'd lied his way into Reyes's office, for fear the truth would break the tightrope he was walking.

"You play, huh? Acoustic or electric?"

"Both."

"You have a piece ready to audition?"

"For you? 'Cause you don't exactly look like you sign the checks around here."

"This is just a temporary job. I'm a songwriter, for your information, uh…"

"Trent."

"Right." She licked her lips. "I'm new on the music scene, but I have backers. You met Reyes. He's behind me one hundred percent."

"You betcha."

Her faux nonchalance didn't fool Trent, but he didn't call her bluff either. He really didn't have anywhere else to go that would be an improvement on the company of a nutty little lady whose tight pink dress made it look like she was smuggling honeydew melons in her underwear.

Chapter Three

After she sat in her car in front of her house for ten minutes, while Trent sat in his truck and watched her, Caroline felt sure that he'd become just as wary of her as she was of him.

On the phone with Reyes, she explained that she hadn't intended to take him home with her. "I tried to return him to your office. Where were you?" She made a face when Reyes put her on hold. Caroline crossed her eyes, jabbed her fingers between her eyebrows, and emitted a hollow whistle like she'd drilled into her head and found nothing there.

Behind her, Trent stuck his head out of his window and craned his neck to eyeball her.

"Ugh!" Her fingertip tapped a hole into her skull while she waited for Reyes to come back on the line.

"Sorry, *querida*. That was the singer that Trent impersonated."

"He pretended to be someone else?" Caroline asked. Reyes elaborated on the circumstances of Trent's appearance that morning, and she tried not to panic. It had occurred to her, unfortunately only after she'd driven across Atlanta and halfway to her home in the urban sprawl, that she hadn't told Trent not to follow her further than Reyes's office building. She glanced at her car mirror and saw Trent staring at her. His not being a redneck assassin didn't mean that he wasn't a redneck at all. "And you thought the best thing to do with an impostor was to send him to me?"

"I only do one favor a day, and I still have to fake an interest in Whitmore's son whenever he shows up, but the risk that the hillbilly took amused me and seemed worth rewarding."

Caroline's hand switched from worrying her brow to slapping her lips. "He is a hillbilly, isn't he? I knew it."

Reyes chuckled. "You sound terrified."

"Shouldn't I be? Didn't you see his hands?"

"Hadn't noticed them. Why?"

"Either he shape-shifts into a knuckle-dragging Neanderthal at night, or he's been in a fight recently," Caroline said, her fingertips moving back to her brow and then down the bridge of her nose as though to hide the concern in her eyes from Trent, who'd stuck his shaggy head out the window again.

"Why would he have to shape-shift into what he already is?" Reyes laughed, but she didn't. "I won't have you uncomfortable, Caroline, but I know that you won't just kick him out. Tell him that I've summoned him, and I'll deal with it when I get back from this late lunch with Janet."

"Jackson?"

Reyes laughed again. "If you like, I can call security and have him escorted out of your office."

"Well, I'm not exactly in the office anymore; that's why I called you." She slumped down in her seat, away from Trent's prying eyes. "I might have let him follow me home."

"*Tonta*. Why, Caroline?"

"It was an accident! I could blame you, since you sent him to me to audition for a music company that I don't even have. Now that he's here, I have to listen at least." Caroline bit her lip.

"Wait for me. I'll come over. You shouldn't be alone with a man in your house."

Caroline snorted. She hadn't had a man over in so long that it would probably be a nice change of pace. "No, don't bother. It's an hour drive from downtown. I can't stall him that long. I'll handle it."

"Really?"

His dubious tone annoyed her. "Yes! I don't need a babysitter, thank you very much."

Reyes poured an aching *"Querida"* down the line. "At least allow me to check on you later, to make sure that you've eaten and that you're still alive." He chuckled, and Caroline did too, nervously. "I only wanted to please you with this, Caroline, so promise to call me if he upsets you in any way, okay?"

And once again, Reyes was a prince among men.

"Okay."

Of course, even Machiavelli had probably been charming.

Once off the phone, Caroline climbed out of her Jetta and heard the door of Trent's truck squawk before she made it around her hood to the mailbox. Three days' worth of mail filled her arms, and a couple of magazines shielded her chest when she turned to Trent.

"Sorry about that. It was, um, important."

All of the lashes around his eyes didn't make his gaze any less penetrating. "You betcha."

"Well, this is my house, temporarily." Caroline waved one hand toward the small, red brick structure that stood in a sea of dead sod. Trent nodded. "Not that I don't know the neighbors. We're all very, very close. The walls are paper thin; they can hear everything."

The warning in her tone might've carried weight had there been more than four houses sparsely situated on her tiny street way in the back of the obviously new Sturbridge housing development. She lived in a cul-de-sac only because the street abruptly ended where the woods began, right at the end of her lot, which put Trent just a few feet from a good place to hide a body.

"Noises echo off of the woods too. I can hear leaves falling in my sleep." She realized too late how little sense that made. Caroline waited until she'd spun around to cross her eyes in an admission of stupidity, and then she led Trent up the concrete walk to her two-bedroom rental.

The living room into which they stepped was huge, yet, notwithstanding the twelve-foot ceiling and row of skylight windows across the right wall, the house was unimpressive. An eggshell-colored partial wall on the same side as the skylight blocked off the kitchen and what there was of a dining area. An archway in the left wall, also matte and white, led to the one bathroom, her bedroom, and another much smaller bedroom in which she stored the living room furniture that had made way for a Kawai upright piano and the assorted instruments she'd liberated from Nez. Two Fender Stratocasters, their amplifiers, and speakers were usually kept covered right in front of the fireplace that she never used, as well as a vintage Lyon & Healy four-string teardrop tenor. On stands sat a Dobro resonator guitar, a pretty Seagull acoustic, and a six-string Robert Johnson "signed" Gibson, the last two being her song-writing weapons of choice along with the piano, near which a no-frills keyboard sat neglected.

"*You* play slide guitar?"

Caroline whipped around, one eyebrow up. As devoid of emotion as his conversation had been so far, the disbelief in Trent's tone hit like a slap in the face. "Well, I'm not using it for a coat rack," she said of the Dobro resonator.

"Doesn't look like you use much of anything at all."

She followed his gaze around the living room and the visible bit of the kitchen and noted, as Trent had, that there was nothing to see but a low, brown suede couch, a small table, and a floor lamp. There was no television, nor were there pictures, papers, or random articles of clothing. Even the kitchen counters were bare but for a chrome paper towel holder.

"Your boyfriend must not let you make the trek from the city a lot," Trent continued, "'cause it's as still as a graveyard in here."

"He's not my boyfriend." For the second time in five minutes, the idea of her corpse came to mind. And for the second time that day, she found Trent staring at her in an almost sly way, probably because her protests implied she was either lying about Reyes or wanting him to know that she was single. Her eyes crossed in a way that was kind of painful. "It's just that I recently moved in here, and I hate living alone, so I hang out late with Jacks a lot. It's like a hotel. I only sleep here."

"Jack?"

"Jacks, or Jackie. It's a girl," Caroline explained and bit her lip against the certainty that she was digging herself in deeper. "Uh, why don't we do your try-out?" She side-stepped into the kitchen and dumped the mail on the white tiled counter. "I try not to play between three and five when Sheila's twins are down for their nap. That's my neighbor, Sheila. She's home *all* afternoon after she picks them up from preschool. She and her husband Nelson live *right* next door."

"And they hear it all. Paper thin walls."

He hadn't moved from standing in the living room with his hands in his pockets, but Caroline's eyes narrowed, unsure whether he was on to her. "Right. So pick a guitar and warm up."

"Mind if I use the phone first? I need to check in with my sister."

Caroline pulled out her cell phone, the only means she had of calling Reyes to come to her rescue. "You should stay in the kitchen. It doesn't get good reception anywhere else."

"You got a land-line I can use?"

"No, sorry." Biting her lip, she handed over her phone, and reluctantly retreated to the far end of the counter. Caroline sorted through the mail, but kept her eye on him.

Tight-lipped at the lack of privacy, Trent retreated to the far corner of Caroline's kitchen in front of a short, white refrigerator. He dialed his sister, who, like the twins next door, should have been out of school by then, but his home phone number rang an alarming five times before she picked up.

"Hello?"

"Ginny, it's me."

"Hey! How's it going in Atlanta?"

"All right so far." Trent pitched his voice to as quiet a register as he could manage clearly. "How'd it go on the short yellow bus?"

Ginny laughed along at the concessions made ever since her disability had been ruled permanent. As callous as it seemed to outsiders, making fun lightened her mood more than pity. "Better now that I got these fancy new wheels. It goes so much faster than the old one, I keep stubbing my damn toe on the cupboards."

Trent stifled a laugh to say, "Watch your damn mouth."

"Think you could paint this sucker for me? I'm thinking lime green with a little bit of glitter and a yellow racing stripe right down the back rest."

"Sure, Gin, whatever you want. You find what I left under your pillow?"

"That hundred dollar bill that I can't get change for anywhere in Bibb City? Yeah, you're one hell of a tooth fairy."

"Genevieve Buckney!" Trent glanced over his shoulder at Caroline, who seemed too engrossed in one of her magazines to have heard him. Still, he continued in a whisper, "If Mama hears you talking like that, she'll take it out on the back of my head."

"Mama barely knows what day of the week it is. I doubt she'll notice a 'damn' or a 'hell' here or there."

Beneath the sarcasm, Trent could sense his sister's mood had slipped a couple of notches. Being a disabled teenager must have been hard enough without a disabled adult who needed almost constant minding.

"She's been giving you a hard time?"

"Nah, she's been quiet as a lamb." Ginny cleared her throat. "I like it better when she talks nonsense to herself, though. At least then I know she's alive when I pass by her on the couch."

Trent couldn't find the laugh he knew his sister was fishing for. "I'll be back this evening, Gin."

He heard her exasperation over the phone. "I told you, she's fine; no need to hurry back. I'd much rather you take your time and bring home this 'Caroline Curran' so I can meet her."

He blinked. "Say what?"

"Caroline," Ginny sang with the same pronunciation for which he'd been corrected earlier that day, "the fancy Atlanta lady that you're visiting."

Goddamn caller ID. "I'm not visiting. I'm here for a job."

"Whatever you say, hoss. See ya when I see ya."

"Tonight. So you'd better have your homework done and your laundry folded up."

"Sure thing, *Daddy*. Have fun." Ginny hung up.

God, she was a great kid, and it was a damn shame that Trenton Buckney Senior hadn't stuck around to find that out, that a hospital visit and a five-hundred-dollar check was all it had taken to clear their absentee father's conscience. As Trent had recently learned the hard way, remorse wasn't something that could be taught; it either waited years under the skin for the right reason to break into blisters, or else it was just a gnat easily swatted away every day. Either way, the people who waited for remorse to turn into an apology were the ones who suffered, and Ginny, thank God, wasn't waiting like he had for so fucking long.

After a stint of picking at the scab on his chin, Trent returned the cell phone to Caroline.

"Thanks." He slid the tiny device alongside the magazine that had consumed her attention. The lines of her face were so tense and her bubble gum lips so puckered and sour that for a second, he was sure that she'd overhead his entire conversation. "Caroline?"

Her eyes flitted to his, flitted away, then she scrubbed the palm of her hand across her sable eyelashes like a teary-eyed and tired little girl. "Do you think she's pretty?"

Trent looked down at two glossy pages of some fashion magazine, across which were spread the long bare legs of one Milan Taylor. According to the title of the article, she knew what it took to "Win Big in the Industry." He could only assume from the photo that it took lazing around half-naked in a pink fur stole and diamond-studded heels. Trent looked up and found Caroline staring at him expectantly. Shit, she really did want him to answer what he was sure was a trick question since she'd already made it more than clear that she suspected him of being a thief, a chauvinist, or a serial killer.

"Uh." Trent scratched the back of his neck, trying to recall where else he'd heard the name Milan besides the couple of times he'd begged Ginny to turn down the volume on *Entertainment Tonight*. "I think she looks like that model who beat somebody with a cell phone a couple years ago."

Honesty without a real personal opinion seemed like a safe enough answer until Caroline's face crumbled.

"She does, huh? She looks just like Naomi Campbell! A younger, taller, *younger* Naomi Campbell." Caroline held up a centerfold for his inspection.

Sticking a photo of Milan Taylor's breasts in his face was surely a test, possibly part two of Caroline's quest to make sure he knew she was single. As adorable as Caroline was, Trent didn't have the time to pursue her, whereas not-her-boyfriend Bardem clearly had the time, the means, and the interest.

"Uh." Trent took the magazine from her hand and slowly folded it shut while he tried to drum up the right words to put an end to the awkward interrogation. "Well, I'll tell you what, Caroline. Showing all that skin doesn't make her look any older than my baby sister, and that pretty much puts the nail in that coffin for me."

"Really?"

"You ever bit into a half-cooked cupcake? It's sweet and all, but it ain't done yet? It ain't frosted. Young'uns are just like that, and the younger they come, the gooier they are in the middle." He laughed when she looked down and looped her arms around her waist, seemingly to conceal her little bit of belly. "By 'middle,' I mean a woman's interior, not her abs."

She kept her arms where they were. "Oh. Well, I'm not gooey or young. I'm thirty-one and thick, but only because I'm short."

Lips twitching, he replied, "Well, that's good to know."

Her cheeks turned raspberry. "Sorry." She crossed her eyes. "Umm, why don't we —"

"Audition?"

"Right! Just, um, go for it." She shucked her thumb in the direction of the stash of instruments. "I'll be there in a minute." Caroline took Milan Taylor from his hand and gave him a strained smile.

By the time Trent warmed up her Seagull acoustic, Caroline joined him in the living room, feeling newly crestfallen. She set a glass of tea that he hadn't asked for on the brick hearth behind him and took a seat on the black lacquered piano bench.

"You ready?"

Sipping her own tea from a straw, Caroline nodded and tried to focus her eyes on his face, but the plaintive and familiar little melody that Trent's fingers pulled out of the Seagull turned her gaze to the corner of the room. She tried to listen but could barely hear over the drone of her emotions. Nez had always said that she was too emotional, and maybe that was why when she heard an unfamiliar baritone instead of her ex-boyfriend's playful bass, Caroline snapped, "Stop."

Trent grimaced. "That bad, huh?"

"No, I just can't listen to 'Landslide' right now," she said of the Fleetwood Mac standard tucked inside her piano bench. "I've been playing it a lot lately." *And downing Chardonnay*, she thought, but he didn't need to know that.

"I figured as much when I saw it in your stash. I figured you'd like it."

"Well, I don't." Caroline cleared her throat. "I'm sorry, can you just try something else? That one doesn't suit you anyway."

"What's that mean?"

Caroline really wasn't sure. She hadn't been paying enough attention to know more than that his performance had been off. She shrugged. "Maybe it's just my Stevie Nicks bias. Please try something else."

Trent strummed and idly hummed a little of "Edge of Seventeen," but Caroline cut him off with another rough clearing of her throat. He shot her a look, and she shook her head violently, her lips tightly pursed against any mention of teenagers.

"You betcha," he mumbled under his breath and then started Weezer's "Say It Ain't So."

When Trent sang, Caroline frowned. His smooth baritone wasn't off-key or rhythm, but it was *off*, lifeless somehow just like his face earlier in the day.

"Stop." Having only made it a few bars further than he had with "Landslide," Trent's brows went up. "What did you sing for Reyes?"

"He asked for Keith Urban. Actually, he said, 'Go, country,' and I took a chance that he was talking about a song and not asking my country ass to show myself out."

"Okay, let's hear that." However, Caroline didn't let him get past the first chorus of "Tangled Up in Love" before she shook her head. Technically, his voice was more than fine; it was resonant, fluid, and oddly without any trace of the twang that coiled around his vowels when he spoke. Caroline nonetheless let out a quick sigh. "Don't you have a song that you, well, care about?"

He blinked. "My sister loves Keith Urban, not as much as Sugarland, but more than the High School Musical soundtracks."

"I mean, that you care about for yourself. A song that reflects you personally."

"Can't you just tell me what you'd like to hear?"

She looked deep into his dull eyes, which was unusual for her. "I'm trying to hear you, who you are."

"That's easy. I'm nobody."

Something hard shifted into his jaw. Trent's gaze skated away from her but quickly snapped back, and the red-blooded man that had slowly crept in under the radar was replaced by the lifeless stranger from before. Caroline couldn't help but cringe. "Why did you lie to Reyes?"

"Because I'm nobody from Nowhere, Georgia, lady, and I'll try pretty much anything that might have a paycheck in it."

Unnerved, Caroline stood up and flipped up the top of the piano bench to rifle through her sheet music. She hazarded an occasional glance at Trent's face, and the harshness she still saw there led her to a thick batch of Jonny Lang songs that were never far from the top of her collection. "You can read notes, right?"

Trent nodded. "You betcha."

Caroline reached around by her keyboard and retrieved a sheet-music stand that she then placed in front of him. A lot of dog-eared pages flipped before she found "Wander This World" and set it up in front of him.

"Try this."

He took a minute to scan the tabs and mouth the lyrics, glancing infrequently at both Caroline and her resonator guitar with a little twitch around his lips. He played, and she noticed the halting and unsure-something that came into his fingering, something surely due to unfamiliarity with the song that managed to match the contemplative mood of the tune. He sang, and she had to catch her breath. His baritone had grit without a hint of strain, a huskiness that never bottomed out or ran hollow. He picked along the edge of an almost vulnerable phrasing that never quite gave in and which was exactly what the lyrics called for. A round tone that she could only describe as Michael McDonald-esque gave flesh to what would have been sparse had Trent tried to mimic Jonny Lang. Instead, his voice ribboned between both of those singers on its own almost too-perfect path. As soon as "Wander This World" was done, Caroline threw "Breakin' Me" in front of him, and she was torn between Mofro's "Lochloosa" and several Gov't Mule tunes clutched in her eager little hands when Trent snorted. She snapped out of the thrall of his voice and looked at him.

Trent gave another laugh, low in his throat. "Just for my peace of mind, does this mean that I passed the audition?"

"Oh my God, yes! Flying colors. I'm not letting your voice out of my sight. Or I guess, out of my hearing?" Enthusiasm illuminated her giddy smile.

"Uh…yeah, that might be tough to do since me and the voice are a package deal, and I gotta hit the road home pretty soon."

"Oh! Well, where do you live?"

"Bibb City."

Disdain flooded her expression. When he rolled his eyes and sighed, she apologized.

"Sorry." Caroline smiled again, glad that there was any expression on his face. "The Blues suit you, which is too cool for school because that's what I do. Well, what I want to do, kind of like a Blues fusion thing right where Rock and R&B used to intersect."

Trent looked skeptical. "Where'd that be exactly? Outer space?"

Caroline laughed. "Okay, yeah, Sam Cooke and Led Zeppelin are on two different planets to most people, but to me, it's like plate tectonics. They used to be the same thing. They used to be Robert Johnson." She tipped her chin at the Gibson guitar perched next to Trent's leg. "The Black Keys, Raphael Saadiq. The retrofit sound is in right now, and I'm about to put my name on it."

"Retrofit Blues? That's the kind of music you write?"

Caroline nodded eagerly. "That's what I write now. I used to write 'kicky crossover R&B.'"

"For Milan Taylor?"

She nodded. "Those were good songs and would have been about something if—*anyway!*"

Through a row of white teeth, Caroline emitted a little bumblebee hiss while her eyes crossed, and an angry tremble shook her round shoulders.

"Anyway," she primly repeated and pushed back a shiny lock of side-parted bangs. "Would you mind if I record you singing before you go?"

He seemed to hide a laugh behind a smirk. "Singing what?

After a few minutes' deliberation, Caroline settled on Mofro's "Lochloosa." JJ Grey and Mofro were a bunch of down-home Florida boys who loved all things country with the same tangible tenderness she'd heard in Trent's voice when he spoke of his sister. He seemed skeptical of her request that he stand in the bathroom shower stall to sing, but after she cut on the recording equipment in the spare room, dragged a quality microphone to the bathroom, and hooked it to the ceiling, Trent seemed willing to believe her claim about the great acoustics.

Caroline recorded both his third and fifth takes, and then she talked him into another round of "Breakin' Me" and recorded that, at which point Trent said he wasn't leaving until he'd heard her novice slide guitar skills. He didn't laugh as much as he could have, but what she saw of his smile beneath the facial hair seemed genuine and drew attention to the baby smoothness of his lips. Wide with a perfect cupid's bow, his lips didn't have the lines and puckers and pits that her bubble gums did, yet his voice made the same sense coming from that mouth that her gnarled contralto did coming from hers. Two tries into a duet of Tracy Chapman's "You're the One," the doorbell cut into Caroline's silent speculation about what else he might be hiding beneath his disguise.

She excused herself to the front door and peered out. Her eyes widened. "What are you doing here?"

Wedged in the threshold of the glass storm door, Reyes's six-foot-two inches of perfection smoldered at Caroline.

"Checking in on you, as agreed. Clearly you're still alive, though you could have picked up the phone to satisfy me on that score, *querida.*" Bright flecks in his navy blue eyes glittered at her. "Left to my own devices, I settled on Chinese to make sure that you've eaten."

He held up two paper sacks and smiled, good as ever at cutting off her avenues for complaint, and since Caroline had sort of agreed to everything he'd said, she really had no choice but to let him in. Reyes brushed by her in draped gray pants and a long-sleeved T-shirt that would have looked like sweats on anyone else and definitely felt like silk against her arm. For reasons she didn't really want to ponder, Caroline winced when he stopped short at the sight of Trent.

"Up late on a school night? Tsk-tsk." Reyes gave Caroline a chiding glance and winked at her.

Across the room, Trent checked his watch at the same time Caroline looked to the clock, and, shit, it was eight thirty, which was not particularly late but meant they'd been at it a solid six hours. Caroline's smile seemed sheepish when he looked at her. She shrugged and mouthed, *Sorry.*

He wasn't. Those six hours were the most fun he'd had in months.

Reyes broke up their silent communication by putting one hand on Caroline's back and ushering her into the kitchen.

Since Reyes hadn't even spoken to him, Trent took the hint that he wasn't invited to dinner. He went to the kitchen threshold and cleared his throat.

"I'm about to head out." Caught between Caroline's glare and Reyes's pleased smile, Trent didn't know who to explain himself to. "Gotta get home to my sister, like I said. I'll call you, Caroline, and thanks to you both."

"No!" She hustled to the door and grabbed his arm. "You must be starving too. Stay for dinner." Caroline pushed him backward into the living room and all the way to the keyboard in the corner. "Stay." She smiled, but seemed uncomfortable after she glanced over her shoulder.

"I don't think I ought to."

"He's not my boyfriend!"

"You betcha."

"Really! He never drops by like this."

Trent sobered up fast. "Is him being here some kind of problem for you?" he asked with a soft I-kick-ass-on-demand undertone.

"No! No, Reyes is…Actually, I don't know, and I'm not angling to find out tonight. Anyway, we still have to talk about our plans."

He raised a brow. "What plans?"

"I haven't figured that out yet, but if you stay for dinner, I'm sure I will."

Her winning smile was pretty but not convincing. "I may be from Bibb City," Trent said, "but stupid doesn't run in the water. You've got no kind of operation here, and I don't have time to wait on you writing a song that Bardem may or may not back depending on how territorial he gets. Like I said, I'm looking for a paycheck."

Caroline bristled. "I can do that. I can get you a gig."

"In a month."

"Try Thursday."

Trent's eyes narrowed.

"Really. If you give me the hours between now and then to pull together a short acoustic set, I can get you a club gig Thursday night."

"What kind of hours are you talking about?"

"Same as today. Meet me after lunch, and —"

"There's this little thing called work that you might have heard of?"

"I have to work too."

Trent played his stone face.

"Ugh!" Caroline glared at him. "If you aren't committed, why'd you waste my time today?"

That was a good question, and Trent could only answer by explaining that of all the bad things he'd expected to happen, he'd come across Caroline the same way as that one lucky day he'd found fifty bucks when he was younger. "For the same reason you're not ready for me to go, I reckon."

Caroline's expression clouded, and she turned a scowl to the kitchen.

"Fine, you're right. I've had a crap day, and I need a break, especially from Reyes's beautiful bossy behind." She crossed her eyes. "All right, give me your cell number, and we'll work something out around your schedule. If you stay for dinner."

Though he'd been sure that shame had worn out for him, Trent swallowed hard at the prospect of admitting he couldn't afford to keep a cell phone number. He took the pen that Caroline pulled from the piano bench and wrote his home phone number across the palm of her outstretched hand, though he knew from the glint in her eye that she wanted it there to ward off not-her-boyfriend. He also knew he'd be spending the next morning diving for the phone before his mother or Ginny could get to it, but when Caroline smiled, Trent was all right with that.

Chapter Four

Instead of taking I-85 to 10th Street NW, which eventually led to Jackie's office building, Caroline joined the Tuesday morning commuter traffic on Peachtree that for most purposes was the carotid artery of downtown Atlanta. Having not slept the night before, she was grateful for the twenty minutes it took to travel three miles so she could think up an exit plan should she see a police cruiser out in front of the building. Caroline could only imagine how many threatening messages Nez had left in the night. She'd turned off not just the ringer but the phone as well after Reyes, outlasting both Trent and her better judgment, had invaded her bedroom to cuddle through half of *Muriel's Wedding*. Lately, Caroline hated being unable to resist a warm body and a kind glance, but she hated even more waking up alone and burrito-wrapped in a blanket as she had at dawn, a parting gift that made her hate Reyes for knowing exactly which line to walk to stay in her life.

A heap of mail adorned her much-resented secretarial post outside of Jackie's still-vacant office, mail that Caroline ignored in favor of starting up the coffee maker, opening the blinds, and setting the thermostat to sixty-eight degrees as her best friend preferred. She peeled off a black trench that covered yet another knit dress in mustard yellow. Caroline loved colorful stretch fabrics, even though they made traffic cones of her massive rack and rear and seemed to attract bossy men to her five-foot-three inches. Had she been taller than a teenager, aloof, and angular like Jackie, surely she wouldn't have to hide behind a phone she was still reluctant to turn on even after double-checking that the office door was locked and the hall free of cops. Cramped down in her desk chair and cringing, Caroline powered up her cell, plugged in her personal headset, and gritted her teeth.

Reyes had left the most recent message, thanking her in his usual suggestive Spanglish for a good night, wishing her a good morning, and reminding her of their date Friday. Groaning, Caroline pressed on to a yesterday-evening message from her older brother Hector:

"C.C., what is Nez doing calling me?" Caroline gasped as she listened. "Call me back so I know you're all right before me, Phil, and Dizzy show up on that punk's doorstep like we should have done months ago. Dizzy's flying back from London for Easter, and me, Linh, and Julianna expect you home, too, not holed up somewhere crying over the son of a bitch like you did at Christmas. Call me back, girl."

There was a second, earlier message from Hector along those same lines, though perhaps more frantic and threatening as befitted a U.S. Marshal, and hours before that was a hang-up from Nez that he'd replaced with an email:

> I'm not giving you the money under the table, for both our sakes. Should be a check on your desk in the morning and a tally of how much I paid you for your assignments and how much I got from Milan's people. The royalties haven't changed, so you need to make peace with that and get that seventy grand you came up with out of your head. Milan was hot and everybody was writing for her; I cut your costs to get your foot in the door, and you know that. So the way I see it, I owe you little more than twenty-six grand, and if you get me some kind of invoice, I'll pay it off, we both pay taxes, and we're done, all right? Cut a brother a break this time, C.C., like you should have before. You didn't even give me a chance to explain, but I think it's too late now that you went and turned into this kind of girl.

There was no parting remark just as there had been no greeting, no apology, and no pleading to ease the vertigo that came with Nez playing nice. Caroline's nauseated terror quickly gave way to fury. Nez had insight into what kind of girl she was, even though he had no idea how long she'd sat on her ass waiting for him to show up and explain why Bratney had called him her man on TV? *After* his nasty tapes had finally freed Caroline from months of being the kind of girl who looked the other way, Nez had the nerve to act decent?

"Oh, no, you will not get away with that." Nez owed her an apology, and she was going to squeeze it out of him if it cost five thousand dollars a letter.

Cheeks hot and temperature stewing, Caroline bitterly tore through the mail until she found a plain brown messenger envelope. The cashier's check inside was indeed for five thousand dollars and was earmarked for "services rendered," among which was presumably second-rate sex that didn't keep him coming back for more.

"Jerk." Her eyes crossed and her teeth ground. *"Jerk!"*

Kit, the paralegal, cut into Caroline's fuming when she fell heavily against the other side of the locked office door. Caroline heard her groan loudly and fish for keys in her bag. Few were the opportunities to make nice to Kit, so Caroline was quick to scoop up the check, her jacket and purse, and run to Kit's rescue.

"Sorry, girl," Caroline said. "I forgot to unlock it."

Kit had a small sour mouth all at odds with her wide blue eyes, and Caroline saw her take in her sunglasses and jacket. "Are you taking off? Again?"

"I don't feel good. I think I'm coming down with something," *like a rabid revenge fixation*. "Tell Jacks, okay?"

"Don't think you can get sick every morning and still have a job here."

"C'mon Kit! You don't need me. You know you loved the overtime before I showed up."

Though she said nothing, Kit looked pacified, and Caroline blew a thank-you kiss on her way to the stairwell in a bid not to meet Jackie in the elevator. She left her car in the garage, walked the couple of blocks to the bank, and then walked back five grand richer and full of plans that were going to make Nez Peterson's head spin when he got a load of what kind of girl she really was. She called Trent.

When he finally got an after-lunch break from babysitting his mother, Trent discovered that Caroline had called four times. He had turned off the ringer to avoid bill collectors, but he'd checked for messages, and she hadn't left any. He called her back as soon as he saw the missed calls, anxious that a few hours' delay might blow his chance at whatever she was offering.

She picked up on the first ring. "Hi. Where are you?"

"Bibb City. Why?"

"Ugh. I was hoping you'd be in Atlanta. Do you have to work today?"

Trent had missed that week's roofing job, a four-day event that had begun yesterday and for which positions were already filled. However, he'd had plenty to do after his mother's panic attack had destroyed most of the drinking glasses and one of the kitchen cabinet doors. He cleared his throat. "No. Why?"

"Come to the city so we can work on your act for Thursday."

"No kidding?"

"You've got a gig at the Red Light Café. Technically, that means first crack at the open mic on Bluegrass Thursday night, but you have to start somewhere. We need to work on at least four songs and your, uh, stage presence, for the cameras, which technically means my friend's Nikon D90." Caroline giggled. "When can you get here?"

With it being a bad day for Margie, Trent couldn't leave her alone until Ginny got home or until Cheryl across the street got her lot in from Head-Start and could keep an eye out. Including the drive-time, that put him at, "Four o'clock."

"Four? That's so late."

"You live damn near in Athens. It's about three hours from here."

"Well, I was hoping you'd meet me by Lenox Mall around two."

"Not gonna happen."

"Suppose there was something in it for you personally?"

Trent wondered if that something came in a sweater dress. "Can't be bribed out of some things, Caroline. Look, I'll try, but I promise three o'clock is just about the soonest I can get to Atlanta."

"All right, fine," she whined. "Call me when you're half an hour out."

"Why don't you just tell me where you want me to meet you?"

"Because I don't know where I might be at three o'clock. Just call me."

"I can't, Caroline. I don't have a cell phone," Trent was forced to admit. "So where do you want me to meet you?"

He heard her suck her teeth. "Please don't tell me that you're one of those anti-technology people."

"I'm one of those can't-afford-the-bill people."

"Oh, uh, wow. Okay. Meet me at a shop across the street from the mall, Voodoo Rue. Do you need help with gas money?"

Though thoughtful, her question irritated him. "What the hell is a Voodoo Rue?"

"Just meet me outside the Neiman Marcus at three, and we'll take it from there."

She sounded plenty annoyed when she hung up, a fact that didn't lessen the shame Trent felt for not having a phone, stagnant shame that had been dormant until he'd met her. Being broke was easy in Bibb City, whereas in Atlanta no personal tragedy was grand enough to stop the steam train of ambition. Trent wasn't even sure that he trusted that train all the way to the end of the line, but he sure as shit had to ride that sucker if he wanted to get anywhere at all.

His mother cried out from her usual spot on the mangy old, tea rose-printed sofa, and Trent sprinted to her side only to find Margie in a fit about whatever Sami had gone and done on *Days of Our Lives*.

"It's all right, Mama." He pried the collar of Margie's purple cotton housedress down from the snotty tip of her nose. "I know that ain't Lucas, but they'll get back together someday, you'll see." He pressed a tissue into her hand. "Why don't you stretch out and get your nap in while you're watching," Trent said, hoping that lying down would make his mother's mood-controlling prescription kick in.

A half-hour into Margie still being inconsolable over the soaps, Trent gave up and retreated to his room to see if he had enough money both for gas to Atlanta and paying Cheryl to start watching Margie right away. It was tough being stuck with someone who lived in a blizzard of reds and blues, the same ones that assaulted Trent right when he was about to lose it, but the sympathy he should have felt for his mother had gone the way of any hope she would get better. It broke his heart to hear all that nonsense coming from her face that, like cracked china, had been pieced back together instead of thrown away, a fact that Margie didn't seem grateful for even on her best days.

A fake smile and a crisp twenty was all it took to talk Cheryl into checking in every half-hour, and then Trent circled the house to the shed to finish scrounging up some new dishes. Sure enough, he found his mother's crystal wedding set way in the back in a box caked over with dust and mouse shit. He'd have to do the cleaning outside with the water hose to keep Ginny's allergies from acting up and had just stripped off his T-shirt when he saw a Wild Turkey bourbon bottle lying by the divot of grass where it had landed. It wasn't unusual for beer bottles to get thrown across their yard on their side of town, but that didn't stop the hairs on his neck from stiffening nor him from rushing into the house and grabbing the phone.

Shane answered after three rings. "Yeah-lo."

"You heard anything new about Courtney?"

"No. Why?"

"I just found a Wild Turkey bottle alongside the house!"

Shane scoffed. "Everybody in Muscogee County drinks Wild Turkey. Hell, everybody up to the Mason-Dixon Line—"

"You know what I'm getting at. How sure are you that he's still out of it?"

"Dead sure." Shane yawned. "Kim's an LPN at St. Francis. I just slipped her my pork sausage last night, and she didn't tell me anything different when her mouth wasn't full."

Trent scowled. Shane was exactly the reason why the word got around. "Suppose folks are putting two and two together. I mean, how'd you even know where he was gonna be that night?"

"Courtney went to that old store regular as a nun to get his check cashed and buy a lottery ticket and bottle of Wild Turkey. Everybody knows that! Only difference was he was running late that night."

"But how did you know that? Who told you?"

"I don't remember; I was drunk. Would you relax? I thought he was dead when I pulled you off him. The boy could barely breathe, much less talk."

"Which is not to say that he wasn't running his mouth all those months he walked around like nothing was nothing. Jesus H. Christ!" Disgust flooded Trent's stomach. "You think he was *bragging* about it?"

"You don't brag about a thing like that."

"You're mistaking Courtney for a man with a conscience, Shane, which he obviously ain't, and chances are that whichever of his boys been throwing bottles around my house ain't much better!"

There was a long pause while Trent tried to stop seeing red, and his best friend let him. At length, Shane asked, "Well, whatcha wanna do about it?"

The thing Trent had done a thousand times in his imagination and then in real life hadn't helped a lick, hadn't fixed Ginny's spine or Margie's mind. He swallowed hard. "I guess a killing spree's out of order, now that I'm just about to get my music career off the ground."

"Are you serious?"

"'Course not," Trent mumbled disingenuously of the spree.

"About the music career? God damn it! I figured it was you who made off with that boy's guitar. That's where you were all yesterday, in Atlanta?"

"Yeah, and that's where I'll be all today, too, if I can count on you to keep an eye on my ladies. Call in and check on them every so often, will ya? I'll be damned if I let anything else happen to them."

"It won't. That's why you did this in the first place."

If Trent really believed that, he'd sleep better at night. "You betcha."

An anxious gut accompanied him to his room for some clean clothes, which simply meant a different wrinkled white T-shirt and beige Dickies. After kissing his mother's cheek and ignoring Margie's inability to register the gesture, Trent checked in with Cheryl and hit the road.

Anxiety collided with the burgeoning sense of shame that he had about all things Caroline, about all things away from Bibb City, from the constant demands for his money and his time, and from the sudden loud ticking of a clock toward retribution for what he'd done to Courtney Vickers. Another man wouldn't have been ashamed of letting go and enjoying himself, but letting go was a grace that Trent had forfeited the first time he'd planted his fist in Courtney's face.

He found Caroline's car outside of Lenox mall and then followed her to a row of boutiques across the parking lot and across the street. Trent became skeptical the second she jumped out of her Jetta. Phone pressed to her ear while she likely faked a phone call, Caroline marched ahead without him until she got to the door and looked back at him hesitating on the sidewalk. Wind whipped back her black trench-coat lapels and revealed her ridiculously kitted-out little figure, the glimpse of which Trent blamed for not reacting to Caroline when she suddenly flashed her pretty teeth at him.

"Don't get mad." She smiled, winningly but unconvincingly yet again.

He tried to pull away from her manicured grasp on the sleeve of his Dickies jacket. "About what?"

"Well, my friend works here, and she's going to give us her employee discount as long as she gets an Ed Hardy hoodie out of it. So we are going to hook you up!"

Trent clarified with suspicion, "Like a makeover?"

"Just clothes for right now! We'll worry about—" The five fingers of her hand drew a circle around his face. "—this, uh, later. Okay?"

"No. Not okay. I ain't bought any new clothes in a year. I certainly don't see why I need you dressing me up like a goddamn Jonas Brother to sing a couple of songs."

"Don't you want to look good on stage?"

"There's nothing wrong with the way I look now." He yanked his hair, and it stood up as though electrified by his irritation.

"Trent, it's not just about a couple of cover songs. It's about paying gigs, right? Well, those require press kits, and press kits require pictures and a list of places that you've played. Now, I know the guy who does the booking for The Earl."

Trent barely blinked at her mention of an Atlanta staple in the independent entertainment scene.

"It's a reputable venue around here, but even with my connection, you are not getting on stage without a press kit, and your kit is not going to impress anyone with you looking like…" Her splayed hand went down the length of his body, and Caroline winced like she'd just scratched a chalkboard. "I'd work with you on building an image if we had time, but for now, we've got to make one up." She tried to push him toward the doors of the Voodoo Rue.

He didn't move. "Doesn't a press kit require a band and some actual tracks?"

"I can get you a band."

He raised a disbelieving brow.

"Trust me when I tell you that I know tons of out-of-work musicians, okay? And I have songs; I've just been waiting for someone to lay them down the right damn way. My ex — " She stopped and rubbed her temple. "Image sells, Trent. Okay? *You* sell. Nobody wants to hear blues-rock tunes from some stumpy, thick in the middle Black chick. I tried it, and my ex was the only person who cared. I thought that meant he believed in me, but apparently I was just an investment."

Trent waited for her to look up from her hands. When she didn't, he touched her shoulder. "I see plenty of folks looking beat down in Bibb City, so I'm not taking that off of someone like you."

"What's that supposed to mean?"

Trent tried to think of a way around inappropriately complimenting his boss. What she called thick looked juicy to him. "Well, you're nicely put together. And smart. Definitely smart enough to know better than believing in a man more than you believe in yourself."

"I do." She straightened up to her full height, which wasn't much. "I just refuse to sell my songs to anyone else who will turn them into 'kicky crossover' whatever for the latest incarnation of Bimbo Barbie!" Caroline exhaled on a deep breath. "Look, I know I have to sell these songs at some point. I'd just like to hear them the right way for once and maybe have a better chance of selling them to somebody who really gives a…you know."

"A shit?"

She glared at him. "Somebody who really cares about American roots music before it dies out completely."

Trent didn't know the first thing about "roots music," nor did he care beyond how much his first paycheck was going to get docked to pay for image-selling duds. And he shouldn't have cared about the way Caroline's face fell while he stood there staring at her, but he did because she was sweet, and her sweetness was one of the things he was ashamed of having traveled two hours for. "Fine."

"Fine?"

"Make me repeat it, and I might change my mind."

She rewarded him with a brilliant smile for giving in.

Though he'd seen fancy shopping places in Columbus, Trent had never in his life stepped foot in a place as pretentious as the Voodoo Rue.

Antique-looking skeletons were posed in clothes and had to aggravate the hell out of even the size zero girls. The red velvet chairs, velvet hangers, and velvet curtains he was able to tolerate only from within the confines of his dressing room. Caroline's friend Farah, a cat-eyed blonde who wore an enormous Iran necklace between her breasts, had taken one long look at him, put him in a room, and spent the next hour knocking for him to open up, shaking her head, and shoving new clothes at him.

"The problem," she explained to Caroline on the other side, "is that he's too leggy for his height. He's flooding in an average, but the tall sizes cut too low in the crotch, and even his junk can't fill up that trunk."

"Farah!" Caroline exclaimed.

"What? Rock and Roll fits snug and not saggy, right?"

Trent peeked through the dressing room slats, and, from the way Farah kept swinging her arm like an elephant trunk between her knees, he was comforted to think that they were laughing with him instead of at him.

"Trent, come out!" Farah hollered, then immediately continued to Caroline, "These are not velvet pants! They're moleskin, which means a similar sheen under the lights but lower friction, less weight, and less cost. Plus, you can just throw them in the wash afterward, and they'll still cling like *cha-ching!*"

Trent opened the door to Farah making jazz-hands toward his crotch, and, unfortunately, she bade him swivel his ass toward Caroline, who was as red as the velvet chair in which she sat.

"See how this brown is almost cinnamon?" Farah tugged on the pants pockets over his ass. "It doesn't wash him out, see, whereas that olive under-tone I tried before…" She drew a line across her neck and smiled at Trent. "And this mauve does the same thing," Farah said of the silky thin V-neck sweater she'd put on him. "I know you're thinking it's too pink, but that's just opera mauve. You could go with a mauve taupe or a light mauve and get the same result as long as it's a cold undertone. Hell, you could go deep blue if you get the right hair color."

Nodding, Caroline then suddenly snapped her neck toward her purse. "Forgot to call Sharona about his hair." She whipped out her cell phone. "But show me that blue you were talking about."

Farah shuffled off, and Trent sat down and waited. They obviously didn't want his opinion, and he didn't care as much as he could have about the metro-sexual colors and fabrics they were choosing. He hadn't felt any-thing so soft against his skin since the last woman that he'd had, and if being metro meant being primped by two pretty women, Trent was all for it. And he loved it when Caroline stepped between his legs and tipped her breasts toward his face to study his hair.

"Brown. Yeah, he might've been dirty blond as a child. Super thick, like—oh! Oh my."

Trent's eyes rolled back into his head from the pleasure of her fingers casually tousling his hair. "Uh, what?"

"I just thought—" She stepped back when their eyes met, seeming to realize how close she was standing to him. "His hair isn't greasy. It's glossy, like…I don't know, but not that icy shine everyone gets from products. It's as slick as ribbon."

He winked at her. "Slick as a snake striking."

Caroline snatched her hand from his hair. "Were you blond as a child?"

"Yeah. I'm dirty," he drawled in a really wrong way.

Suddenly weak-kneed, Caroline stumbled a few steps back from him. "Um, yeah, but mostly brown. And greenish," she said of his eyes.

"Sometimes. They change to blue and back depending."

"On what?"

"The color of my tie." He winked at her again.

He was the furthest thing from a suit-and-tie guy that Caroline could imagine. She kept quiet until Farah reappeared with the second choice outfit. It took Trent just a few seconds to change into the slightly iridescent, teal, button-down shirt and second-skin indigo jeans, but he came out of the dressing room looking like a different man, urban but dashing somehow in the closely cut clothes. As white as pearl in the cold new colors, Trent bypassed pasty and went straight to a translucent creamy color that his beige Dickies would never inspire. Alabaster, she thought it was called, or maybe marble like Michelangelo's David. Either way, the color made sense of his constantly rosy cheeks and lips, the perfection of which rendered Caroline speechless about his eye color.

"Great! It looks great. Wrap it up, Farah," Caroline said, and she retreated to the checkout.

She was leaning against the front counter, trying to get a grip on her newfound sexual awareness of Trent, when he emerged in his own clothes. Now that she knew what he could look like, the tattered Dickies didn't conceal his sex appeal. She tore her gaze from him and pulled out her phone to call Sharona, the friend who had asked about his hair color with the intention of changing it.

After he approached, Caroline avoided touching his hand when she took the blue outfit from him and laid it on the counter.

Unfortunately, Trent laid that hand over hers as she held her cell phone. "Caroline, about all this…"

His fingers were hot and heavy and coarse against hers when he pried away her phone. She hung up on her friend.

"Sharona's not going to turn you into a Jonas Brother, okay? She's just going to warm up your color a little bit so that, well, so that your color pops. I mean, you've got good, uh, color." She was babbling badly. "It would just be better without the mousy brown hair."

She was relieved when he let her go with a grandmotherly pat on the back of her hand.

"Yeah, all right, press kit," Trent grumbled. "I get it. But I just realized these clothes are a hundred dollars each. So one outfit or the other, all right?"

Caroline decided not to mention that while plain-old cotton cost a hundred dollars, silk and moleskin cost more. "But Farah is giving us her discount."

Trent shoved his hands in his pockets and fished around. "Nope. 'Discount' ain't a magic word that puts cash in my pocket. That must only work for girls."

Annoyed, Caroline waved off his crack with one hand. "I'll take it out of your pay for the gig."

"I need that for something else."

She attempted to blow out her frustration in one breath. "Look, I have a charge account here that has an extra ten percent off," Caroline lied, "so I'll charge it, and we can negotiate later, all right?" She chummily clapped him across the shoulder, but hadn't expected electricity to zing her fingertips. Trent was hard all over, and imagining what his marble behind looked like made a bead of sweat pop out on her lip à la Whitney Houston, though what Caroline felt surging up through her stomach was definitely not a song. "This is a business expense anyway," she said a little breathlessly.

"Yeah, and what business would that be exactly?"

"The Caroline Curran — no, Curran-C Music Group. Band! Get it?" Caroline flashed her fingers like headliner lights. He didn't look impressed. "Or we could use your name." She tried to remember what it was. "The Trent, uh…I mean, Trent and —"

"Buckney."

"—the Curran-C Ba — Buckney? Your name is Trent Buckney?"

He nodded. "Trenton Michael Buckney, Jr., at your service."

While Caroline stood stymied for a polite reaction, Farah chipped in, "How about Trent Buck? You can call his album *Saddle Up.*" She winked at Trent.

"Not helping, Farah." Caroline shoved the clothes across the sales counter. "Exactly what we don't need is for him to come off like a country singer. Not," she gulped when Trent suddenly hovered over her shoulder, "that there's anything wrong with being a singer from the country."

"I thought we talked about this." Trent pulled the blue outfit away from Farah's scanner.

"Well, can we talk about it again later? Like, after we have a press kit in which you are not wearing the same exact thing for three months? Yeah." She tried to shove him toward the door and failed. Caroline should have known that his back was made of the same sculpted marble as his shoulder and fingers.

She also should have anticipated that the low whistle Trent made over the sales total would turn into more than just talking when he proceeded to grouse about the cost during the hour drive to her house.

All the way up her front walk, he explained five different ways that anything only he was going to wear couldn't be called a business expense and therefore ought to be returned if he said so. Caroline nodded very politely, through the front door and on to her kitchen. She set the bag and the mail down on the usual counter next to the doorway, pulled a pair of scissors out of the junk drawer, and clipped the tags right in front of his face.

"There, that's settled. Now, I need to run to the store to get some supplies for Sharona. She's pregnant and does not do favors without snacks. Do you want to come, or do you want to stay here and stew?"

"Maybe I'll just hit the road home."

Caroline's face fell, and her first instinct was to apologize for pushing him too far, but then she remembered that she wasn't that kind of girl anymore. "Fine. But before you go, take a look through the music that I pulled for your gig Thursday and pick out something you like, since you'll want to practice after you've done your sulking for the night." She faked a patronizing smile that lasted until Trent's frustrated fingers fanned the pages of Milan's centerfold, undercutting Caroline's tenuous ability to hold her own with men. "Whatever. I'm going." Caroline snatched her purse and turned heel.

When she made it back from Publix with chips, dip, baking soda, rice flour, and a bottle of Chardonnay slipped out of the grocery bag and into her purse, Caroline was embarrassingly relieved that Trent's deep green Chevy was still parked at the curb in front of Sharona's suv. She found them in her kitchen already hard at work. Trent was perched on a step stool with his back to the stainless steel sink and a towel wrapped around his whole face. In front of him, Sharona smiled from behind a wooden butcher's cart draped with parchment paper and covered with little glass bowls of her organic beauty treatments.

"He has the tiniest pores I've ever seen," Sharona said. "I just gave him a quick lemon and honey facial, but I'll make up some strawberry mask for you since you brought my rice flour. And dip, God bless your soul." After yanking a rubber band around her unruly black curls and washing her hands, Sharona tore into the bag of chips and continued talking just about as fast as she ate.

It was fairly easy then for Caroline to sneak a corkscrew and pour a red plastic tumbler full of wine without her friend noticing, but drinking without commentary was a feat that required keeping talkative Sharona on topics other than Caroline's increasingly obvious funk.

"How's Aaron?"

While squinting as she whipped up a concoction of what would be Trent's new hair color, Sharona rolled her eyes. "He swears he'll die if I don't give Hannah a brother. This is why I won't tell him the sex. I don't want to spend the rest of my pregnancy getting over his disappointment. Of course, the second Leah's born, he'll cry tears of joy, I know. I'll show you the video."

Caroline rather hoped not. Sharona's last medication-free, earth-mother birth had been enough to last a lifetime. Sipping at intervals, Caroline watched Sharona go over to Trent, peel the hot towels from his face, and pinch his skin.

"Like a baby's butt! I'm going to set your color, and then I'll send you to shave, unless you've changed your mind about letting me do it for you."

"No, thank you, I can handle it." Trent propped up and let Sharona stuff towels behind his back. He was pink as a piglet, and peered at Caroline from behind the wet hair in his eyes. "What's the matter with you?"

"Nothing!"

Trent gave her a once over. "Doesn't look like nothing. You're flushed. You ain't been crying, have you?"

Beneath both his and Sharona's gazes, Caroline set down the tumbler of yumminess that was heating her cheeks. "No!" She picked it up again as soon as they stopped looking and tried to excuse herself to the living room.

Before she could escape, Trent called, "I checked out that music," from behind the towel that Sharona rubbed all over his face. "What's up with all the country? I thought you didn't want me to 'come off like that.'"

"Bluegrass isn't the same thing as country."

"Bonnie Raitt ain't bluegrass."

"That one doesn't count; it was just, um, you just need four songs ready. Red Light's regular band doesn't much sing, but they always do Flatt and Scruggs's 'Don't Get Above Your Raising,' and if you learn it, they'll probably let you sing it."

He looked skeptical.

"Don't knock till you try it, okay? It's a really cool rockabilly version of the London cover that Ricky Skaggs did with Elvis Costello." Caroline scoffed at Trent's raised eyebrow, but she wasn't about to protest him being impressed with her if it shut him up. "Then somebody's always going to sing 'Drink Up And Go Home,' so that might as well be you, and I kind of think you'd kill 'The Boxer' in an Emmylou Harris *Roses in the Snow* kind of way."

"You think I sound like Emmylou Harris?"

"I think her phrasing will suit you and the Red Light Café a lot better than Simon and Garfunkel's original," she retorted, but when he smirked and the lyrics of "The Boxer" ran through her head, Caroline longed to hear that song from the heart hiding behind Trent's perfect stone lips. "Or you can try to wow them with your heartfelt and moving Keith Urban. Whatever." She quickly refilled her tumbler from the bottle that she'd tucked into the cereal cabinet and retreated to her room.

With "The Boxer" playing on her computer on repeat, Caroline made an unremarkable and slightly tipsy attempt at, first, emailing Nez, then writing that invoice he'd mentioned. She failed at both. She was supposed to know that she'd been worth more to him than twenty-six grand that he could easily afford. She was supposed to know that she was precious, priceless somehow, and not easily replaced with an eighteen-year-old who, covered in cake frosting, could twist her ankles behind her neck and give head simultaneously.

Melancholy kept Caroline's chin on her knees for a long time and, combined with Chardonnay, kept her from hearing the first few bars of Bonnie Raitt's "You" that Trent invented in the other room. Sharona knocked on the door in the same second that Caroline opened it, and they both walked gaga-eyed into the tender thrall of Trent's baritone filling up the living room. Still lacking the twang of his speaking voice, his throat made the song seem a lilting Irish love song that was entirely too appropriate for the handsome rover Sharona had wrought from him. His eyes had turned a pretty cornflower blue in the shadow of his new auburn hair color. Sharona had painted russet and bronze tones through his thick locks and cut just enough to keep it out of his eyes. His hair still shot out in cinnamon spikes that suited him like Farah had said, maintaining a wildness that made something sly of the sharp cheekbones cutting toward the corners of his narrow, hooded eyes.

Caroline had only pulled out her favorite song from nostalgia and from the hope that one day soon, Nez would die and release his hold on all the songs she'd wrapped his name around while they were together. She remembered the Valentine's Day when he'd turned up his nose at the dulcet front-porch thrum of the song "You." Caroline's album hadn't taken off, and he'd been too worried about losing money to care that she'd been naked behind a guitar and playing her heart out with a red bow tied around her neck.

Trent hesitated to smile when they exclaimed over his looks, mostly because, with his beard gone, his cheeks easily betrayed his every shift of mood. Instead, he watched Caroline while he played. She'd seemed relieved when he moved on from "You" to "The Boxer." Like all of the other songs she'd picked out, the lyrics spoke to the injured man within that she'd only glimpsed in their first meeting. Of course, she was glamorizing him. Of course, she had no real idea about what fighting had gotten him, but when he came to the end of the song, Trent gave up a little ghost of that pain and blew it to Caroline like a kiss. She looked overwhelmed, shiny around the eyes like she'd been drinking, and he wondered what was in her red cup.

After Caroline excused herself to the kitchen and didn't come back, Sharona went to her, and Trent stopped playing. In general, he wasn't a fan of women who made attention-getting gestures, but a little attention seemed to be the only thing standing between Caroline and a pity party. He hung around after Sharona eventually, after many kisses and a demand to see Caroline in temple for Shabbat, left to go home.

"Shabbat?" Trent inquired and leaned into the kitchen doorframe after seeing Sharona and all her gear safely to the Highlander.

Caroline flicked a wrist. "It's the Jewish—"

"I know what it is." Trent watched Caroline hunch over the counter nearest that damn Milan Monthly. She hummed softly to herself and nursed what he felt sure was something alcoholic. "You're Jewish?"

She didn't look at him nor did she straighten up, though her butt stuck out like a gaudy advertisement. "My stepmother, Julianna, is. She kind of raised me, part-time, after my father died."

"How did he die?"

"Prematurely." Glassy-eyed, she stood up straight and studied him over the rim of her tumbler. "You know what? You haven't actually changed all that much. I think I just didn't notice before that you were fine. I mean, you look fine. Not literally a redneck at all."

He laughed. Hers was the slightly too-loose conversation of a tipsy woman. "White neck, in fact."

"Like a pearl. You have a pretty complexion. Er, handsome. *Nice.*" She crossed her eyes. "Thanks for putting up with everything today. Really, I'll make it worth your while. I'm serious about my business." Her black boots sloppily stomped back to the cereal cabinet, and Caroline swiped her empty tumbler in front of his face. "In fact, I'm thinking about hiring you as my employee since I'll need you here to practice every day anyway. Then we won't have to worry about whatever it is that you do. You know, for a living." She tipped the wine bottle over her glass. "And we can get… these…songs out."

Caroline frowned at the bottle from which no Chardonnay was forthcoming despite insistent shaking, and then she frowned at Trent when he took it from her.

He uncorked the bottle, poured what was left of the wine, and edged the tumbler toward her with the corner of the Magazine of Doom. "I got a present for ya."

As she raised the tumbler to her lips, Trent pulled a pen from his pocket. "That's a Magic Marker," she remarked. "That's *my* Magic Marker."

"Yeah, well, I'm about to show you the magic." He flipped to Milan's centerfold. "Say you see something in these magazines that you don't like. Me personally, I'd just stop getting them, but for you, maybe you could do a little decorating."

He squared up the centerfold against the edge of the counter and stood back, arms crossed, to consider it. Caroline stood back, too, and watched while Trent, with a flourish of the pen, drew a handlebar moustache on Milan Taylor.

"Now if that doesn't get it done for you, you might move on to some Mickey Mouse ears or some buck teeth. Freckles across the nose." He drew each item in turn while Caroline fell into a fit of giggles that turned to hiccups. "Obviously, she needs some clothes on." He drew a big polka dot granny dress over Milan's svelte body and then covered her diamond-studded heels with combat boots. "And there you are." His deadpan was gravelly and tender. "My baby sister's, uh, in a wheelchair," Trent confessed with much less difficulty than he'd expected, "and she draws crazy patterned stockings on the legs of all the girls in her magazines. I figured something like that might work out for you too."

Caroline pointed to his artwork. "With this kind of talent, I definitely need you on my staff. What do you say?"

"You don't even know how I'll do yet," Trent scoffed and regretted it once he realized that Caroline was just barely holding her emotions in check. "But I guess if you just *want* to be blinded by my good looks, that's fine by me."

"I can't deny that you clean up pretty good, Trent Michaels."

"Trent Michaels. That's what you're calling me, huh?" She nodded eagerly, and because the sliver of a smile that she gave him was sweet enough to carry down the road for the night, Trent acquiesced with a clap of his hands. "Then I guess I'll catch your act tomorrow, boss lady."

He chucked her under the chin and left before he could do anything else.

Chapter Five

Of all the things that Trent could have gone into denial about, being sweet on Caroline Curran was the one he chose, mostly for its potential to wreck everything else he'd come to care about in four short days. Denial was precisely the reason why he was so high on her. In a month of Sundays, he'd been too pissed, too busy, and, lately, too guilty to do anything worth calling pleasurable, but then her smile had brought with it things that hadn't been more than flimsy dreams since he'd been the mama's boy with an angel voice in Shiloh Baptist's choir stand.

More than just the singing, every little thing was no longer a Solomon-sized decision now that he knew for sure where his next paycheck was coming from. What she'd given him Wednesday to "seal the deal" had been two jobs' pay plus the added incentives of reimbursing fuel, being fun, and hinting at a future. Trent had even loosened his fist from around his meager savings to buy some badly needed new tires for his truck, and he'd had a ball installing and muddying up those suckers so Ginny wouldn't get suspicious of what he was up to. Good things didn't come in droves, and no way would he ruin what little he had to steal kisses from Caroline, who was not just high-strung, but also his boss and could fire his ass. No way would he reach for even more than he deserved when Ginny, who deserved a miracle, was already bearing more than her fair share of Margie so that he could work.

Overwhelmed with guilt for keeping up the pretense that he still had three jobs, Trent had taken off Thursday to spend with Ginny after Caroline had hired him and stopped lying about open mic night involving a paycheck. He'd driven his sister to school to beat the short yellow bus and then, before buying his tires, had turned back on the cable so that she could watch *America's Skinny-Bone-Jones Runway* or whatever the hell it was that had always had her on a diet before she'd ended up in a wheelchair. Whereas he'd been dirty, Ginny was bright blond and had been an eye-catching girl in a Robin Wright Penn-not-Madonna kind of way, but these days a jaunt down the romance novel section of the grocery store was the only highlight of her week. She stayed holed up in her room with books and magazines and the silence that surrounded long-term tragedies when the pity was over.

Standing outside the back kitchen door of their glorified trailer, Trent watched Ginny's yellow ponytail switch back and forth while she beat a bowl of cornbread in her lap and snapped at Margie to cut down the gas burner under the lima beans. He took a second to slump as though instead of installing tires and playing in the mud out back of Shane's house, he'd had a long day at work. It just didn't seem decent to walk in looking cheerful on them.

"Hey" was all that Trent actually choked out while he beat a hasty path behind both his ladies to the shower. Twenty minutes later, he came out clean in his usual ensemble and then paused just outside the kitchen with his new clothes folded inside the Dickies jacket he held death-gripped in one hand. In the other hand, he had one of the *Twilight* movies that he hoped would get him out the door without too many questions asked. On a deep breath, Trent swooped behind his sister and dropped the movie between her stomach and the cornbread bowl. "That's a present for ya."

"Where do you think you're going?"

She didn't even glance at the doggone DVD.

"Uh, out?" Trent retorted with as much older-brother authority as he could muster. "But Shane and Kim are gonna stop by later to, uh, drop off some stuff."

"Uh huh." Ginny arched a brow as high as their mother's used to reach in her heyday. "And do you really think I'm gonna let you gallop off to Atlanta looking like that?" While Trent silently freaked out, Ginny rolled to the small pantry at the rear of the kitchen and rolled back with one of his white church shirts neatly pressed and on a metal hanger. She gently shook her head at his expression. "Save it, bud. I'm on to you, with the haircut and the shave and the glint in your eye lately." They both shot a look at Margie who wasn't having a bad night, but wasn't exactly having an aware night either. "You're off to see Caroline Curran, and I can tell you right now, you ain't getting a second date looking like that." She glanced disparagingly over his Dickies outfit and thrust forward the shirt. "Go change."

Freaking out was probably the top reason why Trent tore the buttons off his shirt cuffs during the ten minutes he spent in the bathroom. He couldn't cope with both being so transparent to his baby sister and running late, but he figured that chasing a woman was an easier lie to cop to than the truth. All kinds of nervous, Trent rolled up the cuffs and tried to splash water on his face that instead ended up in his hair, on his shirt, and across a sensitive part of his beige pants. When he finally made it back to the kitchen, he was wearing a white T-shirt and his best blue jeans, except for the ones Caroline had bought him. DVD in one hand, Ginny was smiling wide until she took in what he was wearing and made a chiding sound at him.

Trent demanded, "What now?"

"Well, if she'll take you like that, she must not be as fancy as I thought." Ginny looked really disappointed. "Just don't bring home another Paris or Jessica, all right?"

Trent rolled his eyes, though he was grateful for an easy out toward the back door. "What have I told you about judging people, Gin?"

"Telling the truth ain't judging," she hollered after him. "Those broads give us natural blondes a bad name!"

Though five grand was nothing to sneeze at, Caroline only had to make a few calls to friends who didn't do favors to realize she would need another transfusion from Nez in order to push whatever business she was starting out of its infancy. A record label was totally out of the question, but she had to put some kind of letterhead on the invoice she was writing, and "Trent Michaels and the Curran-C Band" didn't have quite the same ring as it had under the influence of, well, Trent. It had been hard to see past his amazing talent before when he'd looked one peg-leg shy of a pirate; now that he had the face of a star and the hair of a shampoo model, Caroline had to come to terms with the facts that he deserved some proper management and she wasn't an agent any more than she was a record executive. She was a songwriter planning to build a band that would make hits from her music, a dream that gave Caroline the courage to simply write her name at the top of the invoice.

Settling on an amount to bill Nez was another, angrier matter, one that was interrupted when Jackie, in a sleek black pants suit, breezed out of the office at a quarter to four.

"Looks like I'm the one leaving early today. Dinner meeting," Jackie said.

Caroline frantically mouse-clicked to hide her invoice. She answered Jackie's teasing with a wan smile.

Jackie shook her head. "I know that fetching and carrying are not your career aspirations, C.C., but can you at least pretend like you're happy here come Monday? Tomorrow won't count because it's payday."

"Hardy har." Caroline's brow furrowed over what she was going to do with her own employee come Monday. "Um, but I might need to take some time off next week, too, Jacks."

"For what?"

Caroline bared her teeth in what she hoped was a winning smile. "Songwriter's convention?"

"Why are you lying? And what happened to needing money 'so bad, Jacks, please, please, please?' Is this about Wolverine? Oh, my Jesus!" Jackie clapped one horrified hand over her mouth. "Is that hillbilly your new sugar daddy?"

"Uh, ouch."

"Don't play wounded with me. If you hadn't let Nez take care of you, you would have left him sooner."

"How about saving your brilliant commentary for the open mic tonight?"

Jackie made an ugly face, no small feat for a former model. "Do I have to go to that? I thought you only needed my camera."

"I don't know how to use it, Jacks; I need you to take the pictures too."

Jackie blinked. "See, there's this button you push —"

"You know what I mean! I need some good pictures, and I'll be busy chatting up Jarvis and maybe talking Marlon and Minerva into playing with Trent. They said they might come check it out."

"Wendy's still calling herself Minerva?"

"Yeah, and her dreads are blue now, but the girl can bang a drum." Caroline's eyebrows shrugged. "Ten thirty at the Red Light Café, Jacks. Please."

"All right! What's the attire?"

Caroline considered that for a long time before quizzically replying, "Rockabilly chic?"

Unsure herself what that entailed, Caroline spent every last second between her commute to and from the city on her own appearance, after she'd loaded the necessary instruments and sheet music into her Jetta. Though her expansive wardrobe was due mostly to the pleasure Nez took in a well-dressed woman, Caroline wasn't about to blame the clothes for him being a cheater, and she selected that evening's ensemble from a stash of vintage dresses that she'd worn for Halloween costumes. A red and white polka dot halter dress was a bit summery for January, but she'd made a fine Dorothy Dandridge in it and needed the same eye-catching power for that evening. Over half of an image was attitude, and she would have to charm if she wanted to hold anyone's attention after Jackie walked in the room. After painting on a classic red lipstick and pushing back half of her hair with a rhinestone comb, Caroline pulled on a cropped leather jacket, slipped on a pair of patent leather peep-toe heels, and grabbed her purse on the way out the door.

She arrived half an hour early, as planned, and realized she had severely overdressed like a sexed up Minnie Mouse. From the front door to the bar, she waded through a sea of men in jeans, plaid button-down shirts with cowboy yokes, and the occasional Stray Cats tee. They all gaped at her much like the café's owner, Jarvis, who went wide-eyed at the sight of Caroline and her cleavage.

"If you're angling for your boy to open next Friday night, I'm just about convinced."

"Very funny." Caroline leaned in to kiss his sun-weathered cheek and then peeled off her leather jacket. The additional eighty bodies in the room made it a lot hotter than it had been when she'd stopped by early Tuesday morning. Before that, Caroline hadn't been to the Red Light Café since before Nez had upgraded her from favorite haunts to all the trendiest places. "Looks like a good crowd tonight."

"Yeah, and they won't really start pouring in until halfway through open mic. Sorry, doll," Jarvis said when she winced, "but I already know you didn't exactly come here to build a fan base."

"Jarvis, an opening set on one of your regular nights is worth as much as three months on the open mic circuit. Please. Pleee —"

He put up a hand. "Stop. I already heard this sob story Tuesday morning. I said I'd think about it, and that's only because I know you care about good music, Caroline."

"Just fifteen minutes before the Friday night headliner, or Saturday —"

Jarvis cut her off with a chuckle. "What do you want to drink, woman, before you drive me crazy?"

"Water?" Caroline joked, but she knew that one took shots in Jarvis's company or one went to sit somewhere else.

He let her slide with half an ounce of rum while he downed a whisky, but only "because she looked so fetching," and then he left her alone with a plain Coke on the rocks to wait for Trent. Ten o'clock rolled right into ten minutes to open mic, during which time Caroline had only the tipsy flirtations of a barstool cowboy to distract her from watching the front door. At five minutes to show time, she pulled out her phone and pretended to take a call in order to fend off Mr. Tipsy and Persistent. The hope that Trent would actually call died right at ten thirty when she remembered he didn't have a cell phone.

Open mic had already started when Trent rushed into the Red Light Café. On the stage to his right, a girl in a fluffy pink Sandra Dee dress pumped an accordion while she sang rather sweetly despite the five piercings in her lips. On his left, mostly men filled the two-top tables lining the café's brick walls, and the sight of them looking so shiny and clean in what they thought was country attire temporarily distracted him from searching for Caroline beneath the dimmed house lights. Trent looked good in his new brown pants and pink shirt, but Caroline looked amazing in polka dots at the end of the main bar nearest the stage, and he felt intimidated. Behind her, a drunk man flicked at Caroline's tulle-plumped skirt, and a different color red than her dress stained Trent's vision while he made his way over.

Facing him and not the handsy man behind her, Caroline moved to meet Trent halfway. "You're *late?*"

Disapproval glinted in her eyes, not that he noticed much in the first few seconds besides her crimson lips and the pretty pearl sheen of makeup around her lashes. Then there was her cleavage and the amazing way she smelled to consider.

"Trent?"

"Thirty. I mean, I ain't late; it's ten thirty. Ten thirty-four," Trent stammered after successfully switching his gaze to his watch.

"Yeah, but you missed your mark! I put you on the sign-up sheet as soon as I got here, and then Accordion Girl got bumped up because you weren't here." Shaking her head, Caroline dug in her purse and retrieved her keys. "Go get the Gibson and warm up, okay? Quickly. And please try to stop looking so…petrified."

Without even acknowledging her, Trent spun around and stalked outside, shoring up his resolve not to kiss Caroline along the way. It wasn't like he hadn't gotten laid at least occasionally in the last few months, and it wasn't his place to rip the fingers off Handsy who'd touched her skirt.

"You stupid son of a bitch," Trent cursed himself after he'd unloaded the guitar from the trunk of her car. He was being downright greedy for a man who'd just had the life poured back into him, life that was overflowing into feelings Trent thought he'd lost, restless, uneasy feelings that didn't make much sense. He just had to think about something else, like Ginny and how unhappy she'd be if he fucked this up and had to get the cable cut off again, or Reyes who had insinuated himself into a place in Caroline's life that wouldn't be relinquished without a fight. Trent already had more battles than he could handle.

"Don't be stupid." He popped the hard guitar case off of his thick skull before returning to the club.

On the pretense of warming up, Trent left Caroline at the bar with Jarvis, who had bought them each a shot. Handsy seemed like the sleazy type who only hassled sweet girls who were alone, so Caroline was safe with Jarvis there, and Trent relaxed a little on the stool that he occupied right next to the stage.

He was one more of Accordion Girl's Janis Joplin arrangements away from going on when Caroline's friend strolled in and blew her safety to hell. Trent had only ever seen pictures of Jackie on the desktop of Caroline's computer, and the former model had been beautiful, but not in the sex-on-legs way that she took over the Red Light Café. In person, Jackie was a walking dare with skin and hair the color of candy, and every other woman in the room would have to deal with the injured egos and rabid libidos that her presence wrought. Trent watched Jarvis drag a stool from clear on the other side of the bar for Jackie to sit on between him and Caroline, and he watched the rest of the buzzards close in around the women, including Handsy who took that opportunity to get within perfume-sniffing range of Caroline.

Trent couldn't do anything but stew about that after the MC called him up on stage. Barely a fart's worth of welcoming applause trailed him up the steps, so busy was nearly everyone trying to get another glimpse of Jackie. Trent toted the Gibson past a full band accompaniment that was set up for the headliners, and then he was alone under bright lights both beneath and above him that made it hard to see past the front of the empty, checkered dance floor. Even squinting didn't help him to see the sheet music Caroline had tucked into the guitar case, not that there was a stand for it anyway.

"Shit." The mic amplified his cussing, and the crowd's laughter came dangerously close to heckling.

Annoyed as all hell, he launched into what he could remember of "The Boxer." When Caroline crossed the empty dance floor to stand in front of him, he was pleased to see her until she snapped his picture, rendering him even blinder and ruining his concentrated effort to remember all the lyrics. Caroline's glares also didn't help the way he fumbled, nor did her lips, ruby in the bright light, help him to understand the advice she kept mouthing.

Another almost relieved fart of applause sounded when Trent finished singing. He stepped to the edge of the stage, and finally he could understand what Caroline had been saying.

"Use the sheet music!"

"I can't. I can't see!" Since they both knew that "The Boxer" was the song he'd known best, they were really in a pickle.

Caroline chewed on her juicy bottom lip, further distracting him. "Well, I signed you up for three songs, so play something else!"

"What?"

She threw up her hands. "Anything that you know all the words to! But don't bust out your Keith Urban, *please.*"

Stalling for time, Trent crossed to the bottled water on a small table at the corner of the stage. Three swigs later, he came back to the mic with one of the band's electric Fender Squiers slung in front of him. With one foot, he tried to forge the rhythm for Queen's "Crazy Little Thing Called Love."

Caroline's gasp nearly threw him off the rhythm, but then she slipped out of Trent's line of sight when a gaggle of girls flooded the floor. When he found her red dress again, he was not happy with what he saw through his squinty vision. That handsy man from the bar had followed her to the dance floor. Trent's unhappiness switched to being plain pissed off as he watched Caroline draw closer to the stage in trying to get away from Handsy, if shrinking could really be called 'getting away.' Before long, she stood flush against the stage next to the other girls and was thus captive to Handsy's gyrating dance in the vicinity of her ass, but all Caroline did was cringe.

Pissed gave way to incensed, and red flooded Trent's vision.

Staring up at the stage, Caroline had temporarily forgotten her unwanted admirer while she listened to Trent's creamy voice pouring through the mic. Queen wasn't bluegrass, and the band's Stratocaster wasn't nearly as nice as hers, but the song worked for the venue and won over the crowd, judging from the girls and few couples who got up to dance. Trent put a little more Elvis into his rendition of the song than was really necessary, but the impression helped to cover the hole, the off-something in his style that Caroline had heard on Monday. He looked delicious, but all the smooth crooning in the world couldn't compensate for what sounded like a man with a hole in his heart. For the first time in four days, Caroline moved past merely noticing to actively wondering why the hole was there.

Her musings were interrupted by Tipsy and Persistent.

"You wanna dance, dumplin'?"

Caroline didn't want anything from a man who thought calling her a gravy-covered lump of dough was a compliment. "No! Thank you," she refused with a nervous flash of teeth. He stood so close that she could smell not just his beer breath but his breakfast.

"C'mon! Let's see that skirt twirl." He grabbed her hand.

"I can't. I'm, um, working." She snapped a haphazard picture in Trent's general direction.

Like a record scratch, she heard Trent skip the second refrain after the instrumental interlude. She made a face when he rushed to the end of the song, but she was too busy inching away from Tipsy to say a word. When the crowd broke into applause, Caroline looked up and saw that Trent had abandoned his guitar and was exiting stage right.

Caroline's face fell, as he was still due to play a few more songs. She turned to intercept Trent but ran smack into Tipsy, who took full advantage of the opportunity to grab her.

Ogling her cleavage, Tipsy panted, "You all right?"

"Fine," Caroline said through her teeth and twisted away from one of his hands on her waist; his other hand was still clutching her upper arm. "Excuse me, please."

"Feel free to fall in my arms any time, dumplin'."

"I think what she meant was get your goddamn paws off, *please.*"

Caroline spun toward Trent, who from behind her removed Tipsy's other hand by shoving the man hard in the shoulder. Tipsy staggered.

Her mouth fell open. "Trent, what—"

Tipsy, of course, shoved back, and Caroline, caught between them, got her head clipped in the process, but she'd barely had time to register the jarring sensation before Trent had Tipsy doubled over from a punch in the gut.

"Trent!"

Time moved even faster after that. One second, she had a ringside seat for the first bar brawl she'd ever seen in her life, and the next, Jarvis was literally dragging her across the dance floor and away from a sudden influx of men pooling like platelets around a wound.

"Girl, are you all right!" Jackie asked frantically the second Jarvis deposited Caroline beside her.

"Fine! But what—" She was cut off by the sight of Trent who, with murderous eyes and a big rip down the front of his new mauve shirt, was being jostled and pushed toward the front door. She followed Jarvis's gaze across the room, where a bartender piled ice on a towel for Tipsy's bloody nose and fat lip. They both heard the words *police* and *sue* loud and clear.

"Aw, shit." Jarvis pointed a finger at Caroline while he moved that way. "We'll talk payback later. Right now, get your pit bull off of my property."

"Jarvis—"

"Good night, Caroline," he harshly hollered over his shoulder.

"How? How did this happen!" Caroline shrieked. "Jacks, can you get my guitar? I have to—"

"Go put a leash on your hillbilly?" Jackie's head wagged. "I got it. I'll meet you outside after I pay our tab and try to make sure this guy doesn't press charges."

Caroline didn't remember to say thanks in her haste to get out the front door. She burst through several men who were crowded around the entrance watching one of Jarvis's bouncers physically block Trent from going back into the Red Light Café. The men dispersed after she grabbed Trent and hauled him across the street to her car.

"What is *wrong* with you?" Caroline let go of his hand and smacked it. "Are you out of your mind, coming off stage like that and throwing punches? You didn't even finish your set! Look at your shirt!"

He did, and it was hanging open like a half-buttoned cardigan. Trent yanked it together over his chest with one hand. "You're yelling at me for being chivalrous?"

"Can you even spell 'chivalrous'? Do you know what it means? Because the last time I checked, it does not involve brawling like a Neanderthal!"

His eyebrows shot up. "What was I supposed to do, *let* him grope you? You didn't do anything but stand there and wilt, Caroline."

His drawl didn't sound smart, but *wilt* was an uncomfortably perfect description.

"Carol. Lynn. Caroline," she bit back, suddenly pissed at the sugary way her name dissolved in Trent's mouth. "And you were not supposed to ruin this night and possibly start a lawsuit with your backwoods attitude!"

"Backwoods?" Trent shifted on his feet while his eyes narrowed. "Every time I open my mouth, you expect me to spit out a chaw of tobacco and start whistling fuckin' Dixie, don't ya? Well, you got me. I'm as country as they come, and way out yonder in the big piece of this state that ain't Atlanta, we still hold that you don't grab a woman or stand idly by while someone else does. Pardon me for not knowing that was an antiquated notion. 'Antiquated,' a-n-t-i—"

"Attitude! A-t-t-i-*tude*, which explains why you were wasting away in Bibb 'City,'" she cruelly finger-quoted. "I wondered why your talent hadn't been tapped, and now I guess I know." Her five fingers drew a circle around his worked up expression. "You don't even put half of this into your performances!"

Her breath caught at her tone and animated gestures while she waited for Trent's reply. It was the maddest that Caroline had been since she'd left Nez, and yet it felt good to be in an argument rather than just taking a verbal beating. She straightened up and lifted her chin, ready to pounce on the first thing that the hillbilly said, even if it wasn't fair to him.

Trent kept his mouth shut and stared at her while he pulled the reins on his temper. Since they'd met, he'd put her in more than one kind of distress, and he'd been raised better than to treat a woman like that. There was a saying about bottling things up that Trent should have paid attention to months ago when he'd apparently started doing it. He hadn't lost his feelings; he'd just compressed them, and Caroline Curran had been the right kind of occasion to pop that cork. That didn't exactly explain why he'd just busted a man's face, but Trent didn't want to be jealous or do something really stupid like fall for her. He spat a laugh.

"You're *laughing?*"

He tried to sober up, but she looked so adorably appalled that his effort only produced a genuine chuckle. Caroline's eyes crossed, and that made him really crack up.

"Fine!" she said. "Laugh at me. It's fine."

"Not at you, with you. Caroline, wait," Trent called, but she was in her car before he could straighten his face, and she shot off with a squeal of tires and an angry flash of taillights.

"Good work."

Trent turned to the slow applause coming from across the street and from Jackie's hands. She smirked at him before picking up Caroline's guitar and jacket, and she cut across the traffic-free one-way street to smirk at him again.

"I'm actually surprised that you managed to wait until the song was over to jump the guy." Jackie looked him up and down and frowned. "I bet Jarvis ten bucks that you were going to pull a Superman after the first verse of your serenade."

"It wasn't a serenade," Trent protested in the same way Caroline constantly claimed that Reyes wasn't her boyfriend.

"Right. And I'm sure when I give you this stuff, you won't jump at the chance to follow her home." Jackie shoved the guitar at him.

Trent tried to laugh that off but ended up just coughing. "I was already planning to go after her, to apologize."

"You better." Jackie draped Caroline's jacket over his shoulder and strolled back to the bar.

It was after midnight when Trent finally got to Caroline's place. He stood on her porch for a while, thinking about what he'd said earlier and what he *hadn't* said about his ulterior jealous motives, motives that put a crimp in his desire to actually step inside her house, with her in that red dress. After beating up Handsy, Trent's hands itched to claim her like a prize. He'd be better off sorting out what he wanted to say before the door opened. When it did, Caroline's gaze switched from angry to startled at the sight of his shirt, as though she hadn't noticed it before.

"Two things." Trent kept her guitar for leverage in case she wouldn't hear him out. "First, I'm sorry. Really," he added when she didn't react at all. "I'm sorry, Caroline."

"Carol. Lynn."

Trent grinned. Her correction of his pronunciation didn't pack the same punch as usual, probably because she was staring at his chest. "I said I was sorry."

"Uh, sorry. Right. Well, you should be."

"You should be, too, which brings me to the second thing." Trent cleared his throat. "You cracked on me being country about five different ways, and I think maybe you ought to go on and get it out of your system so we can clear that out of our working relationship."

"What?"

"Oh, c'mon, Caroline. I mean, I'm sorry if I ruffled Jarvis's feathers, but you're not gonna let one ruined open mic night throw a wrench in the works, are you?" He tried not to sound as worried as he felt about that. "I promise not to go off like that again, all right?"

"How do I know that? I can practically see an L for 'loose cannon' emblazoned on your chest because you're ripped." She licked her lips, then clapped a hand to her mouth. "I mean, your shirt is ripped."

She was blushing so much that he risked asking, "Would it get me out of the doghouse if I take it off?"

Caroline shaded her eyes with her hands and shook her head. "No! Because I saw your hands on Monday, you know. I had halfway convinced myself that you'd busted them up shucking corn before this happened."

"And that's exactly what I'm talking about. 'Shucking corn,'" Trent quoted, deftly changing the subject away from how he'd really busted his knuckles. "If you're gonna talk shit about me being from Bibb City, it's gonna be a long however-long you spend being my boss. I might even have to sue you for harassment," Trent joked, not of the kind he would have preferred, but he'd successfully terrified Caroline just the same. Her pretty mouth fell open. "So I think you ought to go on and spit it out, all the different ways that you want to call me a redneck. Go on, have at it. Call me a redneck. A yokel. Hick. Hillbilly. Clodhopper. Country bumpkin. Cracker—"

"Okay! You've made your extremely uncomfortable point. I'm sorry too."

"I got a lot of things to be ashamed of, Caroline, but being from the red dirt side of Georgia ain't one of them. You, more than most, ought to know what it's like to get dealt a difficult hand. What can I do but mind the way that I play it? Call me a Neanderthal if you want, but..." He faltered over an odd shift in her expression; she looked through him while her mind seemed to be somewhere else. "But, uh, don't equate that with being from the country. Are you listening to me, Caroline?"

"Yes! But could you say that again?"

"Caroline?"

"Before that."

Sparkling and intense, her eyes glowed garnet in the bright porch light, and Trent's mind ran amuck with reasons why she was staring at him with fever in her eyes.

"Neanderthal? You need me to spell it? N-e—"

"No, not that. Shh!" Her hand fluttered in front of his mouth and nearly touched his lips. "Dang it! What did you say?"

Her fingertips smelled like vanilla soap or lotion or something, and Lord above, he almost slipped and called her Sugar. "S-say what?"

"Oh! Now it's going to worry me all night." Caroline turned heel and ran to her piano.

Trent remained on the porch to keep curiosity and arousal from getting the best of him. Through the open front door, he saw her bend over the piano bench. Her skirt inched up in the back, revealing the lace band of a thigh high stocking that had slipped down. He had to go into her house then. That lace was calling his name.

He toted her guitar to the fireplace and held her jacket while Caroline stood silent, eyes shut and arms folded. One finger tapped a familiar hole in her skull, and one hand clutched a notepad and pencil that she had pulled from the piano bench.

"Ca—"

"Shh. I'm trying to remember. I heard it."

"What?"

"Shush! Just go to sleep thinking about what you said, in case I don't remember myself."

Trent watched Caroline thump her head with the notepad instead of her finger. She crossed the room to a low brown couch on which sat a pillow and blanket that he hadn't noticed before. "You knew I was coming?"

"Jackie called. There's no point in you driving three hours home when you'll just have to turn around and be back in the morning for Marlon and Wendy. Minerva. Ugh, whatever, and now I totally lost it."

She stomped into her bedroom and shut the door, leaving Trent itching with enough curiosity to kill ten cats.

Chapter Six

Roofing generally required that a man get up before dawn, so startling awake in the dark on Friday morning temporarily convinced Trent that he was late for work and had only been dreaming the past week with Caroline. After he'd oriented himself to the reality of the strange surroundings and her short but cushy suede couch, he dragged his tired self to the bathroom, closed the door, and snapped on the light.

Five days of fun hadn't much lightened the luggage under his eyes, though they were bright at least and bluish from his hair color. He hadn't put on any weight either, but he'd always been lean and mean except in the face, which, despite the improvements, Trent still didn't quite recognize as his own. The last time he'd really known himself had been before the accident, and the joker he'd been back then wasn't much to miss, always out of town on construction jobs and always phoning it in when it came to caring about the women in his life — except for Ginny, who had the soft spot in his heart. He feared that Caroline's influence would make him too soft before he faced the wrath of Courtney Vickers's boys.

He took a piss, washed up, left the bathroom, and paused outside of Caroline's door out of curiosity about whether she really did have a snore like a hog call or if he'd just imagined that. Disappointed not to hear a peep, Trent cut back into the living room and caught sight of a dull light coming from the kitchen.

He found Caroline perched on a step stool in front of the white-tiled island and her keyboard. Molasses hair pulled back into a little pug of a ponytail, she wore headphones, a worn out *Purple Rain* T-shirt, and, God willing, nothing but panties if the bareness of her gymnast-thick legs was any evidence.

Caroline caught him at the tail end of a good hard stare.

"Ooh!" Startled, she clutched her hammering heart. She'd been too deep in the trumpet samples on her keyboard to hear Trent coming, and then suddenly there he was, wide-awake and without a shirt. "Sorry, I was trying not to wake you."

"You didn't. I'm used to popping up about five-something, is all."

Caroline glanced at the microwave display and, sure enough, it was a quarter after. She hesitated to turn back to Trent who still had nothing covering his sinewy body down to the sagging waistband of his slept-in moleskin pants.

"I was just working. On a song. I couldn't sleep trying to remember what you said," she explained to his almost too-taut pectorals, and she quickly raised her gaze.

"Well, please tell me what it was. It was on my mind too. All night." He winked at her.

"Um, I don't remember verbatim." Her hands fumbled for the notepad on which she'd tentatively begun some lyrics. "But it incubated while I was falling asleep and ended up being, 'It isn't the hand that you're dealt; it's the way that you play it.' A chorus opening, I think? Because I've got this too." Her fingers went to the keys with smooth certainty, but then she snatched them away to yank out the headphone plug. "Actually, are you *awake* or just passing through? Because I can't quite get this timing nailed down, and the Kawai helps keep my meter natural."

Trent put his hands up and gestured toward the living room. "Please, don't let me keep you." He picked up the keyboard after Caroline stood.

Up close, with his hair a wild russet mess and barely a trace of stubble around his pink cheeks and lips, Trent looked like he'd just had a good long roll in the hay.

"Thanks." Caroline tried not to envy that imaginary hay. He followed her to the piano and put her keyboard in its usual place while she arranged what she had of the song, music partially composed in pencil on fresh white sheets and lyrics in scrawled pieces on her pad. "I'm hearing an organ and interspersed horns keeping the rhythm with a bass guitar, but here's the basic chorus."

She tapped out a melody that was mostly eighth notes and quick progressions down partial chords, but when she sang the lyrics, what had sounded basic took on shades of calling out the gospel.

"'It isn't the hand that you're dealt; it's the way that you play it,' and then something." Caroline repeated the melody. "'I know you've got a love game' — " She kept playing, but stopped singing, shaking her head. "And wow, that already sounds like crap. I picked the wrong meter."

"I don't know about that." Trent grabbed her notepad and eased down beside her. "Yeah, see, I heard this hitch right here, at 'It isn't.' *Ain't.* 'It ain't the hand.' Try one syllable."

Intrigued, Caroline said, "Sing it out."

She played the melody, and Trent launched into the chorus, "'It ain't the hand that you're dealt; it's the way that you play it. It ain't' — what?"

"Skip that," Caroline said to his finger pointing at words she'd crossed out.

Trent nodded and waited for the melody to swing back around. "'I know you've got a love game…that you say is your favorite'?" Caroline positively glowed at him and handed over her pencil. He shrugged while he wrote down his suggestion. "It rhymes, kind of."

"And then something punchy." She improvised a saucy but foreshortened next measure and glanced at Trent. His lips pursed in thought, and, to help him, Caroline flipped back three pages in her pad. "Let's start over from the first verse, but can you turn on the keyboard and press F2?"

He seemed to dance to the keyboard to fire it up, then Trent sat back down so close to Caroline that she could feel the warmth of his leg through the fabric of his pants, and not just on the outside of her thigh either. Like the rest of his body, his thigh was rock hard, making her feel gooey for all the right reasons.

Caroline cleared her throat and focused on playing.

Her synthesized organs and horns hit hard on the first beat of each measure, and Trent had a good two bars to get into the brass balls of the tone:

Quiet girl, sitting over there,
Won't you let down your hair on my shoulder?
Tell me why, somewhere behind your eyes,
I can see the flames but I don't feel the fire?

"'Tell me who told you…'" Trent bellowed, then skipped some strike-outs before ending with, "'…dance?'" There was another chicken-scratched void for two lines, and then:

… look at me and smile, because
it isn't ain't the hand that you're dealt;
it's the way that you play it.
~~You more than most~~
It ~~isn't difficult~~ ain't ~~much~~ too late?
I know you've got a love game
that you say is your favorite
PUNCH!!!

That was all she had of lyrics, though of music there was almost an entire song waiting to have a life poured into it, just like she'd done to him. A mystified smile crept into Trent's lips while he looked at Caroline. True excitement looked a lot prettier on her than the glassy-eyed high of wine.

"I don't know what I said to get this out of you, but…" He really didn't have the words and hoped that his smile would suffice.

"You said almost exactly that except — Oh! I hope you don't think I'm stealing! I already co-signed you just for that phrase." Caroline flipped to the first page of her sheet music where, underneath the song title "The Way That You Play It," she'd written, "By C. Curran and T.M. Buckney" — not Michaels, but his real last name.

Trent was out of both words and air for a few seconds. "You don't have to do that."

"Yes, I do. Unlike some people I might mention, I respect an artist's rights. And it's your song, in a way. Yeah! It's your *way.*"

"My way is like a quiet girl?" Trent joked of the song's opening lyrics.

"No. I mean the way you sing it. The song makes so much more sense to me now, coming out of your mouth." She blushed and looked away, then looked at him again. "And what a fine mouth it is, smiling at me so openly! I wish you would more often. It looks good on you."

She nudged his shoulder with her own, clearly trying to put a chummy spin on what had almost been a provocative moment. Trent bit his lip, restraining the urge to kiss her.

"Plus, you know, this gives you an official employee title: Co-Songwriter."

"That's a title a man can be proud of." He tried just to grin and stay within the boundaries of friendship, but warmth stretched his lips into a smile that seemed to dazzle Caroline. When he nudged her thigh with his own, she nudged back. He nudged again, and they were practically rubbing against each other. "I love it."

"Well, I loved that Tom Jones thing you did with 'let your hair down on my shoulder.' I mean, you sound great when you're…trying. Interested."

"You've definitely got me interested, Caroline Curran."

For the first time in four days, Caroline not only liked the way her name sounded in his mouth but wondered how his tongue would feel dissolving her like a sugar cube too. As Trent sat there on the piano bench in the dim light, his pupils were dilated, and the shifting hues of his aqua irises glittered like a brass ring offering promises she had but to reach out and grab.

Trent said something that Caroline didn't understand at first, focused as she was on willing him to kiss her.

"Hmm?"

"Do you mind if I use your shower? And your phone."

Willing, like wilting, was a stupid enterprise.

"Sure." Caroline snatched her gaze away from his. Embarrassment stained her cheeks. "There are towels in, uh…the thing, the wicker thing in the spare room."

"Thanks."

He hesitated, and hope ballooned in the pit of her stomach again, but nothing came of it after he stood up from the piano bench.

His pants were still sagging a little low, exposing two deep dimples where his lean back ended and an ass deserving better than being sat on began, and Caroline craned a crick into her neck watching it go. A man with such a pretty face had no business with a body hard enough to do so many different kinds of damage.

After checking in with Ginny, washing his urges down the shower drain, and putting yesterday's t-shirt between him and Caroline, Trent settled in for a strained day of trying not to snog his boss. Though they both carried on like the piano bench moment hadn't happened, it was clear from the way Caroline reduced her eye contact that he'd bothered her, and yet none of that helped his plight since she didn't stop being sweet. Just making him breakfast put her in peril of a good necking, and then she had to go shower, change, and come out smelling like something that ought to be licked off her belly.

When proposed band mates Marlon and Minerva turned up, Caroline touched Trent's arm and lied very nicely to them about how well he'd sung at the Red Light Café. Trent had to stick his hands in his pockets to keep them from straying toward her lower back.

All the way through an encore of Queen with Marlon on bass guitar and Minerva doing what she could with the snare and hi-hat from the spare room, Caroline smiled at Trent, and she whispered that if Marlon phoned Kyle the Twelve-String Wonder (which he did), that meant Trent was *in*. He could have kissed her just for making the effort after the way he'd ruined things the night before. She deserved a sound smooching for not giving him any more lip about it despite taking at least two calls from Jarvis and one from Jackie before turning off her ringer.

Trent hadn't been that gracious when Margie and Ginny had sunk his life; he'd shown them the true meaning of resentment before he'd shut down completely, and it figured that a lesson in regret would be the first of his newly opened state.

By lunchtime, Caroline was happy to send Trent on a food run with vegetarian Marlon and Minerva. While they'd spent the morning waiting for Kyle, she'd noticed that Trent had avoided her piano bench and stiffened whenever she came near. Caroline wasn't good at confrontation, and ignoring his withdrawal had been hard ever since apparently *not* wanting to kiss her had turned Trent back into Stiff Lips McStonyface.

Dragging her feet to her bedroom and her nail polish box (at the bottom of which she'd hidden her phone after Jarvis's angry calls and Nez's last unpleasant text message), Caroline dismally reminded herself that Trent was well within his rights not to like her *that* way. One man's dislike did not mean that being short, stumpy, and thirty-one condemned her to a life of reaching even for men who were beneath her league. It did not mean, as Nez had said, that she'd been lucky to have his cheating-behind. She did not have to wilt, charm, or appease her way into a man's good graces just because she wasn't Jackie.

"I am an extortionist," Caroline told her bedroom mirror before remembering she was failing even at that.

There were four voice messages from Nez on her phone, demanding his first tape, the corrected invoice, half of the tapes before he would pay "one red cent" of the next five grand that she'd requested, and, finally, a four-exclamation-point text ordering her to check her "damn" email. Calling him back to prove her prowess proved a bad idea.

"Just because you want to pay twenty-six grand doesn't mean that's what you owe me, Nez!" In fact, his willingness to settle on that sum hinted at how much more he could really afford.

"Just because you want more doesn't mean you're gonna get it! You think I don't know why you won't settle something on an invoice? Do you really think I'm gonna let you milk me dry until you get tired of it and then send my tapes to the press anyway? Don't make me get ugly, C.C."

Caroline gasped. She'd never had any intention of sending Nez to jail over a girl who obviously wanted his boorish behind. "What does that mean?"

"If you don't want to find out, send me half my tapes and you'll get half your money, ten grand first thing Monday morning."

"I did not agree that ten grand was half!"

"Then what, bitch? What the fuck do you think I owe you? Spit it out!"

Caroline never used to tolerate that kind of talk, and her throat burned to realize Nez had lost his last shred of care for her. It was aching and unfair that he'd moved on so easily when she'd been wronged, and having that wrong made right was what she waited for.

Primly, Caroline replied, "Nez, you owe me an apology," a deep and sincere remorse that didn't have a dollar value.

"Yeah. Right. How much do you want, C.C.?"

"I want it to hurt you. How much is that going to take?"

"Like I ain't hurt already? Milan's been busting my balls about those tapes! She'll kill me if I don't get every last—"

"You're doing this for *her?*" Caroline's shriek was so piercing it broke her voice. Hoarsely, she continued, "You *want* this filth back?"

"Nasty don't make it wrong, if you know how to enjoy yourself. Not every woman is a goddamn Puritan! Some of them don't play frigid to get attention—"

A toilet flush cut him off.

"You hear that? It's the sound of your filth disappearing down the drain in a waterproof case. Hope it doesn't end up in the wrong hands."

While she waited for him to react, Caroline threw another of his memory sticks into the toilet and then another. Lightweight and buoyant in clear plastic, they only floated when she flushed the toilet again over Nez's yelling. She listened to his insults for a long time, mostly to get into her head the sound of the kind of man he'd become or perhaps had been all along underneath the patronizing way he used to treat her. She'd been so insecure about her talent that she'd let his attempts to toughen and teach her slide into browbeating. Caroline was ashamed to realize that she'd waited until she'd been cornered to fight back, instead of standing up for herself.

"I'll take your ten grand on Monday, and then we'll renegotiate when you remember who has the upper hand!"

He screamed back, and she threw his voice in the toilet to drown since he'd bought that cell phone for her. Flushing still accomplished nothing, so Caroline piled some toilet tissue on top of the gadgets and tried again. When the toilet clogged, she was crying too hard to care.

Though she'd declined, Trent still brought Caroline a chicken salad back from the deli where he'd eaten with Marlon, Minerva, and Kyle, who'd joined them toward the end of lunch. After the three of them lit up cigarettes on the porch, Trent went in to take the salad to the kitchen, where the sound of the bathroom door abruptly slamming shut distracted him.

"Caroline?"

"Just a minute," she hollered over the toilet flushing.

There were four more flushes back to back between Trent stowing the salad and returning to the living room, an occurrence partially explained by the bathroom door flying open and a squealing Caroline sprinting out wearing rubber gloves and holding a purple plunger.

"*Ew*, ew, it's on my feet, *gross,*" she chanted hoarsely and did a barefoot sliding dance across the carpet.

Trent tried to speak, but couldn't help cracking up. He eventually chortled, "You need some help?"

"Yes," she croaked and kept rubbing what he assumed was toilet water off the bottoms of her feet.

"Uh, is this a number one or a number two situation?"

"No! I mean, no, I'll call a plumber."

"I can fix it. Not with this." Trent took her purple plunger, which looked like a sex toy. "But I'm sure it won't take a minute. No need for you to spend—"

"No. Really."

"—or be embarrassed about—"

"No! I'm sure if I just let it, uh, settle for a while, it'll be all right."

Her insistence made Trent suspicious. He cocked his head ever so slightly, and glanced at the bathroom out of the corner of his eye.

"Really!" She took back her plunger and retreated toward the bathroom.

Fate loved to crucify a liar. Trent was about to inquire, but Kyle burst in the door fresh from his cigarette break and almost breezed right by Caroline. "Just gonna use the john."

"No!" She cut in front of Kyle. "It's broken."

"Badly?" Kyle's scrawny legs shifted in his skin-tight black jeans. "Because I can't really cut around back of the house on this one."

Trent raised a brow. "Yeah, how bad is it, Caroline?"

She ignored him.

"Sheila! My neighbor. You can go over there. I'm sure she'll let you. I'll call."

Trent watched her pat her pocket for her cell phone and then glance at the bathroom. When their eyes met, he had a pretty good idea of what was stuck in the toilet.

Caroline asked Kyle, "Can I use your phone?"

Kyle looked pained and pranced again. "It's in my car."

She blew out a breath. "Fine. I'll just walk you over." When Trent stuck out his hand for the plunger, she rolled her eyes and handed it over.

"Don't laugh at me," Caroline muttered as she passed by him.

"*With* you," he called after her, but she didn't look back from leading Kyle to the front door.

Trent made short work of recovering her cell phone and several memory sticks from the toilet. Unlike her ruined phone, the sticks were still safe and sound inside their plastic cases. Trent was so tempted to stick one in her computer that he carried the lot to the kitchen and stuck it in a zipper storage bag. His burning curiosity almost got the better of him before Caroline returned with Kyle twenty whole minutes later.

Trent waited for Kyle to saunter off into the living room, then held the bag up to the light and squinted at the items inside. "Evidence found at the scene suggests —"

Caroline snatched the bag. "Just shut up."

"Marlon and Minerva went to get me an auger and pick up her drum kit." He tipped his head toward her bag. "How many of those suckers did you chuck in there? 'Cause if that's what's stuck in your S trap, I can't get them back without tearing out the toilet."

"Don't bother. They're trash." Caroline carried the bag to the microwave. She slung the bag inside and hit the Popcorn setting.

Trent pressed the Cancel button. "There's metal inside that plastic. You don't want to fry your microwave, do you?"

"Who cares? I took it from *him* anyway," Caroline muttered and hit the Popcorn button again.

Trent jabbed Cancel, unplugged the microwave, and pushed it across the counter. His fingers rubbed thoughtfully across his lips while he studied Caroline's swollen eyelids and sticky lashes. "Would this be the same 'him' that you were hollering at on Monday?"

Her eyes crossed while she emitted a buzz as loud as a saber saw. "His name's Nez. He cheated on me."

"With Milan Taylor?"

Caroline's head jerked an affirmative. "And recorded it for posterity!" She snatched the bag and flung it across the room. "It was like a car wreck in slow motion. I saw it coming, but I just sat there and wilted, just like you said. Literally wilted on the floor at Jackie's house, when I was inhaling bacon cheese fries and beer, and I saw Nez and Milan walking the American Music Awards red carpet on tv. I stayed on that floor for *four days.*" She let out a weary sigh. "Why was I so weak?" Caroline shrugged and scrubbed tears from her eyes. "Wow, it's really lame that I'm telling you this. Again. I'm sorry."

"Don't you dare apologize to me." Trent walked out of the kitchen and then out of the house to his truck. He couldn't stand the sight of her pretty brown eyes filled with tears; it reminded him too much of his sister. When he returned to the kitchen, he held out a hammer to Caroline, handle first.

"Kyle's on the porch getting high, and Marlon and Drummer Girl won't be back for a good fifteen minutes, so I think you ought to bust those suckers into tiny little pieces." That was a better solution than him getting Nez's address and going over to bust the fucker's face into pieces. Trent ignored his itching palms. "Just don't start crying again, or I'll have to come in here. Don't hit your thumb either."

Trent gave her the hammer and left instead of wrapping his arms around her. His hands could not be trusted under the circumstances.

Two hours later, a silent and puffy-eyed Caroline was curled up in the corner of the couch and staring off into space while Trent and the gang cranked out one blues cover after another. He'd fixed the toilet while Minerva had set up her drum kit and Kyle, despite being a pothead, had demonstrated his magic touch on anything with strings. Marlon, shorter than Minerva and sporting braids, one gold tooth, a tuxedo jacket, jean shorts, and red velour house shoes, brought some business sense to their session and made lists of songs that would go over well at clubs where he and Minerva were known. Every so often during the jam session, Caroline scrambled off the couch and ran to her bedroom, then came back looking more puffy-eyed than before. Finally, she left and didn't come back for a half-hour, prompting Trent to break off from playing to go knock on her bedroom door.

"I think she fell asleep," he reported back to the group.

"Don't worry. We've seen this before." Minerva shook her blue dreadlocks. "Fuck Nez! I knew his ass was evil. You see how he made her jump the white picket fence." She looked Trent up and down even though her skin, tattooed up both arms and across the neck, was just a suntan darker than his.

"Hey," Marlon sang in his funny Smokey Robinson tenor, "if C.C. don't talk about the brother, we don't talk about the brother."

"Nez ain't my brother, and for that matter, I ain't letting him claim Black no more either. He's nothing but a blot on the butt of manhood!"

Marlon sighed and turned to Trent. "We gon' get up outta here before my girl starts grilling you, dude. Holla at ya tomorrow, I guess. It's been real." Real *what* he didn't say, but Trent took Marlon's offered handshake for a compliment and assumed the same when Kyle repeated the gesture before following his friends out the door.

Though he was at best a guest, and not Caroline's boyfriend as he'd let Minerva believe, Trent wasn't comfortable leaving Caroline to wake up in the dark, disoriented and without any way of calling to find out where they had all gone. At least that was what he told himself when he went to her couch and sat down. Getting up and going to her piano bench was another, stickier choice, having something to do with loving the way his name looked on her sheet music and being sure that the second he stepped out the front door, the joker he'd been before would jump back in his body and drive his ass a year into the past.

Since he didn't play the piano, Trent grabbed her Seagull acoustic and picked out enough of the notes to get the gist of things. Half an hour later, he had Caroline's melody committed to memory, but it took him hours to repeat the little bit of success he'd had earlier with some of the lyrics. By six o'clock, his legs, folded tailor-style across the floor on which he'd sunk, had all but fallen asleep, and it took Trent three tries to get up and answer the doorbell.

It was Reyes A. Bardem, whose smug mug was actually a relief compared to the snarling ex-boyfriend face Trent had been halfway hoping to see all afternoon. Choosing to forego a greeting as they had the last time, the two men passed several silent seconds sizing each other up. Reyes looked dapper as usual in an expensive second-skin leather jacket, and he didn't seem interested in Trent's improved appearance. He switched a hand containing an exotic bouquet out from behind his back to check the time.

"Aw, you shouldn't have," Trent couldn't help but joke.

Reyes's voice matched the cool briskness of his demeanor. "Caroline's expecting me."

"Well, I'll go get her." Trent gleefully shut the door in Reyes's face and went to Caroline's bedroom. He knocked and then pounded, but she didn't answer. Finally, he turned the knob and called out, "Caroline," in a warning tone as he opened the door.

She was curled up in a ball on top of a plum quilt. A pillow as big as her body covered her head and left her legs, stripped of their denim skirt, as bare as they'd been that morning but for a pair of knee-high socks featuring Animal from *The Muppets*.

"Caroline." She didn't stir, and Trent's reluctance to move further into her room gave way to necessity and an itching curiosity about her private life.

As with the den and the kitchen, Caroline's room featured no furniture except a bed, a big mirror, and a floor lamp with a pink glass shade. Mirrored doors were slid away from a long closet on the left wall, behind which heaps of clothes, shoes, and plastic storage bins spilled over onto the beige carpet, but there were still no pictures or trinkets or half-empty boxes of cheese crackers, all the little things that made a room belong to someone.

"Caroline?" Lips twisted, Trent pried the pillow off her head. Beneath the mussed and tumbled locks of shiny hair covering her ears, she had foam plugs deeply inserted. Whether they were to block out the band's playing earlier or her own snoring, he wasn't sure, but he had definitely heard one or two hog calls in the quiet hours since the band had left. Trent shook her shoulder, and, as expected, she startled awake.

"Ooh!" Caroline backed away from Trent and into the wall above her bed where there was no headboard. She yanked her flailing legs up and into the confines of her *Purple Rain* T-shirt. "Uh…what—"

"You have company." When her still-sleepy eyes cast around the bedroom for other uninvited guests, he amusedly explained, "At the door." Caroline's eyes abruptly went wide. "It's only Bardem. But I think he might be here to take you out, unless he always shows up with flowers and a chauffeured town car."

Her hands clapped over her face. "Oh my God, I forgot! Oh my God." She launched herself across the bed past Trent, and hit the floor at a dead run toward the closet. "Tell him I just need a minute. Twenty! Twenty minutes. And can you please do me a favor and throw this—wait, no. Ugh, no…"

The rear view of Caroline in knee socks and a T-shirt distracted Trent for a long time from the double-fisted dig through the closet she was doing at warp speed. Shiny slips of silk and bright gossamer skirts kept falling over her shoulder and cutting across what looked like a juicy sliver of Caroline's plum behind. When, finally, with a loud "A-ha" she had settled on a plain pewter-blue wrap dress, he spent a minute wondering why all of the rejected clothes on the floor looked a hell of a lot more revealing, flimsy, and expensive than that one.

"Can you throw this in the clothes dryer for me? On low, just to knock the wrinkles out," Caroline clarified and pressed the cool, slick fabric into his hands. "Pretty please with whipped cream and a cherry on top?"

Trent had no business thinking, much less asking, on top of *what*. "Sure thing."

"Twenty minutes," she hollered, grabbed a clear cosmetics bag, and sprinted to the bathroom.

Though he would have loved to do otherwise, Trent let Reyes in after explaining the delay. A little too obviously well-bred, Reyes didn't show any more than the previous briskness when he came in and trailed Trent to the kitchen. After stuffing the dress in the dryer and wondering how long exactly he was supposed to leave it in there, Trent emerged from the pantry to find Reyes arranging Caroline's bouquet in a tall glass vase.

"What happened there?" Reyes asked of the hammer and thrashed gadget bits piled on top of a wooden cutting board.

"Uh…spring cleaning."

"Is that her cell phone?" Reyes's black eyebrows twisted with incredulity.

"What's left of it."

"What happened?"

"I—" A door opening and then another slamming shut cut Trent off. "I couldn't say." He retrieved Caroline's dress and escaped to the bedroom. He found Caroline in a sleek black slip that clung to her curves, with heated rollers in her hair and a ton of black makeup around her eyes. He must've winced because she crossed her eyes.

"Is it too much? I was going for a smoky eye to cover the puffiness." She unraveled a roller with one hand and put in earrings with the other. "I look like a raccoon or a whore, don't I?"

"Nah, it's…kind of…" *Dramatic*, which she was, but also dark and daring, which she wasn't, especially in her pewter blue dress after she'd slipped it on. Except for the Cleopatra eyes, Caroline looked simple and pretty, like a teacher on the first day of school or a new girlfriend at her beau's family Thanksgiving dinner. If she thought that looking sweet was going to dissuade not-her-boyfriend's libido, she was dead wrong. With her eyes like that, all Trent could think about her dress was getting it off. "Yeah, it might be a little too much."

Caroline moved to the floor-length mirror and grabbed a tissue and a small bottle of lotion. "But I don't want to look puffy!"

"Don't worry about it."

Trent was all right with puffy if it would keep Reyes securely in sympathy mode.

After Caroline was dressed in pewter sling-backs and a dove-gray trench coat that she tied closed over her dress, she turned to Trent and smiled. He had waited patiently through the whole process, just to keep her company.

"Thanks," she said. "And I'm sorry about everything today."

"Don't be. I'm not."

"Yeah, but—"

"Please don't apologize for letting me know you better. It might hurt my feelings." He grinned, and she laughed. "And as far as I can recall, you ain't backed down from me once, so you're not weak. You're just hurt."

Caroline beamed at him. "Thanks."

"Anytime."

"Will you be coming in the morning?"

"If you make me, boss lady." He winked at her.

Perhaps because she'd been dreaming of him when he woke her up, everything he said hinted at the sex they'd had in her fantasy. Caroline laughed at herself, and rolled her eyes. "Well, I promised, so."

She tipped her head toward the door Reyes was waiting behind and wondered why her feet didn't start moving, wondered what she was waiting for more than a "Goodbye" or a "See you later." Then, of course, Caroline remembered. She hadn't just dreamed of illicit kisses; she'd nearly asked for one on her piano bench, and ever since it hadn't materialized, she'd been running around half-dressed and hideous in front of Trent who didn't like her *that* way.

"Okay!" she at last said. "Bye."

All the way to the city in Reyes's town car and beneath the soothing drone of his velvet voice, Caroline wondered why she was on a date when she'd wanted to stay at home. She had needed friends after her break-up, but she didn't need a faux boyfriend. She turned to Reyes who had given up trying to talk to her a while back and simply had his arm draped across the seat behind her head. A few of his fingers idly toyed with her hair in a soothing gesture.

"What are you thinking about?" she asked.

"Your boy. He cleaned up rather nicer than I would have thought on Monday."

Caroline laughed. "Yeah, it's hard to see past the hill—" She cut off *billy* and substituted, "harsh exterior at first."

Reyes, who noticed everything, pinned her with his gaze. "You don't think his behavior at the club last night was that of a hillbilly?"

Caroline gaped at him. "How did you know about that?"

"Some people enjoy telling me their secrets," Reyes prompted, presumably for her to explain the mess that she'd left in the kitchen, but she didn't. His fingers moved to brush back her bangs and continued down her temple and under her eye to the evidence of her crying. "You were to call me if he upset you in the least, *querida.*"

In the darkness of the car, Reyes's blue eyes were as midnight as the sleek raven hair framing his face. He constantly tried to reel her in with his intensity, and before Nez, she might have found Reyes magnetic. She used to fantasize about the attentions of powerful men like him before, but in the aftermath of her ex, Caroline was shy of affection that came as an undeserved and lavish gift so easily given and surely just as easily taken away.

She turned her face from Reyes's touch. "He didn't upset me. Nez did."

"Would you like me to send a mohel to Nez's next grooming appointment?"

Caroline faked a laugh at his circumcision joke and kept her eyes trained on the window. Sometimes she was sure that the grace with which Reyes retreated when pushed away was the reason why she never outright told him no. Most of the time, though, she knew she was both selfish and a coward.

"Or perhaps it's time to engage a better kind of revenge," Reyes said. "A successful career, for instance."

An envelope brushed the back of Caroline's hand. She glanced at Reyes, who encouraged her to open it with a smile, and she took it. Inside was a printout from the "Tales from the Moshpit" section of the *Atlanta Music Guide*, an online periodical of all things pertaining to the city's music scene.

"It's just a mock-up," Reyes said of the short story about Trent's brawl at the Red Light Café. "But I figured a little press with a carefree spin, let's say, would make your first foray not an entirely wasted evening."

Somehow the article even quoted Jarvis as saying Trent "was an energetic and brassy new voice in the blues revival movement." Caroline kissed Reyes's cheek for the effort, and besides being silky smooth, his skin smelled downright sinful.

"If I had a photo, could you get it in?"

"Perhaps. If I had a weekend free sometime next month, would you spend it with me?"

Caroline declined with a silent stare. Dropping eye contact was her preferred means of making him back off, but doing so would have felt immature now that she was aware of wilting.

Reyes grabbed her hand and kissed it. "I'll see what I can do," he said.

He didn't hide his disappointment, but Caroline reacted with an elaborate display of gratitude that, probably because she held his hand, Reyes allowed through the ride to the city and all during the dinner they shared at City Grill. In their private room of the restaurant's gorgeously restored 1912 downtown building space, Reyes was cordial and attentive as always, but he did not press her to go out for drinks at the end of dinner like he usually did, a change that didn't raise an alarm until they'd returned to her house and were standing on the porch.

"Can I come in? *The Colbert Report* is about to come on."

Caroline's eyebrow twitched. Much as she knew that he liked that show, Reyes never mentioned TV at her house unless he was looking for a reason not to go home. "Umm, no thanks. I'm tired." She faked a yawn. "Didn't get much sleep last night."

Caroline caught the slight shift in Reyes's posture from elegantly upright to rigid. "Up late on a school night again, were we?"

Caroline ignored that. "I was working on a song."

"I'd love to hear it. Or maybe we can watch a movie."

"Maybe later." He wasn't being very subtle in his desire to get in her house, and specifically in her bedroom, where the TV was, which only made sense if he was on the lookout for something like Trent or evidence of the same having slept over last night. "I really have to get to bed. Good night, Rey—" He cut her off with a kiss that came and went quickly, probably because Caroline's eyes were wide open and her lips stiff with surprise. "Umm—"

"*Discúlpame.*"

"No! I, uh—"

"You're not ready; I can see that. Forgive me, *querida.*" He kissed her again on the forehead, then backed away toward the town car with a little smirk playing across his lips.

Caroline retreated into the house, shut the door, shucked off her heels, and walked to the kitchen for a glass of water before she realized that Reyes had just assessed her lack of a sex life. His smirk suggested he felt sure she wasn't ready to kiss anyone if she wasn't ready to kiss him, and given the browbeating she'd taken that day, Caroline probably would've stewed about that had she not spied Trent's hammer on top of her piano on her way to her room. He'd moved it from the kitchen and had laid it on top of a plain sheet of paper that contained both a second verse and a finished chorus for their song:

> Who told you them two legs wasn't good enough to dance,
> Told you not to take a chance on a man like me?
> Luscious, lovely girl, I like everything I see
> If you'd only look at me and smile...'cause
>
> It ain't the hand that you're dealt; it's the way that you play it
> It ain't the size or the cost, but the way that you rate it
> I know you got a love game that you say is your favorite
> So c'mon, play it with me

And instead of stewing, Caroline carried Trent's lyrics to her room and tucked them under her pillow, thrilled about what kinds of dreams they might inspire.

Chapter Seven

"Don't mess with Tex."

All the way from Caroline's house to a return engagement at the
Red Light Café, Trent muttered those words under his breath to keep himself
from rear-ending Reyes's fancy-ass sports car. He was driving Marlon's cargo
van while Marlon was on the phone trying to talk his preferred harmonica
player (instead of the one they'd practiced with on and off) into attending
the band's first paying gig. Caroline had Minerva and Kyle in her Jetta,
leaving Reyes sandwiched between them and just one toe tap away from
a forced acquaintance with the asphalt. It was extremely lucky for Reyes
that his '67 Shelby Mustang was an important piece of automotive history,
since no amount of trying, sincere or otherwise, had stopped Trent from
feeling a jealousy he'd been denying on a daily basis.

In the month that had passed since his disastrous solo gig, he'd had
heaps of opportunities to think well of Reyes. Instead, Trent had taken up
calling the band's smug benefactor "Tex" the way Marlon and Minerva did.
Despite Caroline's claims that he never used to do so, Reyes dropped by
her house all the damn time with food and flowers, or food and wine, or
wine and some PR item that he'd pushed on Caroline's behalf. Getting Jarvis
back into the *Atlanta Music Guide* and then into a luxury box at a Hawks
game had gotten them two Thursdays' worth of time between open mic and
the house band. They'd had drinks with booking agents from the Variety
Playhouse and the Tabernacle just for getting caught in Reyes's company.
As much shit as he talked about Nez, Reyes also seemed to care about the
precarious state of Caroline's self-esteem, and she never complained of
him behaving badly whenever Trent's staying late at her house turned into
keeping Trent up to gossip.

Since the piano bench moment that was not to be mentioned, Caroline had put her own PR skills into making a chum of Trent, and perhaps it was that, more than Reyes himself, that Trent couldn't quite swallow. Every time she smiled, he had to suffer through the bitter taste of only being friends to smile back. He had to remind himself not to fuck up his increasingly good luck, to nod his head at the right time and never touch Caroline, an effort that jealousy was definitely not helping.

Trent pulled the van into the café's small alley and alongside of a loading door through which they would haul all of the instruments. It was several hours until show time, and he was not at all surprised when Caroline came over to tell him that Reyes was taking her to dinner since it was Valentine's Day. Careful to keep his gaze disinterested, which pretty much meant not looking anywhere in the vicinity of her face, Trent took her instructions about how to keep Jarvis happy without getting drunk on all the shots that would be handed out. He nodded at the right times just like he was supposed to, kept his mouth shut and his hands in his pockets, but he couldn't convince his eyes not to watch her ass jiggle and jive behind a coral sequin dress all the way to Reyes's equally shiny car.

Marlon was staring dead at him when Trent got back to unloading the cargo van. "Why'd you give up tapping that if you can't keep your eyes off it?"

It was probably a good thing Trent wasn't Caroline's boyfriend. He would only get into trouble with an open-ended license to tell her nosy friends to shut the hell up. "I ain't so much as touched that," he grunted through the exertion of slinging an amplifier onto a rolling cart.

"Just 'cause you two cooled off don't mean you gotta let him all up in your cookie jar, dude. Every time I see Tex, he's smacking his lips."

Trent's teeth clicked together and not because of the cold winter air. "Correction: I have never laid a finger on anything of Caroline's except this." He held up her Gibson guitar. "So. Not my girl, not my problem."

"Oh. Min was under the impression that you been staying late for—"

"Yeah, well, I wasn't." Minerva was under a lot of impressions, chief one being that she could dress him and Kyle down for not being Black enough for the Blues whenever she felt like it, even though she wasn't but a quarter Haitian herself.

"Sorry," Marlon said, not with snippy sarcasm, but with apparent sympathy that only made Trent's deprivation that much more painful.

Over the next few hours, though, he did a fine job of not thinking about it. After setting up their gear slightly behind the stage's blind spot and practicing a few times, Trent bought his band a round of beers, over which they had a rowdy argument about the set list. Besides warming up Minerva and giving the men a means to dish back some of the bitching she did at them, the argument killed time and kept Trent from checking both his watch and the door for Caroline's return.

They were to start with Mofro's "Dirtfloorcracker," which gave the musicians a chance to get groovy while Trent adjusted his attitude through the irony. Marc Broussard's "Rocksteady" was next, to get the girl contingency on the floor, and by then Trent was supposed to have a smile on his face for Jonny Lang's "(Ain't No Woman Like) The One I Got," Queen's "Crazy Little Thing Called Love," and a version of "My Babe" with a pinch of Elvis and as much Little Walter as he could muster for Minerva's sake. After that, they all had a ball with The Doors' "Roadhouse Blues," and usually that was as far as they got before Jarvis cut them off.

Tonight, however, the headliners were running almost twenty minutes late, and Jarvis was going to give them a chance to push past what was popular with the crowd. Marlon, Minerva, and Kyle insisted on Bo Diddley, Muddy Waters, and Stevie Ray Vaughn respectively, which was funny since Willie Dixon actually wrote all of the songs mentioned. Trent had learned that from Caroline, of course, for whom he wanted to channel Howlin' Wolf and sing another Dixon classic, "Spoonful," because it was in her top ten and because he who did not ask for a spoonful of sugar did not receive. Since that thought put him right back in the wrong headspace with less than ten minutes to go before they performed, Trent rose to get the gang another round and some water for himself.

"Don't mess with Tex," he hissed under his breath.

Cody, the bartender, extremely busy with the Friday night crowd, evidently didn't mind Trent filling his own water glass while he waited for three drafts of Rogue's Mocha Porter ale. In less than a minute, Trent actually polished off two glasses in the attempt to distract himself from watching the front door.

"What'd you do to get so thirsty, handsome?"

Trent's gaze dropped down to the blonde at his elbow and then down further to the enormous rack she had surgically attached to her chest. Whereas Caroline's breasts had an enchanting gravity that reeled him in, Blondie's jugs ballooned up and out almost to the point of bursting. It was grotesquely fascinating, not that her vanity took more from his wide eyes than a compliment.

"Heavy lifting."

"You work out, huh."

"No, I *work.*" His hand jutted out like an afterthought. "Trent."

A blink was the only sign she gave of noticing his reluctance. "Summer."

Though neither a Paris nor a Jessica, Summer still said her name with a plastic perkiness that matched her jugs. Her tiny hand was freezing cold inside of his and made more fakery of her sunny yellow hair, spray-tanned skin, and tissue-thin leopard-print dress. Complimenting her on how great she looked for her age might have been appropriate if she'd been more than twenty-four.

After waiting for him to try some kind of line on her, Summer said, "It sure looks like you work out."

A good-fitting shirt would do that for a man, and Trent took a second to appreciate the teal number that Caroline and Farah had picked out for him. "You betcha." Trent signaled Cody. "Can I get you something to drink?"

She smiled. "Jack and Coke."

Since he'd given her the proper cue, Summer didn't hesitate to start prattling on about herself, and Trent was happy to let her do it while he wrangled a spare stool from behind the bar. He sat her down between a regular named Josh and two attorneys who would be sure to pick up the slack after Trent left Summer to their attentions. She appealed in the same way that McDonalds did when a man was famished, but after a month on the Caroline diet, Trent was pretty much spoiled for fast ass.

Consequently, Summer's points of interest, so to speak, did not keep his attention from drifting to the damn door. He was almost relieved when Caroline finally arrived in the wake of Reyes, who, for all that he was trying to play bodyguard, couldn't help being a superstar like Jackie. More than one man cleared a path for the obvious air of importance Reyes wore with his public face and a jet-black Armani suit. By the time they made it over to Trent's side of the bar, Jarvis was there with a bottle of Johnny Walker Blue and an invitation up to the VIP room.

"Caroline?" Reyes asked with a courteous flourish of his hand.

Busy drinking in her strapless, coral cocktail dress, Trent almost missed the sharp tone with which she dismissed Jarvis and Reyes both.

"You go," Caroline said. "I won't be able to see from up there."

"Well, then—"

"No, really."

Trent raised a brow. He could tell she was unhappy from the way she didn't make eye contact with anyone.

Less sensitive, or perhaps less interested, Reyes went with Jarvis, who'd promised them one of the coveted tables along the brick wall near the stage. They moved toward the bar to talk shop, giving Trent a chance to get a word in with Caroline.

"You all right?"

"Fine." Her tone was curt. "How are you?"

"All right. How was dinner?"

She pursed her lips and nodded her head, like that was any kind of answer. "I see you've been making the most of your practice time." Caroline raked him with a gaze that included Summer.

Trent's eyebrow jumped. Either the deprivation diet was making him hallucinate, or Caroline was jealous of Jelly Jugs. The urge to ask made his stomach ache, but he didn't need one less reason to keep his hands to himself. "We practiced all the way up until the doors opened, Caroline."

"Did you practice your manners? Half the people here came just to see who you're going to beat up next. That guy from before brought all his friends to heckle you."

There was much more skepticism than sympathy in her tone.

"Thanks for the warning," Trent curtly replied.

"Take it to heart, please! We don't need any more bad press."

"You betcha." Trent couldn't resist a last word before he followed the band to the stage. "I reckon the way you're scowling at me will keep me in line. It's not doing anything for your dress, though."

Trent left her alone with nothing but a bad mood for company, and Caroline folded her arms across her chest. She'd just nearly ruined a month of carefully cultivated friendship over a bimbo that Trent had every right to push up on if he wished. As Reyes approached and spoke of champagne before leading her to a small table on the left side of the stage, Caroline further wondered why she should be offended by Trent's taste in women when she had a big piece of beefcake to satisfy her at the snap of a finger. Said beefcake filled a flute for her, but she couldn't thank Reyes because she was gritting her teeth at the bimbo who clapped her hands, screamed, and rushed the stage just one bar into the first song.

Caroline stewed through half of the set before the total lack of charity in all of her thoughts sank in, and she turned her scowl on herself. God, she was turning into one of those women who saw a bitch in every skinny chick and a rival in every kind of beauty that she did not possess. Shamed, Caroline glanced at Reyes, who was concerned but silent, and she struggled to get her attitude in check. Several sips of champagne helped the effort. She was not going to turn into a hater; there was nothing down that road but a hatefully ever after.

Unfortunately for Caroline, fate also loved to tempt the repentant. One rousing chorus into The Doors' "Roadhouse Blues," the crowd was still singing along with Trent at an impossible decibel that they'd been keeping up since Queen, during which the hecklers had done their worst. Instead of ignoring their taunts for him to put down the guitar and be a tough guy, Trent had improvised a saucily self-mocking verse of Lazy Lester's "(I'm A) Lover Not A Fighter." He'd won over the crowd, so when a fresh ripple of noise started in the far corner of the café nearest the door, Caroline at first was sure the hecklers were up to some kind of end-of-show revenge, and she urged Reyes to stand up and check it out. Both the consternation that flashed across his face and the smirk that followed put a twist in her stomach.

"What? What is it?"

Reyes sank down beside her. He shrugged his eyebrows and poured her another glass of champagne. "The end of your improved mood, no doubt."

Blowing trademark peace kisses that had the added benefit of suggesting oral sex, Milan Taylor slunk across the Red Light Café in thigh-high silver snow boots that might have been appropriate for the February weather without a bedazzled red romper that looked ridiculous even on Valentine's Day. Long waves of honey-blond horsehair hung down to her pert ass and floated to and fro while she made love to the fans. Her trailing entourage handed out DVDs, hats, T-shirts, condoms, and other bits and pieces of the cloying sexual teasing that Bratney embodied.

Caroline felt an aneurysm forming at the base of her brain. "What is she doing here?"

Reyes nudged a champagne flute closer to Caroline's fingers. "Stealing your press, I think. Drink up. Brave face, *querida*," he added when it became clear Milan was headed straight for them.

Despite knowing that Milan was one of his artists at Island Records, Caroline was thrown by the cordial way Reyes received the wench. They were from Texas and Detroit respectively, but exchanged European air kisses on each cheek before Milan greeted him with an enthusiastic, "Rey-Rey!"

Caroline barely had time to regret ever calling him that when yet another endearment was sullied.

"*Querida*, what are you doing here on a school night? How did you even get in?"

"I have my ways."

Caroline rolled her eyes at the sticky falsetto that the girl maintained even when she wasn't singing.

Reyes and Milan continued to talk from a script that Caroline could have written, Reyes in particular wielding a familiar charm that wounded her to hear lavished on someone else. Milan was equally easy to anticipate, even though she'd never met her before. In person, the girl was doubly lovely beneath the heaps of make-up, and she didn't seem at all as dim-witted as Nez had suggested. In fact, there was a knowing gleam to the way Milan kept glancing at Caroline while she monopolized Reyes's time and never introduced herself. Shock was the only thing that kept Caroline sitting still as long as she did.

When at last Caroline jumped away from Milan Taylor, Trent's blood pressure went down and the baser parts of his brain did a jig at the sight of his sugar throwing off Reyes's restraining hand. Though he'd seen the trouble coming, Trent had hesitated to sing some kind of warning in hope that Reyes would intervene. When he didn't, under other circumstances that didn't involve Caroline's hurt feelings, Trent would have been pleased to have such a good reason to think less of Tex.

"Roadhouse Blues" and "Spoonful" having come to an end, the band was deep into their first public performance of "The Way That You Play It," which, though still a first draft, struck Trent as an appropriate soundtrack for Caroline's halting and frustrated push through the Milan-loving crowd toward the restrooms. Voice aching with an exhortation that earned him a thumbs-up from Marlon, Trent cried out to Caroline, "It ain't the hand that you're dealt; it's the way that you play it," but she was obviously too busy trying not to get trampled for the second time that night to listen. She was always too busy being a castoff to carry herself with a confidence that would have made jewelry of her gorgeous coral dress. And she'd been too busy complaining through a month of late nights to listen to the man who was on the brink of being irretrievably crazy about her.

The set ended, the stage changed, the headliners tuned up, and while the crowd rejoiced in another opportunity to hit up the bar, Trent kept himself as close to the door of the women's restroom as possible. Caroline had gone in a good fifteen minutes before and no doubt would come out puffy of eye. What he saw when finally she jostled past two drunken sorority girls was the portrait of a woman in deep distress. Caroline came straight to him and just stood there, nose raw and red and mascara-ringed eyes averted to hide her shame and seething.

"You wanna get out of here?" he asked. She managed to meet his eyes after a couple of tries. "Marlon's got Minerva helping him pack up, mostly to keep her from 'snatching Milan bald,' so I can drive you home if you like. You're in no condition, as much champagne as you had."

Caroline swallowed several times. "I left my—"

"I got it." Trent handed over her purse while he cut behind her to drape a little pale gold jacket over her shoulders. "And your boyfriend's been told to kiss your grits, so feel free to reinforce that the next time you see him." After she failed to respond, Trent took it upon himself to guide her through the throng and out of the club, but instead of hovering in front of her like a bodyguard, he took her by the hand like a friend.

Fifteen minutes into the drive to her house, she finally spoke to him. "You really told him to kiss my grits?"

His gaze flashed from the Jetta's rearview mirror to her face and back. "Well, to tell the truth, it was Minerva who let him know, in no uncertain terms, that you were put out with him. Then she threw your stuff at me before Marlon dragged her away." Trent chuckled. "She's really starting to grow on me."

Caroline didn't say anything right away. In fact, the long delay between his prompt and her response reminded him so much of Margie, another poorly pieced-together woman, that Trent's throat closed up.

"*He* asked to be my Valentine. And he was going to come over tomorrow and cook for me." Caroline's voice broke, and she snapped her eyes away from his and back to the window. "I *know* he works with her. I know he's been so nice to me all along, and I'm just too emotional. I'm just so *mad*, though!" Her voice shook like her fingers clutching her throat. She made a fist and banged the car console. "I can't stop being mad."

"You sure you ain't just looking for an excuse to brush him off?"

"No, not at—God, I'm pathetic. I'm still mad at Nez when good sense keeps telling me to get over it like everyone else does."

Trent touched her fisted hand. "Being mad stains everything, doesn't it?"

Caroline looked at him, and the whole sordid story of how he'd shown up with busted knuckles was right there on the tip of Trent's tongue. He swallowed hard.

"I get it, with you and your boyfriend. Sometimes you need somebody to remind you that you're worth the effort." Since she'd done that for him, his eyes laved gratitude over Caroline's face, and his fingertips tried to coax the anger out of her tight knuckles. "Who better than Prince Charming himself? But Tex is invested in you, and trust me when I say that you don't want to wake up in a month and realize that being hurt made you hurt somebody else. You're too sweet, Caroline. That'd just ruin you."

Trent's sound sense still didn't shock her broken heart out of its stupor as they drove along in her car.

Caroline sniffed. "He's not my boyfriend. I guess I should tell him that, huh?"

"Only if you're gonna start telling yourself that you're worth it on a regular basis. If you're not, keep him handy." Trent shot her a grin and a wink. "I couldn't care less about him being ruined."

Caroline laughed a little, but the effort shook loose some of the tears she'd been holding in. She snapped back to the window, trying to escape his notice. "I don't even know why he bothers." She smeared mascara across her index finger trying to stop crying. "I'm a hot mess."

"A big hot mess usually tastes the best."

Caroline's first laugh was automatic. The second was short and shocked after she gaped at him and her cheeks ran raspberry.

"Something wrong?" he asked.

"No! Not wrong, I guess. I mean, I'm sure you didn't mean anything by it, but it sounded like you meant—"

"I did."

In the darkness of the car, his eyes were pearl bright and lustrous, but they gave nothing away while Trent stared at her. When finally he turned his attention back to the interstate, Caroline didn't know whether to trust his suggestive words or his stony expression. She erred on the side of self-doubt, as always.

"You didn't have to say that."

"I wanted to. Unless you didn't want to hear it."

"No. I mean, yes! Well, thank you, I mean." Caroline crossed her eyes and stifled the urge to smack her mouth. "Sorry, I just didn't think you noticed me. Like *that.*"

"All I do is notice you, Caroline Curran."

She recognized his tone of voice from the piano bench moment that they did not mention. Caroline's head reeled, and she didn't know if it was the champagne or the sudden realization that trying to hide that he liked her had been what made Trent stiffen up. Perhaps literally; he had just made a sexual reference, after all.

"You know, you're not my boyfriend either. Maybe you could, um, not be my Valentine. I mean, it *is* the fifteenth." She glanced at the dashboard display that read one twenty-one a.m.

Trent glanced, too, then pinned her with an inviting gaze. When he licked his lips, Petula Clark's perky version of "Downtown" did a lap around the dirty side of Caroline's mind.

Damn it, he thought. "I can't stay, darlin'. I have to give Ginny's date, Hank, a talking to. He's taking her to a scary movie instead of the school dance." Trent choked out the words, aware that they would save him from the very mistake he'd been avoiding for a month if he just shut his mouth and left it at that. He then added idiotically, "But if you want to give me between here and your house, not-Valentines it is."

He told himself that he couldn't get into trouble in a car, yet remembered exactly why he was planning to threaten Hank's life.

When Caroline looked over, Trent grinned. She looked away, and so did he, feeling silly and much like a nervous teenager on the way back from the high school dance himself. For a gesture that seemed intended to free them of expectations, being not-Valentines put into Trent's heart a fantasy of staying and playing for her until she fell asleep on the couch, just as he had a couple weeks ago. Only then, he would carry her to bed and get in with her.

They made it to her house, and he was slow to get out of the car and let go of the sweet silence that had ruled the last half of the trip. Feeling silly erased the strain he'd been carrying around since that-which-had-not-happened on the piano bench, but he ceased to miss that opportunity when a different imaginary kiss was invented every time she looked at him. Half a dozen glances passed back and forth while Trent dragged his feet up the single step to the door and she fished around for her keys.

Suddenly, Caroline gasped and tilted her face up to the porch light.

"What?" Trent asked from close behind her.

"Look at my face!" She pointed to her reflection in the glass storm door. "I look insane!" Caroline fruitlessly scrubbed at her smeared makeup and only ended up looking even more like the Joker fresh from an all-night bender. "Why didn't you tell me?"

"You were in a bad way. Didn't quite seem like a good time to say that you looked—" Trent cleared his throat.

Caroline spun around and pointed both index fingers at her face. "I left a club where Milan Taylor was, looking like this! I bet this is exactly what she came for, a picture of me looking hideous to stick on her Twitter!"

Trent knew it would be foolish to insist that Milan hadn't horned in intentionally, though how she'd known where they'd be in the first place did put a fresh itch in his urge to mess with Tex.

"You look fine. Caroline." Trent tried to pull her fingers from her face and then remembered he'd already blown his touching allowance for the night. "It was dark, and I'm the only one who knows that you were crying. So what if there's a picture? For all anybody knows, you partied too hard and then took home a boy-toy, if you play it that way."

She seemed to get the reference, but behind her eyes, Trent could tell that her heart was still broken. He licked his lips and willed her to get better. Maybe it worked because she smiled a little.

"This is not a thank-you kiss." Caroline almost fell out of her three-inch heels trying to plant her lips on his cheek.

Damn, damn, damn. Damn. "No, *this* is not a thank-you kiss."

He'd never liked the taste of lipstick and used that as an excuse to slant his mouth across Caroline's in an invitation for her to open up. He'd never liked champagne either and blamed it for the way they reeled back against the storm door before rebounding into each other's bodies. There was a saying about watching what you wished for that Trent should have reviewed before he'd stood on stage begging for a "Spoonful" of Caroline's sugar. Hot damn if one hit didn't have him addicted and ready to break his diet between the sheets.

"But you are welcome," he whispered. "Any time you feel like asking."

His shirt clipped her nipples when he reluctantly withdrew from her.

He waited for her to invite him in, but when she didn't, Trent didn't push the issue. He was not Reyes and would not be throwing his weight around a delicate flower like Caroline. He wanted to see her bloom, or at the very least, grow up and grope him.

Caroline licked her lips. "Um. Can you not be my Valentine next year, too?"

"Count on it." He grinned and gave her one last chance to ask him to come in. When she didn't, Trent waved goodbye and started staging the Alamo in his head. *Damn Tex.*

Chapter Eight

Though she'd tried to scale down her anger all weekend long, by the Monday after Milan's press theft, Caroline had officially changed Bratney to Bitchney. She might as well not have put a month into appeasing Reyes for all the PR and favors he'd thrown her way. In both the *Atlanta Music Guide* and the paper-and-ink *Atlanta Journal-Constitution*, Trent's first press-worthy gig was not named when the Red Light Café was mentioned in a mere footnote to Milan Taylor's weekend itinerary. Though Nez at first denied any knowledge of Bitchney's usurpation, he was quick to parlay the debacle into a fresh fight over the invoice for services rendered.

Hearing his voice slither through the phone for the first time in weeks had made Caroline sick to her stomach. After replacing not just her cell phone but her phone number, she'd been amazed that ignoring him had cut down her interest in the still-disputed ten-thousand-dollar payment. On top of disinterest had come a check from Nez's company, St. Peter Music Publishing, for her portion of the royalties that Island Records paid whenever Milan performed one of Caroline's songs. The check wasn't much more than the monthly amount Nez had been unfairly withholding, but for him to release it meant that Caroline was winning the extortion war.

Funny, then, that she was standing over her safe deposit box at Regions Bank, fingering the really incriminating tapes and trying to pry her fingers away from a memory stick that would make for the most serious of scandals. Surely she wasn't that mercenary, despite the wild compulsion to rake Nez across the coals that burned bright in her throat. He couldn't just walk away; she wanted to send him away maimed even if she had to withhold the very last thing she had that he still wanted. To that end, Caroline did not put any of the most sensitive tapes into the envelope that she would trade for the next payment. She dug into her purse, slipped a Ziploc bag full of busted memory stick bits into the envelope, and sealed it.

"Chew on that."

She shut her safe deposit box and evil-eyed the envelope on her way out to an account manager's desk where, as arranged, she swapped the envelope for a wire transfer directly to her account.

The satisfaction of being ten grand richer only lasted as long as it took Caroline to push through the bank's glass doors, partially because of a foreboding feeling about Nez's next chess move and mostly because Reyes was standing at the curb next to a black town car. Caroline's eyes went wide behind her sunglasses. She hadn't returned any of Reyes's calls since Friday night's debacle and had let him believe that she was still miffed when really she just didn't know how to draw a boundary between them.

"Um, hi. What are you doing here?"

Brows raised, Reyes swaggered forward to hover over her.

"Querida." He pulled one hand from the pocket of his black cashmere coat and wrapped Caroline's red knit scarf around her neck. "Do you mean to catch your death, walking around in a peacoat with your legs exposed?"

"I'm wearing tights." Caroline stuck out one of the brown booties she wore with stockings and a plaid skirt.

"Tights are not pants, a distinction that matters when it's thirty degrees out. Thank God I came with the car." He moved to the rear door of the still-running black Lincoln. "Come. I'm taking you to lunch."

"Um, no, you're not. I'm picking up sushi for me and Jackie on the way back to the office." She shucked her thumb toward the little Japanese place on the corner of 9th Street. "And I'm leaving after that, so…"

Reyes yanked open the door. "Very well. Get in the car, and I'll take you."

He seemed unmoved by her arched brow, probably because she was shaking slightly in that Monday morning's frigid February air.

"I walked here, and I'll walk back, thank you."

"Querida—"

"Caroline. You're not my boyfriend, so I think you should stop calling me all those other things that you call me."

His eyes narrowed, and he was silent for a few seconds before saying something to the chauffeur in Spanish and shutting the door. The car pulled off while Reyes stepped very close to her. He stared into Caroline's eyes through her tortoise-shell sunglasses.

"I never said that I was."

Caroline felt like scoffing even though he was right. In fact, as often as they'd had dinners and drinks since last November's fateful American Music Awards, Reyes had never once used the word "date." But she also couldn't recall him ever introducing her as his friend; she was always *Mi querida*" or *"Mi muñeca,* Caroline."

"Well, I just want to make sure it's clear that we're just friends."

"Yet another distinction that matters all of a sudden. Since I already knew as much and obviously so did you, to whom did you want to make the distinction so abundantly clear?"

Struck with an urge to apologize, Caroline pursed her lips, and she shrank from both the prospect of bringing Trent into conversation and Reyes's sharp tone, one that he used to go to war with Jackie. "I don't want to fight with you, Rey."

"You'd prefer to punish me — unfairly, I might add — for being courteous Friday night instead of getting ready to rumble as your other friends tend to do?"

He knew exactly what to say to make her feel bad, a talent he had in common with Nez, and Caroline felt a good, strong wilt starting in her stomach.

"Forget it. I can't talk about this right now. I don't even know *what* we're talking about." Feeling stupid for abandoning his favor, she hitched her purse up onto her shoulder and pulled away when Reyes grasped her arm.

Though his grip was firm, Reyes's voice was quite soft when he said, "Don't you think that I'm confused as well? I didn't expect to want you, Caroline." Stopped dead in her tracks, she watched his dark blue eyes grow wary with that revelation. "We went from having a mutual friend in Jackie to having a mutual enemy, and..." Reyes at a loss for words was quite the sight, especially since he still managed to smolder at her while he collected his thoughts. "You just make it so easy to be with you."

"Great. I'm easy."

"No, you're comfort itself."

The wind blew Caroline's bangs into her eyes. He was as quick to exploit an opportunity to touch her as she was slow to turn away from the seductive smoothness of his fingers across her brow.

A small but genuine smile played across Reyes's lips. "I don't know another woman who shares herself so easily. I thought you were blind to that weakness at first. I would be remiss to let anyone else take advantage."

Caroline didn't know if her stomach was fluttering at his flattery or tightening at the condescension beneath, but she was too dumbstruck to resist when he tucked her hand into his elbow to stroll down the street. He cared, but his motivations confused her all the way to their stop at the sushi place. Not until she stepped out of the shop door with food in hand and saw his Lincoln idling at the curb, apparently as instructed, did Caroline pinpoint what bothered her about Reyes's behavior. He wanted her to go weak in the knees and wilt so that he could keep her, like a pretty pressed flower, in the breast pocket of his expensive suits. He never dared to treat Jackie like that, which somewhat explained the mutual and highly heated disgust between the two most beautiful people Caroline knew.

He followed her back to the office where Caroline ate potato chips instead of partaking of the melodramatic snipes that Jackie and Reyes made over the sushi tray. They both wore black and sat on the edge of her cherry wood desk, while she sat behind it and waited for the clock to strike one p.m. Through a battle of strained body language that Caroline couldn't fully interpret, Jackie treated Reyes like the spoiled prince he was, and he, in turn, ribbed her like she was just another one of the guys, though without the profanity that Jackie spat when she was really trying to goad him.

"Since when does your green party have anything to do with the goddamn environment?" Jackie held up one of the coveted invitations to Reyes's St. Patrick's Day affair.

This year's invitation was an origami four leaf clover, which, torn open, revealed the date and time of the party in gold print and, as always, a small gold pin that one wore both to the party and afterward as a status symbol amongst certain company. This year's pin was a recycling symbol.

"The only thing green last year was the men's money and the women's eyes. You didn't even put any food coloring in the fucking beer," Jackie sneered.

"I'm upgrading from mere pleasure to significant experiences, Jacks. Try to grasp that. Assuming you're able to, please bring a guest." Reyes tossed another invitation onto her lap.

"Why not? I'll call…" Jackie snapped her elegant fingers. "What was the name of that chick I did last fall? Oh yeah. Candy."

Reyes went red. He glanced at Caroline, and she pretended not to notice the embarrassment and perhaps fury that mottled his complexion.

To Jackie, he continued, "Is that a pet name or her professional handle? She certainly looked like a pro in the pictures you sent."

"Professional? I don't date whores!"

"I didn't know you looked that pretty on your knees, Jacks."

"If you tasted like Candy, you would have known."

Reyes rolled his eyes. "No woman is as sweet as candy. They taste like oatmeal, actually, with a bit of butter and cinnamon."

"Nutritious and delicious?" Jackie licked her lips. "No wonder I've been turning down dick lately."

Caroline had never approved of their vicious jousting and felt sick to her stomach with guilt for doing the same with Nez. She picked up Reyes's invitation. She hadn't received one. He had asked her to stand at his side and not to stand by herself. Caroline squared her shoulders against being treated like a sidekick. "Can I bring someone?"

Latent anger with Jackie frayed Reyes's fake smile when he turned to Caroline. "I wasn't aware that you had someone in mind. I—"

Jackie snorted. "Cut the crap, Reyes. You know she's talking about the hillbilly."

Though she bristled, Caroline could only bring herself to say, "He's not from the hills; he's from Georgia. Like us."

They both ignored her in favor of a deadly silent standoff. Reyes's complexion was russet with blood, and for the first time since Caroline had known him, his Spanglish wasn't the only thing reminding her of how much Mexican ran through his veins.

"But you would look so lovely as my guest of honor," he said to Caroline. "You could use a coming out party, I think, after all that's happened."

"Wow, Caroline, he's throwing you a fucking *quinceañera!* How does it feel to be treated like a teen again?"

Caroline had grown up a bit recently, but she had not grown above bristling at references to teenagers. She stood up and gathered her things. Reyes let out a string of obscene Spanish, while an apologetically wide-eyed Jackie grasped her gaffe. "C.C., I'm sorry."

"Forget it." Caroline silently reminded herself to do the same, because she had to learn to get through a conversation without Nez and Bitchney battering her thoughts. "It's one o'clock, and I have to go. I have to meet *Trent,*" she snapped, reminding them both that the hillbilly had a name, "for a photo shoot."

"*Querida,* wait."

Caroline swept past Reyes toward the door, and yanked on her gray peacoat as she went. She already had the red scarf wrapped around her tight lips and throat, her sunglasses covering the misery in her eyes.

All the way up the interstate to Atlanta, Trent seethed about having his picture taken for the press kit. He was in no mood to fake smiles for hours, not with his nerves balanced on half a dozen different edges.

Since it was a Monday and the band would practice nonstop until Marlon and Minerva's private Wednesday gigs, he wouldn't be going back home until Wednesday night and wouldn't be there to keep Ginny from coming in as late as she had from her Saturday date with Hank Bassett. For a kid who allegedly spent all of his spare time drawing comic books and watching the Syfy Channel, Hank looked like he could bench-press a shed. A gentle giant, Hank had been waiting with a big grin outside of church Sunday morning to wheel Ginny to a pew as close to his folks as possible. Gin had been pissed at Trent for removing her to Margie's usual spot, and had slapped his hand for trying to stop her from texting on the new cell phone he'd bought her in conjunction with his own. She was costing him a mint in overage fees, and keeping Shane on baby-sitting duty had been costing Trent an extra fifty bucks a week.

Yet none of that was a distraction from the possibility that Courtney Vickers had checked out of St. Francis Hospital. Trent could barely breathe waiting for Shane to call back and confirm, and he was deeply ashamed of fearing that protecting his family would mean having to give up Caroline Curran.

He'd spent most of Saturday wondering whether, in her mind, their not-Valentine's kiss was something he could bring up come Monday. Most of Sunday had then gone to Trent wondering who the hell he was to even think about trying to keep a girl like Caroline. He didn't have room in his life for another woman who needed taking care of, and yet he couldn't tear his mind away from what it would've been like to do exactly that all Friday night and Saturday morning, too, just sleeping in and screwing like neither of them had a care in the world. Caroline clearly needed a night like that as much as he did, and Trent had just thrown open his legs to settle into a good strong fantasy when a strange vibration broke through the rumble of his seasoned Chevy.

Goddamn cell phones. "Yeah."

"Good news is that he's still in a coma, so you won't be going to jail," Shane reported over the line. "Bad news is that they transferred him to a head specialist in Atlanta, kind of like a last resort before they pull the plug and the drunken boys from his funeral come after your ass."

Ominous Wild Turkey bottles, of which Trent and Shane had seen more than one in recent weeks, came to mind. From the hope of having fingerprints "just in case," Shane had suggested the bottles be kept in the shed. They waited there like land mines for a shoe to drop, waited there declaring that fingerprints didn't matter a damn until after someone got hurt.

Overwhelmed with worry, all Trent could think to say was, "Fuck."

"Maybe you ought to move." Those were terrifying words coming from Shane who usually was quick to suggest rushing headfirst into danger. "Ginny ain't got but a couple months left of high school, and you're already in Atlanta half the week as it is. Find a little apartment and get the hell out of Dodge."

"Gin would kill me if I pulled her out of school. She's actually thinking about going to the prom now that Hank's come into it."

"Thought you were planning on busting that up."

"I was till his folks had us over for Sunday dinner. I ain't seen Gin socialize like that since I don't know when. Hank didn't look at her like she was pieced back together, know what I mean? Hell, he's even got her thinking about getting back on the yearbook committee."

"That ain't all he's got her thinking about. I heard Gin on the phone last week saying something about 'going away' — "

"What?"

"Didn't hear where, but can't you still end up barefoot and pregnant in a wheelchair?" After a deadly silence on the other end of the line, Shane said, "Well! Since I done already put my foot deep in it, I'll let you go. Keep it in the road, hoss," he added with a sympathetic undertone and then hung up.

Apoplectic was what they called it when a man burst a blood vessel in his brain and couldn't get his shit together for anything. As much red as Trent saw the rest of the way down the interstate, he'd probably burst a few in his eyeballs too. Busy thinking up ways to castrate Hank, Trent was quite compliant with the staff at the downtown photography studio who politely handed him off, one after another, to various underlings until he ended up in the hands of a twenty-year-old hairdresser.

"You're early," she mumbled, and Trent wondered how fast he'd been driving the last leg of the trip to arrive twenty-five minutes ahead of time. The hairdresser pushed him down in a leather chair and peered at him from behind wire-rimmed glasses. "And you need a haircut." She clucked her tongue.

While she labored to make his hair look as tousled as it usually did from finger raking, another girl came in with set after set of slick, dark-hued clothes, one of which Trent changed into before yet another little miss put makeup on his face. He was trying to think of a civil way to protest having a bunch of white gunk rubbed under his eyes when Minerva showed up in the doorway of the pretty-up pressure chamber. Her dreads were bluer than usual, as blue as the glitter that was painted around her eyes like a Mardi Gras mask to match her midriff-baring peacock feather vest and leather pants.

Tight-lipped, Minerva demanded, "Why is Sharona inviting Reyes to Purim dinner?"

It took a second for Trent to digest the lack of greeting and then another to remember who Sharona was and guess at what Purim might be. "Beats me."

"Either you were acting up over the weekend, or Sharona doesn't know about you, because C.C. doesn't want Julianna to know who she's fucking. Mind your business," Minerva snapped at the wide-eyed makeup girl.

"Why are all y'all so damn nosy? All of Caroline's friends," Trent clarified before Minerva could get in his ass about "y'all" having a wider racial reference, "always in her business."

"We have to stay in her business. That girl can't take care of herself." Minerva folded her arms. "So are you in or are you out? Because I told Sharona at Shabbat to hold Tex's invitation. If you don't show, C.C.'s gonna get pushed at one of Aaron's friends, and once the word gets around temple that Caroline might convert for the right man, it's over for you, Garth Brooks. Mixed race kosher babies are in right now."

"What exactly are you asking me, Minerva?"

"Are you in or are you out?"

"Isn't that kind of up to Caroline?"

"You're leaving it up to her? Damn, you really haven't tapped that. I thought Marlon was lying." Minerva loudly sucked her teeth, then glared at him. "Forget it then." She stormed out just as abruptly as she'd arrived.

Trent and Miss Makeup attended the sound of Minerva's boots stomping down the hall, and then, sponge in hand, the makeup girl disdainfully informed him, "Purim is a Jewish holiday in March. It's, like, really important."

Extremely tired of being talked down to, Trent rolled his eyes before she resumed rubbing gunk under them.

When finally he made it back to the warehouse-sized studio, shinier, prettier replacements for all of the instruments they really used had been set up in the middle of an umbrella area that was painted a careful shade of white. Minerva was there, behind a bright red drum kit, and so was Kyle, his thin ash blond hair shaved on the sides and slicked up into a circular saw-blade of a mohawk. He wore black just like Marlon, who was across the room holding a clipboard and talking on the phone. The staff hadn't gotten him out of his tuxedo jacket and shorts uniform, but Marlon had been upgraded to a velvet number that put Trent in mind of CD/DC's "Back in Black." He glanced down at his own simple blue jeans ensemble and felt plain by comparison. After they played a few songs for a series of band-in-action shots, the photographer and his assistant separated them for portraits, Marlon and Minerva first. Kyle took that opportunity to wander outside and get high, so Trent was left alone in a set of wooden director's chairs when Caroline finally walked into the studio with a cell phone pressed to her ear.

Caroline would have been pleased that being tardy to the band's photo shoot hadn't held up the process if she weren't still on the phone trying to talk Jackie down from another round of apologies.

"Sorry, guys. Accident. Stay off the bypass." Caroline then resumed telling her best friend, "Jacks, I know you didn't mean anything by it, but don't kid yourself that you were standing up for me. That was about you, Reyes, and *Candy*. And pictures, Jacqueline? Really? I'm not judging your sex life, but that's weird. You came out to Reyes. I think he knows how it all goes down in your bedroom." She smacked her forehead. "I didn't say that."

Caroline didn't hear Jackie's denials; she'd caught sight of Trent and all ability to think ground to a halt. When a professional stylist bypassed velvet, leather, and peacock feathers to dress a man in nothing but low-slung blue jeans and a black tank, it was because that man made nothing much look extremely good.

"Huh?" She almost tripped over a director's chair as she approached Trent. Thank God she still had sunglasses on to hide her ogling. "Fine, Jacks. Can we talk about this later? Jackie. *Jacqueline.* I'm on your side, as long as you leave me out of it. Did you tell him where I was? Because he cornered me outside of the bank like a stalker."

Trent asked, "You have a stalker?

Caroline shook her head to Trent, then continued to Jackie, "I can take care of myself. Now goodbye." She blew out a breath.

"Hey there." He grinned. "Standing up for yourself looks real good on you. So does that plaid schoolgirl skirt and the cute little shoes."

She nodded, still too distracted by his looks to speak. Being dressed in nothing much only made it clearer that he'd look amazing in nothing at all. Though she should have been used to the sight of Trent's diamond-cut shoulders by then, Caroline barely managed to mumble something that sounded like "Hi" while she punched the speed-dial on her new phone.

"Friends don't stalk each other, Tex," Caroline hissed in a voicemail and hung up.

Trent asked, "He's giving you problems?"

"No," Caroline lied and sat down to get her eyes off of Trent. The chair he sat in was in the back and out of the brightest lights, so his voice came from behind and slightly to the right when he leaned forward to speak to her.

"Yeah? 'Cause it seems like you're in a bad way."

He very obviously hadn't said "Come sit on my lap," so it was funny how she managed to hear that. "I'm fine."

"You sure you don't need a hand?"

She wondered where he might put that hand to work. Her flash fantasy was interrupted by a short brown-haired guy who approached with a notepad in hand.

"Caroline Curran?"

"Yes?"

"Angus Young, *Paste* magazine." He tacked on a disingenuous "Nice to meet you," stuck out his hand, and withdrew it almost as soon as their fingers touched.

Not in any position to turn down even a terse journalist from a reputable entertainment rag with national exposure like *Paste*, Caroline found a fake smile.

"Nice to meet you too." She swiveled one wrist back toward Trent. "This is—"

"Trent. Yeah. I met him while I was waiting." The total lack of expression on his face hinted that he was miffed about that. "I just need a couple things for the profile."

"The...profile?"

"Uh, yeah, for our 'Artist Discovery Series'? I'll need a copy of your single too."

Since *Paste*'s "Artist Discovery Series" usually debuted full albums from established bands that had earned the exposure, a profile for a single that hadn't been recorded yet could only mean that Reyes had flexed his pinkie finger. Angus's thinly veiled resentment suddenly made a lot more sense. "Right! Um...well, it's still in, uh, the process. Can I send it to you later?"

"When later?"

Caroline quickly did the math for how long it would take to arrange, record, produce, and release the song after she and Trent finished writing it. "April?"

"Upcoming release from Island Records," Angus quoted as he wrote the words. "What's the name of the band?"

Curran-C just wasn't going to cut it. "It's...eponymous."

"So it's the 'Trent...'?"

"Michaels. The Trent Michaels Band."

"Cool." Angus leaned to the left to ask Trent, "Where'd you guys get started?"

"Here in Atlanta," Caroline answered.

"You're from here as well?" he tried again to ask Trent.

"He's from, uh, out west," Caroline supplied, which was true, geographically.

Angus blinked at her evasive answer. "Like a cowboy?"

Caroline laughed awkwardly, but Trent didn't.

Slumped down behind her with his legs belligerently thrown open, Trent listened to Caroline lie to Angus even for insignificant questions that his real life should have been good enough to answer. Though Trent had never finished college, Trent Michaels had moved to East Atlanta after he graduated and currently lived in a loft where he lazed around all day writing songs when he wasn't performing with the band. Caroline invented a previous band for him called "Shiloh," and Trent was disgusted that she could remember the name of his church but not his real age. When prompted for it, Caroline turned to Trent for the first time in the interview, and he just let her dangle until she guessed, "Twenty-five." She popped his knee for that when Angus wasn't looking, and the undeserved punishment only pissed Trent off that much more.

"I guess that'll do it, except…Yeah, where are you guys playing next? I'd like to send someone to check it out before the profile runs," Angus said with a pained smile, indicating that doing favors didn't totally outweigh his journalistic integrity.

"I reckon we'll be playing up Reyes A. Bardem's ass," Trent piped up. "Since you seem to like it there so much," he adjoined in a pissed whisper against Caroline's ear before brushing past her and Angus to take his place for the portraits.

Galled, Caroline sat staring after Trent for so long that Angus excused himself with a fake apology. Granted, she might have gone a little too far in her effort to build Trent an image, but Caroline certainly didn't deserve contempt for being indebted to Reyes, whose favors benefited them all. In fact, Reyes must've seen something in the band for himself if he was trying to generate buzz for a single. Bits and pieces of publicity were one thing, but spending Island money on a recording wasn't something that Reyes would do unless he was sure of making that money back. Trent should have been able to understand that, but Caroline knew there would be no getting through his McStonyface routine until he decided to come out of it himself.

She let him glare at her from across the studio and tried not to care when the photographer had to spend ten minutes coaxing Trent to look alive. By the time they moved on to the head shots she'd ordered so that Trent would have something to sign for his increasingly female fanbase, an aggravated Caroline threw up her hands and called them off. Trent's frozen, emotionless face would just be a waste of her hard-extorted money.

While she waited outside of the photography assistant's office to see proofs of all the shots she'd missed, Caroline was so furious that her hands shook too badly to text a thank-you to Reyes. Marlon and Minerva had already said their goodbyes and gone since Caroline had called off practice for the night by citing a fake dinner with Jackie that she hoped to make real. It was one of Trent's scheduled nights to stay in town, and not wanting to be trapped in her house with him did not mean that she could rescind the invitation. They all had to get up early to practice for the 40 Watt Club in Athens, Georgia.

As soon as she saw Trent coming down the hall from the studio with Kyle, Caroline turned her back and tried to look really busy on her new Blackberry. He called her name, and she scooted along the wall away from him until she collided with a big potted plant.

"Caroline—"

"I'm busy."

"I can see that, but I just need a minute to—"

"Hello? Jacks?"

"Unless your phone rings in dog-hearing frequencies, you and I both know that you didn't just get a call. You don't have to lie, Caroline."

"You didn't have to be a jerk, Trenton! And since I don't like talking to jerks, I'm not talking to you!"

"Is it all right if I talk, or are you not listening too?"

She didn't appreciate him getting smart and shot a scathing glare before darting around him and back toward the assistant's office. He grasped her shoulder.

"Caroline, wait. I'm trying to apologize here. I'm sorry about what I said, all right?" He blew out a breath. "I know Tex is your friend, and I know I should be grateful. But when you went on like that about Trent *Michaels*,

I couldn't help but feel like you don't really care to know anything about me. And frankly, I couldn't help but wonder if Friday night was a mistake."

She spun around then, and Trent added, "Not because I didn't want to, but because I'm not sure who you were kissing, me or just the next guy who was nice to you."

Caroline bristled, but there was no point denying that she never declined the benefits of Reyes's company.

"Yeah, well, it's hard to get to know you when you petrify before my very eyes, and that's more often than not."

"You're right. Trent Buckney ain't all that nice," he admitted.

"I'm not all that nice either."

"If it's possible, I reckon you're too nice, Caroline. That's part of the reason why I don't think—Well, I just…" He raked his hair back, raked it back again, then buried his fists in it, leaving his elbows up in the air.

Trent at a loss for words was much different from Reyes. He really looked lost and not merely perplexed that he was running short on subtleties.

Caroline offered, "Reyes is throwing a party next month. I'd like for you to be my guest. Date, I mean. Not because I'm being nice or you're being nice, just because." She left the rest up in the air like he had, satisfied that they had both anted up. "I'm tired of nice anyway."

Something sly came into his eyes. "Is that so?"

"Yeah." She tried to act nonchalant about the way he'd woven sex through those three little words. Nonchalance failed as soon as Trent licked his lips and stepped closer to her. "Yeah, I'm gonna call right now and tell Reyes." Caroline whipped her Blackberry into the space between them.

"I dunno about that." Trent laid his hand over hers. "Might be a good time for the element of surprise."

Like static or sunshine, his invisible intentions registered with feeling where he touched her skin. She'd forgotten since Friday that there was often a big difference between what Trent said and what Trent suggested.

"Why?"

"Because he's sweet on you. I don't think he's gonna take kindly to me horning in on his territory."

"I'm not anyone's territory. Reyes hasn't staked a claim on me."

With the same sly eyes as before, Trent repeated, "Is that so?"

Caroline suddenly understood why women could be done in by three little words.

"I reckon," he continued, "you do seem like the kind of girl who makes a man buy the farm before he sows any oats."

"Not buy. Lease, maybe." Caroline swallowed hard. "I mean, at least, I like to know that he's seriously in the market." Her name was called from inside the office, which provided an easy out from what was rather too revealing a remark, so Caroline wasn't sure why she chose the hard way instead. "Are you?"

His pretty face suddenly seemed to pop into high definition, wary behind the slate blue eyes, cautious around the lips, but focused most of all upon her as his body dragged at her like a magnet.

The attraction trumped the discussion and made silly noise of Trent asking in return, "Are you?"

"Huh?" She hadn't quite heard the words over the heaving of her breast and the roaring of her pulse.

"Caroline," came the voice from the office doorway.

As Caroline spun toward the photography assistant, her ass bumped into Trent, and she wasn't as quick to jerk away as she could have been. "I'm coming." She heard Trent shift on his feet behind her. Seeming to sense that she was interrupting something, the assistant smiled shyly and ducked back into the office.

As soon as they were alone, Trent suggested, "That can be arranged, if you want."

His lips grazed her ear when he spoke the words in a whispered challenge. His hand found the hem of her sweater, then the line that her bikini panties drew across her hip. Caroline clenched when he flattened his hot hand on her skirt over that spot and squeezed. He pulled her back into close contact, and bumped against her tailbone. The definition of close was being able to tell by touch that a man was wearing button fly jeans.

Caroline's breath came in little lurches while his hand, hidden in the thick folds of her sweater, skated along the soft mound of her belly and up to her navel, around which he drew a circle big enough to dip into the waistband of her skirt.

Thrilled, she squeaked, "I lied. I'm gooey, right now."

"Just sticky, or drippy?"

Wet against her earlobe, his accented whisper felt like both. Caroline blushed furiously. She didn't speak, but her belly shook beneath his hold.

Trent slid his thumb around to the back of her waistband and snapped it.

"I guess I'll catch your act later."

"Um. Yeah. After I get back. You know, from Jackie's."

"You betcha." He smirked at her before walking backwards down the hall and giving her a last good look at his *arrangement*.

Chapter Nine

Sneaking off to a bookstore in Columbus without Ginny was damn near a cardinal sin, so sneaking back in the house and pretending like his mug shot wasn't in *Paste* magazine was really more than Trent's conscience could take. In the weeks since the photo shoot, he'd been walking on eggshells waiting for the issue to come out and wishing that he'd told his sister right from the start what he'd been up to in Atlanta. *Paste* wasn't the kind of magazine likely to show up in any of Bibb City's remaining stores, but Ginny wasn't limited to their stomping grounds now that she had Hank who had a Ford Explorer. Even she got out as far as Atlanta lately, and Trent had avoided giving her The Talk as much as he avoided admitting to his extracurricular activities. He couldn't very well expect her to tell the truth when he lied or to remain pure when he was dirty.

Clutching a sack full of recent releases for her romance novel collection, Trent hesitated outside of Ginny's partially open door. Through the crack, he caught her giggling over a text message and shuffling a stack of papers on her lap, papers that Ginny tucked under a pillow at the sound of Trent's knock. Apparently, he wasn't the only one keeping secrets.

"Hey."

"I didn't say come in." Ginny launched a stuffed lizard at his gut.

Trent caught it and launched it back, clipping his sister's ear. "What, am I interrupting something?" Though not at all gooey in the middle, Ginny was still a young'un and not very good at hiding her feelings due to the blush complexion they both got from Margie. Trent cleared his throat. "Something going on that I ought to know about, Gin? Like something with Hank?"

"No." Ginny twisted the pink hem of her Taylor Swift T-shirt into a knot. "Sorta."

Trent cleared his throat again, but his voice still came out as halting and snarled as a water-logged boat engine. "Uh, I don't know how much Mama may have said about this before, but—*ahem.*" He coughed and almost couldn't stop. "I am a boy, if you need the scoop on what to expect from Hank."

Ginny turned so pink that her flushed face could have passed for sunburn. "I've already got the gist, thank you very much."

He didn't like the sound of that, but bit his tongue. "All right. Well. I'd, uh, appreciate you cluing me in if you're planning on…*ahem.* Being out overnight. Just so I know where you are. You know, just in case."

She showed approving surprise of his maturity, letting Trent know that he'd done a good job of not grimacing, but Ginny still didn't elaborate on the secret she'd tucked under her pillow.

"Or let's say you were gonna *go away,*" he emphasized, "maybe after the prom? Don't surprise me with something like that at the last minute, Gin."

Shame-faced, Ginny studied her hands for a minute, and then she reached under her pillow. "I was gonna wait until…well, I don't really know." She slid several glossy folders across her bed quilt. "I doubt anybody will want me as bad as my grades were before, but Hank said…" Ginny shrugged.

Trent scanned several brochures from the University of Here and the School Over There before he realized that Ginny was talking about college applications. She wasn't concealing a sex life; she was hesitating to go after a B.A.

"They're all in the state! It ain't like I'd go far away and leave you alone with Margie. I just…well, Hank's going to the Art College in Atlanta." Her words ran together with the giddy precocity of a little girl sitting on Santa's lap. "And he thinks I could go for something like writing at one of the state schools. I could come home on the weekends and help—"

"Gin." He hated to hear her hesitate, and Trent was convicted of the buckets of resentment he'd been doling out. What else could he call the way he'd withheld any kind of enthusiasm for being at home? Caroline's frequent cracks about *his* impassive expressions suddenly weren't so silly. "I don't care if you want to go to the moon for college."

"Really?"

"Goddamn right. Look, I know we both got the short end of the stick here, but I been doing this for—"

Trent cut himself off from saying *you,* from lying to his sister yet again. Nothing that he'd done recently had really been for her. He'd gone to Atlanta to grasp at anything that even smelled like pleasure, and he'd nearly killed Courtney because he'd needed someone to suffer like he'd been suffering through filling in for his absentee father and out-to-lunch mother. Acceptance brought with it a weight that carried Trent to the foot of Ginny's bed to sit down. He touched her little lifeless toes, each nail painted an amazing purple.

"Gin, remember when I said I wouldn't rest until I found out who did this to you?" She nodded, and Trent bit his lying lip; he hadn't rested before or since then. "It was Courtney Vickers."

Secrets couldn't be kept in a small town, and though Courtney hadn't even been an acquaintance, the story of his hospitalization had gotten around. Trent watched his sister put the facts together, and the picture that emerged enflamed her face.

"*Why?* Why didn't he call for help at least? He just left us out there!"

Trent could only imagine the horror of coming to consciousness on the side of a dark highway, could only imagine how long Ginny had sat there in pain waiting for help before she had tried to reach Margie, who'd been thrown from the car. Ginny had permanently damaged her spine in the process. To have her ask for an explanation instead of an apology said more than Trent really wanted to know about how well Ginny had gotten over it without his intervention, and to not be able to answer her question shamed him. He didn't know why Courtney had side-swiped his ladies off the road and then sped off; Trent hadn't bothered to ask, hadn't bothered even to pause before shedding the fucker's blood.

"I don't know, Gin. He was drunk. It was a hit and run—"

"The old 'Shit happens' defense, huh?" Ginny scoffed and stared at her brother, waiting for him to do better. He couldn't. "I heard he was gonna die."

"Maybe."

Ginny's amber eyes circled to the ceiling and then to the floor before returning to his stricken face. For half a second, she didn't seem to know him, and how could he blame her? He didn't really know himself.

"I don't know what to say," she finally admitted.

"Don't say nothing," Trent said fiercely, as though making her a vow. "You just go to school, and the prom, and you get into a good school somewhere. And don't you worry about money, 'cause when the time comes, I'll have it." He stood up and handed over the bookstore sack, but he did not pull out the *Paste* magazine as planned. "I got something big coming up, for both of us," he said, and he meant it.

Getting his shit together was the only thing Trent had to give his sister, since it was already way too late to lead by example.

It wasn't too late, however, to follow her lead, and all the way to Atlanta for his St. Patrick's Day date, Trent reconsidered his nearly two-month hesitation toward Caroline. What at first had seemed sensible about not hitting on his boss suddenly felt like a fear of being found out, a fear of stirring up the scrutiny of a woman who would surely have something to say about manslaughter. What Trent regretted wasn't what he'd done, but that it wasn't over, and Caroline's sweetness didn't seem at all compatible with his lack of appropriate remorse. Of course, he shouldn't have cared since he still kidded himself that he wasn't about to fall for Caroline Curran, or that he hadn't already done so, for that matter. He couldn't afford to get fired with Ginny's college tuition in the equation.

"No fuckin' way," he barked at Keith Urban who insisted through the car stereo that he was "Tangled Up in Love."

Farah had assured Trent numerous times that the suit she'd picked for him was iridescent not shiny, and caramel-colored not gold. Climbing out of his truck, Trent still couldn't tell the difference and was nervous about going behind Caroline's back to surprise her. The leather soles of his new shoes made a rich man's click up the concrete walk and then the steps. Trying to decide if he was in over his head, Trent took a deep breath before knocking on the door.

"Just a minute," he heard from at least halfway across the living room, and then the front door cracked open just an inch. "One minute! I need to find my other shoe and put on my lipstick," Caroline explained from behind the door, "but I don't want you to see me yet, so I'll leave the door open and then you close your eyes and count to —"

"I'll just wait out here, Caroline." Trent chuckled. "You could've been and back by now."

"Right." She flashed him a smile and sized him up. Trent noticed a competitive gleam come into her eye. "Make that two minutes."

Trent had time to go back to the truck and check that no hair was out of place before Caroline finally made it back. When she called out to ask if he was ready, he did a little drum-roll on the storm door and wolf-whistled when Caroline stepped out all smiles and coltish legs in her delicate gold heels. What he didn't say was that despite the lack of cleavage and nearly knee-length hem, her jade green dress was as heartbreaking as a spring breeze in Hell and painfully reminded him of what he'd done not to deserve her.

"You look nice," she said.

She looked delicious. Trent couldn't even speak.

"Great suit."

"Your friend Farah helped me out. Sent me to a tailor and everything, though she didn't mention that I'd end up being so shiny."

Smiling, Caroline waved that off. "It just has a little sheen. It's very modern."

He nodded, but couldn't tear his attention away from how the porch light scattered across glittery particles of lotion on her skin, as though she were a fairy. Mesmerized as he was, Trent realized too late that he'd been too caught up admiring her to express his admiration.

Her face fell. "Okay, then! We'd better get going." She held up her keys, then turned toward the door.

Trent started to apologize, until he saw the back of her dress. *"Damn."* Technically, there was no back, and his hands started to itch. In front, the creamy green fabric looped over a sparkly choker around her neck. In the back, that choker trailed right down her spine like a diamond leash from a collar. Spring ended for Trent, and he was officially in Hell and in the hottest part, according to his crotch. He honestly tried not to move a muscle, but Caroline kept her back turned just too goddamn long for fiddling with her keys. His dick, technically not a muscle, couldn't help but to move in for a closer inspection.

"Nice dress." Trent's lips brushed the tiny fragrant spiral curls that shot out from her head in every direction. She turned her ear toward his lips, and how could he help nipping at her gold hoop earring? Human lips had more fat than muscle anyway.

Trent's fingers closed over her keys and locked her dead bolt, mostly as an excuse to press against her behind. She didn't seem to mind, and he lost track of time while they shared breaths, half-turned as they both were into each other's faces.

"I was checking the weather report all week, hoping it wouldn't be too cold to wear it."

Though intended as an acknowledgment, Trent's "Mmm" came out more like a moan. He leaned a little forward, trying to coax her into turning her head two inches so that he could taste her pink sugar-stained mouth, but she wouldn't do it. He grinned. She knew how pretty she looked, and she was taunting him, as was the way of Southern ladies.

"Doesn't being your date make me your designated admirer for the night?"

He breathed the words in her ear, and she shivered. "Yes."

"How exactly am I allowed to show my admiration?" His tongue stretched the vowels into salty taffy.

"Did you have a suggestion?"

"Several. None that involve you making it to this party, though."

"Then I think we'd better go."

Trent offered his hand to lead her to the truck, a gesture that would have been gentlemanly if his grip hadn't been so sticky. "Whatever you say, boss lady."

In that same suggestive way all along the interstate, they competed to be charming, and occasionally losing to her admiration incited feelings in Trent that no mere party could improve. Even after they entered an auspicious gray block building, in which Reyes had not just a penthouse but a whole roof, Trent couldn't muster the subdued and intimidated something that was supposed to keep him in line for the night. His fingers stayed just under the hem of Caroline's cropped faux fur cape and brushed across her back whenever he had to lead her in or out of a door. She had skin like a ripe plum, moist enough to cling to his touch, soft enough to give in to his grip, and easily bruised, Trent imagined, by every body part that he had.

Reyes was standing right there when they stepped off of a private elevator and into his place. *"Querida."* He squeezed and complimented Caroline. "Trent." The men shook hands, briskly but no more, before Reyes moved on to the next set of arriving guests.

Wide-eyed, Caroline whispered to Trent, "That went well."

She said it like they'd escaped some kind of punishment, and Trent didn't like the implication that she'd been waiting on Reyes's approval.

"It typically does while you're still playing it close to the vest."

Caroline made a cross-eyed face that he ignored in favor of looking around. The penthouse was nice, like an art museum. Every wooden surface was burled or burnished within an inch of its life and insisted that the owner had good taste instead of suggesting he enjoyed living there. The room in which they stood was about as big as Trent's and Caroline's houses put together, but only about twenty very elegant people milled around drinking from black glass goblets and tumblers. Even past the temporary sound stage in a corner and outside of the mostly glass far wall, Reyes didn't have any extra friends taking in the sunken pool or the view of the city. Money apparently couldn't buy everything.

A waiter came by with a tray of seafood concoctions that Trent was about to sample before Caroline clutched his forearm. "Oh my God, that's Raphael Saadiq!"

"Who?" Trent tried to catch the waiter, but the crab what's-its, sadly, had moved on.

"Raphael Saadiq!"

She pulled Trent toward a little dimly lit nook near the stage where another waiter with a different tray offered them a drink. Trent took two and handed one to Caroline.

"He co-wrote 'Untitled (How Does It Feel).' Hello!" Obviously star struck, she giggled like a teenage girl. "But I've loved him since Tony! Toni! Toné! *Sons of Soul.* I think I'm going to shake his hand. Oh my God, do you think he would play a song for me?"

"I think he's about to play a song anyway." A six-piece ensemble, including Saadiq on bass guitar, chimed in on the extremely smooth first strains of "(Lay Your Head On My) Pillow." As soon as the titular words poured through the microphone in Saadiq's yearning tenor, Trent stripped off his suit jacket. "You wanna dance?"

She looked uncertain as he pulled her across Reyes's thick red area rug and onto the hardwood floor nearest the picture windows. "Umm, nobody else is."

"And here I thought this was supposed to be a party." Trent pulled her into his calculating grasp.

As was the signature of classic R&B, the rhythm of the song thumped like a human heart and cajoled the rest of the body into writhing along. Caroline's hips went wherever Trent's hot hand on her back told them to go. Whenever he twisted or turned her, his fingers slipped further down under her dress strap until he almost had a hand on her fleshy hip. He went wild at the thought that she wasn't wearing any panties, until she slapped his hand away from the string of her bikini.

Trent looked her in the eye to see if he'd gone too far, but she smiled at him. In turn, he pulled back from being so handsy and seduced her with his sly chameleon eyes. Though his cologne smelled more like pine than it did money, Trent hoped that his oak-hard arms wrapped in soft, white cotton emphasized the *man* in *country gentleman.*

The tune changed to "Love That Girl," an up-tempo number that hearkened back to the Motown sound. Besides steering clear of the other guests who joined them on the small dance floor, he had his hands full blending his two-step patterns with her improvisations. They fell into each other as often as not until finally Trent clutched her close to him. They turned in a circle as one, each accusing the other of having two left feet. Such hip wiggling as they did typically involved the tearing off of clothes and proved that the intersection of rhythm, rock, and roll was between two bodies.

Fate loved to test one's resolve to behave, and Reyes almost got cussed out when he tried to cut in. Trent just managed to keep his mouth shut, but the ire in his eyes did not go unnoticed.

"Forgive the intrusion," Reyes replied to Trent's glare, "but I need to speak with you, *querida.*"

With an arm around her shoulder, Reyes drew Caroline away. She looked helplessly at Trent. "Um, I'll be right back. One minute, I promise."

Left aroused and alone on the dance floor, Trent was quick to slip through a side door and out into the cool air that blew across the roof. The scent of chlorine and imported tropical foliage trailed him around a pond-sized pool and past a varnished bamboo shed to the balcony where he unexpectedly encountered Jackie.

"How long you been here?"

She snapped out of an obvious funk. Not a lot of women looked sleek in all white, but in an ivory silk jumpsuit, Jackie's svelte figure screamed snow leopard. "Long enough to see you pushing up on my friend like she's yours for the taking. You'd better watch yourself and Reyes, too, before he hurts you."

"Yeah, I reckoned he was faking that cool-under-the-collar act."

"Reyes might be too cool. He would never make a scene. But his kind of cool is ruthless and holds a grudge, which is a lot worse in the long run than throwing a punch." She drained a black glass tumbler much too quickly.

At the loud clink of loose ice, Trent asked, "Can I get you a refill?"

"No thanks. I'm trying not to get really drunk and do something dumb like confront him."

"Over what?"

"We almost had a thing, before. Well, we were friends, and then… and then Caroline. I don't know why I'm surprised; she's so totally one of Reyes's girls."

"One of his girls?"

"Someone sweet and easy that he can keep in his pocket like a fucking candy bar. After twenty years of friendship, he thought he could turn me into some soft-serve, vanilla housewife type, but I showed him." She didn't mention the pictures she'd sent to Reyes, and Trent likewise didn't reveal that he'd overheard all about them from one of Caroline's unguarded phone conversations.

Instead, Trent laughed, relieved. "So he's chasing Caroline because you don't like him."

She raised a brow. "What's funny?"

Trent rubbed the bridge of his nose and laughed again, at himself. "How far a man will go to pretend like he's not in love with a woman."

Jackie rolled her eyes and slurped the remaining liquor from her ice cubes.

Trent felt uncomfortably sympathetic toward Reyes, who could be a jackass, but even jackasses had feelings, and Jackie seemed like a tough woman to get next to. He looked at Jackie, who glared at him in return. Trent wondered why she was friends with Caroline at all until he recalled that sour people needed sweetness the most.

"Would you like to dance, Ms. Goode?"

"What?"

"You know, where you hold my hands and move your feet back and forth? It's gotta beat standing out here alone, sucking down Tex's booze and feeling sorry for yourself. We could at least go in there and make him jealous."

Jackie measured him with a stare that abruptly turned into a smile. "You're on, as long as you don't expect me to do the goddamn two-step."

Across the roof and behind the window of an ultra-modern office, Caroline breathed a petty sigh of relief when Trent and Jackie crossed past the pool and toward the penthouse. She was waiting impatiently for Reyes; after leading her the long way around the front room and stopping frequently to charm his guests, he had disappeared to take a call that would confirm the urgent and personal news he had to share. Hoping it was about Trent's band and fearing it was about Nez, Caroline had wandered to the window to fret and caught her date in deep conversation with long-limbed Jackie. A lot of image-obliterating eye-crossing had gone into Caroline keeping herself from rapping on the window.

When finally Reyes burst back into the office, Caroline had worked herself into a lather wondering what Trent and Jackie were doing in the front room. "Reyes, what—"

"Milan's here." He grasped Caroline's bare shoulders. *"Querida,* she came as the guest of someone I invited. *Discúlpame."* His eyes seemed to watch her for sudden movements. "She's been drinking, and I didn't want her to catch you unaware. I think there's been some kind of falling out between her and Nez. You wouldn't know anything about that, would you?"

Caroline withdrew from his grasp and his gaze, as though the word *extortionist* were written on her forehead. Reyes certainly maintained a look of suspicion that she was about to make a scene.

"I can have her sent home."

"No. It's fine," Caroline lied because she could already feel herself getting gooey in the middle. "Excuse me."

She brushed past him and turned right only to turn left a second later toward the private restroom at the rear of the corridor. She'd heard Reyes exit behind her and prayed when she found the restroom occupied that he would keep going toward the party and leave her alone. When he did, she doubled her arms around her waist and tried to hold herself together while she waited for the restroom to empty. She wasn't going to fall apart in front of an audience again, and as she was on a date, she also had Trent to deal with. For all that she still considered herself out of his league, he played hardball and would call her out if he saw her mascara smudged, so Caroline tried to keep the frustrated mist in her eyes from becoming actual tears. Funny, then, that she thought she'd caught her reflection in a mirror when Milan burst out of the bathroom scrubbing an index finger under her eyelashes and screaming into her phone.

"You said you'd go to jail for me, and now I'm jeopardizing you? I'm doing this for —" Milan went silent at the sight of Caroline.

In fact, they both went so still with shock that they could hear Nez loudly threatening to dump Milan five different public ways if she didn't "get her interfering ass home in half a damn hour." They stared at each other, two teary-eyed little girls in a throw-down by the monkey bars, though neither of them was the bully to blame for instigating. The hard and unkind truth was that Caroline wasn't the only woman in the world who'd been side-swiped by a brute.

"If you leave first," Caroline said, "at least you won't be the one who got dumped by a man like him." She didn't stay to hear what the girl had to say. Harsh words lashed her back, but did not hurt as badly as the idea of staying on Nez's victim list and keeping company with the Bitchneys of the world.

At the end of the carpeted corridor, Reyes tried to intercept Caroline, but she side-stepped him and cut across the dance floor to brush past Trent and Jackie, which, though not exactly a confrontation, was still an honest display of her displeasure. Trent followed right on her heels all the way around the pool and the little bamboo building, but Caroline waited until they'd made it behind the trees and tiki torches to turn on him.

"What's wrong?" Trent demanded before she could get a word out.

Caroline glared at him for a long time and finally had to admit, "Nothing! It's a party, and you're dancing." She crossed her eyes. "It's fine!"

"What happened with Reyes?"

"What happened with Jackie?"

"Uh, nothing?" Trent replied, his tone seeming to questioning her sanity.

"Nothing. See? Just like I said."

He folded his arms and stared at her, but Caroline didn't elaborate.

Trent shifted his stance. "Usually I don't mind when you do your loony thing, but waiting around for you wore down my patience."

Caroline's eyes flared. *"Loony?"*

"What's going on? Look, I know it's probably none of my business—"

"No, it isn't!"

Anger mottled his expression. "Well, hell. If you wanna file me under strictly pleasure, Sugar, just say the word."

"That's obviously what you're here for." She flung one arm back toward the escalating party and rolled her hips in an ugly imitation of dancing.

"I thought that's what we were both here for. We're on a date, remember?"

"Then what happened to you being *my* designated admirer?"

"Personally, I thought I was doing a good goddamn job until you left me hanging for Reyes!" Scowling, he gritted his teeth before continuing in a tone that was razor-edged. "Jackie was in a bad way, so I asked her to dance, and that's all."

The handsy way he'd danced with her was Caroline's only reference point, and her eyes went wide. She aped his accent to reply, "Yeah, I'll betcha you showed her a real good time."

Trent whirled on her. His scowl had turned into outright glowering.

"Jackie being so tall must've made it easier to grope her," Caroline continued. "I remember how hard you had to work to get your hands down *my* dress!"

"Sugar, you can tell yourself that tale if you want to, but you and I both know that I didn't have to work to get you wet." She blanched when he leaned in to add, "I could smell you when we stepped off the front porch."

Caroline's neck popped back, and she slapped him. She didn't feel justified, though, since he was right, and she was only acting out of petty jealousy.

He showed no reaction, but condescendingly drawled, "Feel better?"

Whereas the first slap had stung, Caroline actually tried to hurt him with the second. He laughed at her, infuriating her further.

"You been waiting a long time for a good excuse to slap somebody, huh?"

Though she wanted to, Caroline had better sense than to try and hit him again. Instead, she puckered up like the Virgin Queen and tried to look down her nose at him, no small feat for a half-pint.

"Aw, fix your face," Trent said. "You're only horrified 'cause you liked it."

Her mouth fell open, way too dramatically. "How dare you! You stupid…stupid—"

"What, you're all right with violence, but you're too good to say, 'Son of a bitch'? Or how about, 'Fuck you, Trent.' Comes easier than slapping, to me."

The hairpin turn into sexual innuendo happened so fast that Caroline wasn't sure whether she wanted to kiss him or kill him.

"Yeah, I reckon a good hard fuck is the real cure for what's ailing you."

"Fuck you, Trent!"

He stepped up to her. "You wanna say that again, or you wanna take me up on it?"

Like a slap in the face, his first kiss hit hard and was quickly gone. The second was a similar kind of angry taunt that Caroline returned, and then they made a bruising game of sucking at each other's lips in between glares until Trent bit her. She shoved him, and he laughed, then grabbed her hand and pressed it to the tented fly of his pants.

"Good and hard." He hooked her fingers in the waistband of his pants and kissed her, suggesting that his dick was a gift for her to unwrap when she was ready.

Teeth cutting each other's lips, they backed away from the pool, into the balcony rail, and then up against the little bamboo house tucked into the imported foliage. Trent turned the knob and grabbed Caroline to keep her from collapsing backward. Tired of craning his neck to kiss her, he snatched her up by the ass and carried her across the little storage room. One of her shoes fell off, and the other she kicked into a stainless steel gas grill before landing hard on her butt on a small wine-chilling refrigerator. Heaving for breath and seething at her, Trent undid his pants and reached for her hand. Caroline grabbed his hand instead, and he didn't need an explicit invitation to reach between her legs. Scoffing at her pushing aside her panties, Trent yanked them off and spread her thighs as wide as they would go. Just a little kneading from his fingers stirred up the overripe spunk of her, sweet and tart just like those small, dark summer plums that country boys ate right off of the tree and sucked down to the seed.

Like the scavenger he was, Trent kissed her in a slobbering, messy frenzy and bruised her lips with his gluttony. He whipped it out, and Caroline nearly pulled it off in her haste to get him inside her. The wine refrigerator's glass door fell open, and the bottles inside clanked and crashed in time to their fucking and his grunting. Her hands grabbed his ass, and his hands were so anxious for her tits that they stretched her dress to the tearing point. Their mouths bashed together, trying to kiss as though they cared about anything more than coming. Thick and wide, Trent jabbed deep inside of Caroline until snug became tight, tight became a vise, and she squeezed a stream of awestruck obscenities out of him. Trent hooked Caroline's knees in his elbows and let the last of her orgasm milk him dry.

Afterward, they lingered still stuck together and gasped for breath. Stretched out on her back across the delightfully cold wine refrigerator and part of an adjoining countertop, Caroline grinned at him. The back of her hand swiped sweat and lipstick from her mouth. She looked dazed, like his good hard fucking really had shaken loose the things that were ailing her.

She propped up on her elbows and kicked her heels into the backs of Trent's bare thighs. "Fuck Nez!"

He liked the way she wielded the cuss word as though it belonged to her, but Trent's face fell to hear another man's name in the afterglow.

"Sorry," Caroline said. "I mean, thanks."

Trent blinked in consideration for a second, then reckoned maybe it was okay to just say, "You're welcome." He was perched on his palms outside of her thighs, enjoying the cold climate that surrounded the wine chiller. Caroline sat all the way up and scraped his sweat-soaked hair off his forehead. She smiled and kissed him like they really weren't going to have a long conversation about what this meant. Trent didn't know for sure if he was okay with that. "Uh, I didn't plan on this happening, so I wasn't wearing—"

"Shh! Don't ruin it."

If coming back to reality was ruining it, Trent was that much less okay with playing the part of Caroline's rebound fantasy fuck. He pulled out of her. "What's ruined is your dress, I think."

Caroline glanced down to survey herself, and he briskly put his clothes back together. When he handed over her panties, she kissed him, and he let her, but nothing more. "Can I borrow your jacket? I can't walk around like this."

"Don't you think maybe we ought to go?"

"Yeah. Fucking on the fly isn't nearly as neat as they make it seem in the movies. I can't just put on some lipstick and carry on like I don't stink of sex." She laughed a little. "I've never done something like this before."

"Don't worry. When the regret comes crashing in, you can blame it on me." Trent found her shoes and handed them over with the same nonchalance as he'd handed over her panties.

Her eyes were wide, and as usual, the sweetness in them pierced his course heart.

"What just happened? Why are you doing your Stiff Lips McStonyface thing? Five minutes ago, I'm sure that was Trenton Michael Buckney being so amazing to me." Caroline's face fell with her shoulders after she shrugged. "Who are you now?"

It wasn't an accusation, but concern; fucking down to his level apparently didn't change Caroline being too good for him.

"I don't know," Trent said.

Caroline stared at him, like she was waiting for him to do better.

"Just Trent." He kissed her. "That's all I wanna be." She was slow kissing him back, but when she did, they both put feelings to it. Trent didn't know what all of those feelings were, but he held her face and kissed her slower and deeper to prolong what he feared was his last untroubled moment before *everything* came crashing in.

Chapter Ten

Every time Caroline tried to get upset about Trent not calling since the party, she remembered that she owed him for banging her into the best mood she'd had in a year. Not hearing from him wasn't new anyhow; he'd gone home as scheduled and would be back that evening for their Thursday gig. While she sat at her secretarial desk watching the clock count down to one p.m., Caroline rehearsed some badass things to say when Trent showed up at her house and tried to put the moves on her.

She, Caroline Curran, had *fucked* a man, had enjoyed the kind of carefree, guttural, shake down to rock bottom coitus that matched the way the word *fuck* hollowed out the mouth. With Nez, after spending weeks in frequent slumps, she'd always overdressed for sex and tried to attach lofty emotions to the encounter that were lacking the rest of the time. With Trent, nothing had been tested or proven with sex. She'd simply enjoyed the way that the rock-and-rolling of his groin had lobotomized all things Nez from her mind. Freedom had come with the friction that she'd felt when he'd pushed into her, had come with the drag of slick wet flesh against her long-undisturbed nerves. Damn it, her vagina had sparkled with tiny flint strikes of lust that crackled up and down her hamstrings and spine, sharper and hotter under the pressure that he'd pumped into her until, finally, Caroline had burst into a violent but quickly dying fire. She'd needed to know that sex would be that good for her again.

"If you have to keep going over it blow by blow at least go over it aloud."

Still enthralled at the thought of her body being a thing apart from her feelings, being a magnificent experience of sweat and skin and smells unto itself, Caroline couldn't get it together to protest Jackie ribbing her for the hundredth time.

"Huh?"

Eyebrow cocked, Jackie smoothed down her skirt and perched on the edge of Caroline's desk.

"As much effort as I put into salvaging your reputation after you left the party, you could at least provide some details about what it was like to hump the hillbilly."

Scoffing, Caroline tried to pretend she didn't know what Jackie was talking about, but two days of similar cross-examination had pretty much confirmed that she and Trent had been up to no good in Reyes's fancy shed.

"No, thank you, because that would be weird."

Jackie primly patted her chignon into place, though the devil was in her eyes.

"Interesting. Because with you, when you like the guy, it's weird to talk shop, whereas when you don't like him, it's gossip."

"Nuh uh!"

"You've been giving me the rundown since you cut your lip on Trevon Hawkins's braces, Spring Fling '93. So." Jackie plucked a piece of chocolate from a bowl on Caroline's desk. "You like him."

"I liked *it.*"

"Good, so you aren't going to do something really dumb like fall in love with a man that you can't handle? And I can save my lecture about having your fun but—"

"Yes, you can save it!"

Jackie smirked. "Because you don't like *him.* You just liked *it.*"

"Right."

Caroline sat up extremely straight and hammered on the computer mouse. She had been striving for strength about as long as Jackie had taken aim at being a nice girl, and neither of them had managed either yet. The office's front door burst open.

"Right," Jackie replied sarcastically and then swiveled her head toward a messenger who carried an enormous bunch of perfect orchids.

Since both of them knew Reyes's peace-making bouquet on sight, Caroline and Jackie exchanged an eye-roll at his exorbitance. The arrangement that the messenger sat on Caroline's desk was worth hundreds of dollars, and she pulled the card while Jackie grasped a pen to sign for the delivery. They were both shocked when the card revealed that Reyes had sent the flowers to Jackie.

"'So sorry about last fall, Jacks,'" Caroline read from the card. "'The pleasure of your company was more significant than I grasped at first. Dinner soon; I'll call you. R.A.B.'?" Caroline's question was meant for the message rather than the initials. She looked up at elegant Jackie and had to blink to keep Reyes's rebuff from stinging tears into her eyes. "Last fall?"

Jaw clenched, Jackie bade the messenger to wait with one raised finger, and then retreated to her office. When she returned, she had a cell phone pressed to her ear and a pair of scissors in one hand. She gave the messenger a twenty while she left a terse voicemail for Reyes.

"If you *ever* try to pit me against Caroline again, you'll end up in the same condition as these fucking flowers!"

She turned her camera phone and took a picture of the scissors snapping a few of the blooms clean off, and just like that, fifty bucks fell to the floor.

"This is why I send pictures. Men like you don't understand the words, 'Don't mess with me!'"

Jackie hung up, and Rod Stewart's "Da Ya Think I'm Sexy?" chimed from both of their cell phones several times while Jackie finished castrating the arrangement. She and Caroline each pitched in an additional five bucks to make sure the messenger returned the arrangement to Reyes's office, and as soon as the traumatized young man was gone, the girls stared at each other.

"You know he's coming over here," Jackie told Caroline. "He's probably already in the car practicing a sorrowful speech on the way."

"Can I go, Jacks?" Caroline's desk chair squawked against the hasty way she shoved back from the desk. Jackie grasped her friend's shoulder before she could pull on her peacoat.

"C.C., I think you should stay and tell him to mind his own motherfucking business."

"Is that what you told him, *last fall?*" Caroline coldly inquired.

"This is going to sound awful, and I'm sorry. But he knew that courting you would torture me because, well, I slept with him." Jackie brushed Caroline's bangs out of her startled eyes. "What he didn't count on was that we're sisters and that we love each other too damn much to get in a cat fight over his ass."

Caroline blanched. "Jacks! You didn't tell me? What if I'd slept with him?"

"He's not your type. That's not an excuse. Fuck!" She slapped a palm to her head and rubbed her temple. "Weren't we talking about you? You were miserable after your break-up, and a spa day and a margarita weren't going to cut it. I knew Reyes wouldn't hurt you, and I thought you wanted a man to…"

Caroline frowned and folded her arms across her chest. "To what? Make me feel better about myself?" That was true, but it was also pathetic.

"Well, you needed a different man, didn't you?" Jackie smiled wryly. "If that's Trent, fine. Like him. Just don't let him hurt you; he's the kind that can. Lasso his ass and tell Reyes to step off."

"I can't! How am I going to look Reyes in the eye after I did the nasty in his backyard?"

"Girl, those flowers were just Reyes being petty because he didn't get his way. He wouldn't be trying to shame you about getting your swirl on if you'd done it with his caramel ass." Jackie stabbed her stiletto through one of the orchid blooms on the floor. "Tell him he's supposed to have your back no matter what. I mean, either he is your friend or he isn't."

"Can't you tell him for me? I think you owe me after this hidden sex revelation."

Jackie cocked a brow and circled five fingers around Caroline's pleading expression. "Weak sauce." She kissed her index finger and thumped the kiss on Caroline's forehead. "Go. But do not spend the rest of the night fretting. Call that hillbilly over and take him for another ride to get your mind off of it."

"He's not a hillbilly, Jacks," Caroline called on her way to the office door.

"The hell he isn't! He's just a hot hillbilly."

By the time Caroline hammered down the stairwell to the parking garage, she'd worked herself into a terror of finding Reyes standing beside her Jetta. He wasn't there, but the terror trailed her into traffic, where she almost sideswiped another car, and then across Atlanta to Smith's Olde Bar, where the band was playing that night. Because she'd mentioned Smith's in the upcoming events part of their profile in *Paste*, The Trent Michaels Band had actual billing out front of the pub. Caroline parked facing a poster of Trent and the gang all lined up like Mount Rushmore, in keeping with his taciturn photos. Shaking her head, Caroline got out of the car and nearly stepped into the path of a black SUV that suddenly pulled away from the curb. She almost said, "Sorry." Instead, she flipped the bird and shouted, "Watch it!"

Though silly, the shout felt good and reminded Caroline of her escapade with Trent. After dropping off a box of band T-shirts, she carried on to her neighborhood in an improved mood. Despite being two days old, the physical memory of sex made the hungry mouth between her thighs wet its lips. She fantasized during the hour-long drive to the Publix near her house where she stopped for pre- and post-coital provisions: condoms, lip balm, flavored water, a mixed nuts assortment for quick energy, and frozen fudge bars to stick in their mouths before they went down. She treated herself to one bar on the way to the car. She dripped fudge on her sweater and stopped short long enough to notice a black SUV parked a few slots away from her car, the same one that had almost run her over before.

Newly terrified of being arrested for making an obscene gesture, Caroline got into her car and studied the suv in the rearview mirror. She thought she was overreacting until she pulled out of the parking lot and the black car followed. She couldn't see the license plate or the driver's face behind tinted glass. By the time Caroline turned into her cul-de-sac, it was too late to do anything about the fact that she'd been followed home except pull up in her tiny driveway and have a panic attack.

When Trent's cell phone rang in his pocket, the nurse behind the hospice desk of Emory University Hospital shot him a look and pointed at the sign on the wall that read, "Please turn off your cell phone," right above, "Please wash your hands." Five fucking times in the past hour, he'd used sanitizing goo to clean the sweat off of his palms in anticipation of actually going into Courtney Vickers's room. The hospice nurse had been sympathetic to Trent's nerves at first and had praised him for bringing a potted plant instead of flowers, but she gave up on chit-chat after he chose to scowl into space.

Trent's cell rang again; he pulled it out, read Caroline's number in the display, and then powered down the phone. No doubt she was calling to pretend like she wasn't upset that he hadn't called, and Trent couldn't explain himself without telling the whole truth about Courtney Vickers. His *Paste* magazine article had made the rounds of Bibb City, and having a higher profile scared him to death. He couldn't imagine Shane and Reyes shaking hands at his next gig or Jackie not looking down on his little sister. Atlanta had been his refuge, but last night he'd had a nightmare about his entire town playing paparazzi in front of Caroline's house.

He was only visiting Courtney to have something humane to tack onto the end of "I beat a man to death" when he confessed to Caroline. Trent's leg bounced, and he leaned forward on his jean-clad knees to stop it. With all ten fingers threaded into his hair, he shut his eyes and tried not to give in to the excuse that he had to leave because Caroline had called. The plain truth was that he couldn't go into that room because God was in there doing the math, and though it would be for entirely different reasons, Trent was sure he'd come up just as short as Courtney. A pain that he was reluctant to call regret pinched his sternum, and he stood up, leaving the potted plant on top of a copy of *Paste* magazine, of course. Wondering whether God had left it there just to fuck with his head, Trent stomped to the elevator and pressed the down button.

He called Caroline twice on the way to her house, and when he got to the jammed by-pass, he reckoned that she'd called to warn him about the traffic. The more time he spent creeping along bumper to bumper, the crankier he got about his failed reconciliation with Courtney.

"What the hell was I supposed to say to that comatose son of a bitch?" he demanded loudly and presumably of God since no one else was there. God didn't answer; He was probably busy coaching repentant people through the difficult process of forgiveness. "I don't even want to be forgiven!" As soon as the words were out, Trent knew that the real issue on the table was him forgiving Courtney and letting the resentment go that the rest of his foreseeable future would be spent on the roller-coaster that was Margie.

After that, he sank into a sullen funk that lasted all the way to Caroline's cul-de-sac. Trent parked at the curb in front of her mailbox, jumped out of his truck, slammed the door, and tried to rein in his temper on the way up the walk. Being pissed wasn't going to change a single one of his responsibilities, but, "Shit fuck fuck motherfucking goddamn it all to hell!" Resentment wasn't humane, but it was human, and he hoped that giving in to it was a first step on the road to getting over it like Ginny had. Trent swallowed hard, tried to summon his stone face, and couldn't. He cleared his throat and rang the doorbell anyway.

It took Caroline five minutes to answer the door, and when she did, she had a baseball bat in one hand. "Why didn't you answer your phone?" she hollered through the glass storm door before unlocking it and hurrying him in with one frantic hand.

Taking in her wild eyes and the paranoid way that she checked all of the door locks twice, Trent pulled at the neck of his white T-shirt. "What's gotten into you?" She was wearing her comfort clothes, knee-high socks and a worn red T-shirt as long as a dress, but Caroline looked anything but comfortable. While she peered at him from beneath furrowed brows, Trent pried the wooden bat out of her hand. "Caroline? What's wrong?"

"I think someone followed me home! I mean, someone did follow me home, and I think it was Nez."

"*What?*"

"I was at the grocery store. H-he was right behind m-me."

Though his face was pinched and serious, Trent spoke in a soothing tone to calm her fear. "What'd the car look like, sugar?" He rubbed away the gooseflesh on her arm.

"An SUV. Black with black windows." She watched Trent pull his cell phone out of his pocket. "An old GMC Jimmy, I think."

He dialed some numbers and then covered the handset. "Did you get the license plate?"

"No. Are you calling the cops?"

"Did you already call?"

"No!" She snatched his phone and hung up. "I can't."

"'Course you can. Even if you didn't get the plate, you don't want to wait until something bad happens to start a paper trail. I'll be right here with you." He squeezed her shoulder.

Caroline shrugged off his touch.

"I can't involve the cops." She tried to overcome a reluctance to look in his eyes while she explained what kind of person she was. Finally, she fixed her gaze on Trent's T-shirt. "I can't tell them because I'm extorting Nez, which is illegal. I think that's why he's threatening me like this. He knows I can't do anything about it."

She kept her eyes on the taut way his shirt stretched across his chest. The fact that she was aroused made Caroline feel like even more of a horrible person until she realized that being aroused meant she wasn't afraid. Scared, yes, but not incapacitated with terror the way she'd been while cowering in her car in the driveway. She wasn't terrified with Trent there, and Caroline braved a look up into his eyes.

"Extorting him how? You got something on him that you're keeping here? Is that why he followed you home, because he didn't know where you live?"

"Actually, no. I guess he didn't."

"But what you've got on him, you're keeping here?"

"Not anymore." Caroline watched his expression settle as he recalled the busted memory sticks. "They're all sex tapes. I have the rest of them in a safe deposit box. I was supposed to trade them to him last time, and I didn't."

"Why?"

Done diluting her feelings, Caroline announced, "Because I *hate* his guts!" Like the word *fuck*, the violence of *hate* scrubbed out her mouth.

"All right. Well. You can't stay here by yourself. I'll be around through Saturday, and then I think you ought to go and stay with Jackie."

Caroline waited, but Trent didn't rebuke or scold her. "That's the first place he'll look."

"Not if you're out of town. We'll make a big show of taking you to the airport. I'll drive your car back here and camp out, and you can drive my truck to Jackie's after I'm gone. Let him follow me. I *hope* he follows me."

In all that plotting, Trent never once questioned her motives or her methods. He instead put himself on the line not so much for her right to be hateful, but for her right to be flawed. The difference between those two things left a clean taste on Caroline's recently scrubbed tongue.

"Don't fight," she said. "I don't want you to get hurt."

"I wouldn't be the one getting hurt."

"If you fight, it'll never be over." Alone in her mind, she hadn't been able to escape an obsession with Nez, but Trent had penetrated her thoughts and given her better things to think about than revenge. "And I'm not letting him run me out of my house," she added, not wanting Nez's name in her mouth. "I'll call Reyes; he'll know how to sort this out."

"I told you, I already know how to get it sorted."

Stiff Lips McStonyface was back, and Caroline couldn't help giggling with pleasure.

"You're jealous?"

Trent snorted.

"I think you are," she said.

"You think wrong."

"I know that you don't want me to know that you like me. You've been trying to hide it." Trent didn't say anything, and she licked her lips trying to hold on to her courage. "Why? Don't you want me to like you back?"

Asked bluntly like that, there was no wiggle room around the truth that they both seemed to want a hell of a lot more than a few paying gigs. Caroline was proud of herself.

Trent swallowed. "Do you?"

Caroline's cheeks burned and her stomach bottomed out, but she didn't wilt. She was excited, hanging in a moment like a roller coaster free-fall. "Yes. A second ago when I told you all my dirt, and you didn't even flinch? I really liked you a lot right then."

"What's to flinch from, Caroline? Some numb-nuts hurt you, and you hurt him back." He brushed the bangs from her brow with gentle fingers. "That's called standing up for yourself, the way I understand it, as long as you don't go too far."

She watched the fingers that had touched her so tenderly clench into a mean fist that he tried to shove into his pocket. Caroline caught his hand and rubbed her thumb across his knuckles while she remembered how they'd looked split and scabbed the first day they'd met. "What's too far?"

Shit fuck fuck, she was on to him. "If it stole all your sweetness, it'd be too far."

Caroline flinched from the harsh tone that didn't match his words, but only for a second, and then, just as she had at the party, she seemed to ask with her pretty brown eyes, *Who are you really?* The truth pooled on the tip of Trent's tongue, and he kissed her lovingly for as long as he could stand to admit that he was crazy about her.

"Naw, you still taste sweet to me," he croaked while she stared at him in confusion. His thumb stroked across her cheekbone while he tried to make his mouth move into the story about Courtney Vickers, but instead of those words, Trent's deep truth rose up and kissed Caroline again until her pulse was hammering in her throat. "I think you ought to cancel that gig for tonight."

She looked from his lips to his eyes, which he figured were deep blue with things that he wasn't ready to say. "I can't cancel, or we'll have to pay."

"Then I think you'd better tell Marlon and Minerva to get set up without us." Trent flashed his watch in her face and then stripped off his shirt.

It had been a while since she'd seen his bare chest, and Caroline bit her lip at the sight of the almost extreme way that his body was carved. Muscles, tendons, and veins stood out in stark relief all the way down to the deeply indented hips that barely held up his jeans. With just a little tug on that waistband, he would have popped out rigid and ready.

"Okay." Unwilling to stop ogling him, Caroline back-pedaled into her bedroom with every step that Trent took forward. She found her purse on the bed and dropped it on the floor after pulling out her cell phone. While she dialed, Trent kept coming toward her and unbuttoning his indigo jeans on the way. "Hi, uh…" The extra half-inch at a time of visible crotch stole her sense. "Minerva! Yeah, um, we're going to be—*ahem*—late," Caroline garbled after Trent stuck her hand down the front of his pants. "Mmhmm! Yeah. Set up. Yup. All-righty. See ya."

Trent kissed her as soon as she hung up, and he rasped his tongue against hers in the same tingly way that she danced her fingers over his dick. When she squeezed, he sucked. When she teased, he just barely ghosted his lips over hers. She got the hang of tormenting him pretty quickly.

He groaned and pulled away from her. Then he ripped open the rest of his button fly and stepped out of his jeans. He tugged the sleeve of her t-shirt, flopped onto her bed, and stretched out. "Your turn."

After Caroline pulled her shirt off over her head, she found Trent reclined into her pillows, still amazingly naked and watching her with amused eyes.

"Leave the knee-highs. I think Mighty Mouse is gonna look mighty fine hanging off of my shoulders."

Right then, Caroline fell a little in love with him; it wasn't every man who could make kink out of her cartoon socks. When she was undressed, Trent beckoned her with one hand.

"Come sit up here," he said, and she joined him on her knees at the head of the bed. "Up *here.*" He puckered up his wide lips for a kiss. "Why don't you have a seat?"

Caroline's eyes widened. "Are you talking about what I think you're talking about?"

"Probably so, sugar."

"It's just that I bought props for that!" Caroline scrambled off of the bed.

When she returned with condoms and an unwrapped fudge bar, Trent took the ice cream from her and made a skeptical face. "You do realize this means that my mouth will be cold?"

Caroline nodded, but she hesitated since she'd never tried the idea before and had only read it in a magazine at the grocery store checkout. "Maybe we should give it a trial run first."

His cheeks hollowed and made a nasty noise when he sucked on the fudge bar.

Caroline giggled until he leaned forward and closed his cold lips over her nipple. Her initial gasp became a titillated hiss in the course of his mouth warming to the heat of her skin.

"Works for you, huh?"

She nodded, and he moved to her other nipple. Caroline drew back, took the fudge bar, and stuck it in her mouth.

Trent grinned. "I like the way you think."

Moments later, Trent was flat on his back holding her thighs open to his marauding mouth. Inverted over him, Caroline was caught between sucking the melted fudge bar and licking the drips from him. Busy as she was, Trent made her come much faster than she was able to clean him up, but he didn't seem to mind. He rolled her off of him and snatched the gooey fudge bar before her arms and head fell uselessly over the edge of the bed. Lying there euphoric, Caroline felt the melted ice cream paint her belly with a thick, cold swatch of chocolate. Trent's grainy tongue followed right along to lick and lap at the rivulets that ran between her breasts and toward her neck. He stuck the last of the ice cream bar in her mouth, tucked into her, and then sucked fudge from her tongue while he fucked her right off of the bed and onto the floor. The friction of his pelvis matched the carpet scrubbing against her palms as they went down in a sticky, greedy heap.

Three hours, two showers, a delivery pizza, and a box of fudge bars later, they were on stage together at Smith's Olde Bar and were gearing up for the first song of their opening act set. Trent fumbled with tuning a guitar, because he couldn't stop glancing at Caroline. Dressed in a plain black sleeveless dress, she sat at the keyboard to fill in for Marlon's friend who hadn't been able to make it at the last minute. Her usually straight hair had crimped beneath his fingers when he'd bent her face down over the arm of the couch and loved her a little more, regardless that they'd been running late.

He could make her say any nasty thing in the world that he wanted while he was in her, and every time Trent now looked her way, Caroline's cheeks betrayed the things she'd admitted to him. He'd said some things, too, not about Courtney Vickers, but he was working that way starting with Jonny Lang's "Breakin' Me," which Trent knew was one of Caroline's favorite songs. Minerva led them in with a high-hat count off, and then Caroline's little fingers caressed the guitar melody with delicate piano trills that cracked Trent's voice every time he heard them. Like her kisses and her sighs and the high sharp delighted way that she squealed when he showed no mercy to her magic spot, Caroline's little ways made him bigger than the sex, bigger even than the song when its emotional climax clawed out of his throat.

Trent caught Caroline staring at him, and he stared right back while his heart, healed of that hole and pumped full of blood, ached in time to the song's desperate lyrics. She smiled, and he hoped she understood that even though it wasn't the whole story, love was Trent's deepest, truest part, and would remain after the rest was forgiven and forgotten.

Chapter Eleven

itting on a steel stool in a recording booth at Island Records, Trent stretched out his arms and tried inconspicuously to check his watch for the fourth time in one minute. It was well after two o'clock, and Caroline still wasn't there. She'd been jittery all week, a fact that Trent wanted to chock up to fear of being followed again, but she might've been avoiding admitting that she'd made up with Reyes. Trent certainly hadn't scored the recording session for his good behavior. He checked the time again and saw that the minute hand of his battered watch had swept a whole ten seconds from two twenty to two twenty-one p.m. He scowled.

Minerva, who led the rest of the band in being tired of Trent's pissy mood, did a drumroll that made a bad joke of his down-turned mouth. "What's it gonna take, Garth Brooks? A drink? A joint? A baseball bat to the skull? We don't have all day to get a good take out of you! We've got a gig tonight."

Kyle flicked one of his limber fingers against the guitar tabs for "The Way That You Play It."

"Yeah, dude. This song, though cute, has not improved since *dawn.*" Kyle exaggerated the time that they'd spent recording, but not by much. "Your Muddy Waters, on the other hand, needs some work before we go on tonight." Kyle's opinions carried extra weight since he was usually too high to speak, so Marlon nodded in agreement, though he usually seemed sympathetic to Trent's inclination to bite the hand with which Reyes fed them.

"Sorry, y'all," Trent growled and didn't sound sincere at all. He tugged the neck of his white T-shirt, and slumping, waited for the producer to tell them to try again. A sound tech came in and made adjustments only to

Trent's microphone, though doing so before had not taken the growl out of Trent's voice.

The producer's voice crackled over the intercom. "From the top!"

Minerva counted them off, and since Marlon had never engaged a permanent piano man who met his standards, a keyboardist borrowed from the studio started the song. Through headphones, Trent heard a prerecorded horn section making magic of the arrangement that Caroline had originally envisioned. He tried to get his attitude together, for the sake of her hard work and because an album wouldn't be able to change his ladies' lives if he couldn't get a damn single recorded. Hoping that fantasizing about Caroline would change his tune, Trent closed his eyes and thought about how she'd felt naked against the length of his body when they'd stayed up kissing until dawn Sunday morning. He'd nearly missed church for her, but playing between Caroline's legs was a good way to go to Hell. He sang into the microphone, "Quiet girl, sitting over—"

"Cut!" came over the intercom.

Minerva jumped up from her drum kit and stomped to the sound-proof glass that separated the band from the producer and his crew. "How much would it take to get the real Garth Brooks in here?" She dug into the back pocket of her low-cut pants. "I've got forty-two bucks plus a Visa gift card." Kyle snickered, and Minerva kept ranting until Reyes stuck his perfect mug up to the glass and waved. Minerva smirked at Trent. "Looks like you're fired, Trenton."

"Cut the boy a break, *Wendy,*" Marlon interceded.

"Take ten," the producer hollered over the intercom.

Minerva and Kyle flew out of the room, presumably for a smoking break, and Reyes entered the recording booth in their wake. Reyes went to Marlon first to offer a handshake that Marlon accepted after glancing helplessly at Trent.

"Tex," Trent grudgingly twanged when Reyes approached him.

Reyes neither offered his hand nor addressed Trent by name. "You're doing better than I'd expected."

Considering how poorly he'd been performing, Trent was just as insulted as Reyes probably had intended. "Can't stop thinking about me, huh?"

"I can't afford to. I care too much about Caroline. In fact, over lunch, I'll be warning her that you're exactly the sort of person who attracts the wrong element."

Trent stopped short. The smug motherfucker must've done a background check. "If you're gonna insult me, at least don't be vague about it."

"If you're a good man, you'll back off so that your kind of trouble doesn't follow her. Oh, wait! It already has."

Had Caroline not rushed into the booth right then, Trent might have fainted from fear that Vickers's boys and not Nez had followed Caroline home. He hadn't thought of that before, and he was wild around the eyes when Caroline approached.

Caroline touched Trent's arm. "Hi." He just stared at her. "Reyes?" Reyes's smile was so strained that he looked like he was about to snap her neck with his perfect teeth. "Uh, what's going on?"

"Heard you're headed to lunch," Trent said. "Mind if I have a word with you before you go?"

Trent didn't let her get a word out before he hauled her by the arm toward the recording booth's door. He nearly lifted her off her feet while he dragged her around a corner and into an empty studio down the hall.

Caroline yanked free of his grasp as soon as they were behind a closed door.

"What is *wrong* with you?"

Trent didn't say anything at first. He'd been too blissful lately to pay attention, and unattended information suddenly caused a traffic jam in his brain. Finally, he articulated, "Were you in that article? That *Paste* article? They wouldn't…" *Give out her address*, but that didn't matter when he'd been chasing her for weeks without paying attention to who might be following him.

"Wouldn't what?" After he failed to elaborate, Caroline threw up her hands. The spaghetti strap of her pale yellow dress fell from her shoulder. "Trent! What is going on?"

"Did Tex call you? To set up this recording session?"

"Yes."

"Before or after you were followed?"

"What does—"

"Before or after, Caroline?"

"After, and what difference does it make? He's doing me a favor!"

He scrubbed his face with his hands and took a deep breath. Reyes's lunch date seemed deliberately planned to drive a wedge between Caroline and Trent. However, it didn't seem likely that Reyes would give her address to Vickers's boys just to accuse Trent of putting her in harm's way. Guilt was making Trent paranoid, but he had to warn her regardless. He stared at her, but the words wouldn't come out.

Caroline folded her arms and glared at him. Her anger seemed to mount while he stalled. Her head cocked to the side. "Are you at least going to attempt to explain your boorish behavior?"

Trent licked his lips. He didn't speak, didn't even blink, because he was too scared to lose her with one wrong move.

Eventually, she yanked her purse up onto her shoulder, and her dress strap fell down again. "Give me my car keys." Caroline yanked up her strap and stuck out her hand. "I'm out of here! I'm sick of you, I'm sick of Reyes, and I'm sick of living at Jackie's like a fugitive!" Eyes squinted like she was trying not to cry, she dug Trent's truck keys out of her purse.

"I'm sorry. Look—"

"No!" She threw his keys at his chest, and they clattered to the floor "Just give me my keys."

He grasped her shoulders, rougher than he should have considering that he'd already manhandled her. "Skip this lunch. Please. I got something important to talk to you about, and I don't know where to start."

"How about you don't start because I don't want to hear it!"

"*Please.* I think Tex is trying to get rid of me, and—"

"Jealousy? That's what this is about?" Caroline's eyes crossed.

"I…I, uh…" God, he was hot all of a sudden and completely tongue-tied. "I shouldn't have waited to say this. 'Course it's not the kind of thing you just say in conversation—"

"Give. Me. My. Keys!"

"See, I thought you'd think less of me? Except you already do think less of me, so that was a dumb excuse." He ran the words together, afraid to stop talking. "See, I wanted…well, I wanted—"

Trent grabbed her arm when she tried to sweep past him. He pressed her against the door, and then he backed off with his hands held up since Caroline looked about one second from strangling him with her wayward dress strap.

"See, I just needed a fucking break. And then I wanted this job, and then I wanted you. I *want* you," he pleaded. "'Course, by the time I figured that out, I was scared of telling you the truth." He raised his hand to his mouth to cough and recalled that, though Caroline had noticed his scabbed knuckles when they'd first met, she was still there with him. "See, my sister ain't just in a wheelchair. A man put her there, and I…he—"

"Oh, Trent, I'm sorry. I should have asked about your sister. It just seemed like a touchy subject." She tried to take his hand.

He recoiled from her touch. "Don't do that. I got blood on my hands. I hurt him, Caroline."

"Okay. Well. I'm sure you didn't mean to. Jackie's a lawyer; she can —"

"I *did* mean to." God, his stomach hurt all of a sudden. "I put him in the hospital, and I don't think he's coming out alive."

"Oh. Okay." Her voice shrank, and she looked so startled. "Well…"

Wariness drifted into her gaze, and then Caroline didn't seem to know him. It wasn't natural not to regret manslaughter, and Trent didn't blame her. He was just too hurt to keep looking her in the eye, and his shoulders slumped when he turned his back on her.

Caroline tried to put on a brave face, but even she wasn't polite enough to cover up that much discomfort. Having spent so long held hostage by all of the things she didn't know about Nez, she was frightened of the much deeper uncertainties in Trent.

"Umm, Trent?" She wrapped her chilled fingertips around his bicep, but he didn't turn around. "I'm sorry. I know I should be acting…better. If you could just give me a minute, or sixty." She crossed her eyes and tapped her forehead. Trent was looking right at her when she righted her vision.

He looked pained. "Why are you so goddamn sweet?"

"I'm not really."

A sigh wheezed out of his chest. "Yes, you are. Who apologizes for not taking news like that in stride?"

"You didn't. You didn't bat an eyelash when I told you what I'd done. So I guess that makes you more than sweet."

Trent stared at her, looking desperate to believe that she was right.

Trepid, Caroline bit her lip. It was hard to believe in a man who didn't believe in himself. Rather brisker than she'd intended, she grabbed his hand and squeezed it too hard.

"Umm, I think everything is going to be all right." Her face fell when he slipped on his impassive mask, but she couldn't blame him for not jumping on board that lame platitude. "Okay, no. No. I think you should finish recording your single —"

"I think I ought to go home, Caroline."

She ignored him. "And I think I'm going to go have lunch or something because I need sixty minutes and a glass of Chardonnay, okay? I'll meet you back here, and then we'll go have dinner before the gig tonight. Italian. And we'll talk." Caroline sucked a breath and steadied herself instead of wilting. He didn't say anything. "You don't like Italian?"

His lip twitched, and she wished then that it had occurred to her earlier to kiss him, to speak a language that he understood. Since she was wearing flats, he seemed a giant, and Caroline almost tipped over trying to get high enough on her toes to reach his lips. Embarrassed, she grabbed a fistful of his shirt. "Would you help me out here?"

Trent took her hand, and though Caroline's smile shook a little, she followed when he led her to a small sofa. Trent sat down and invited rather than pulled Caroline onto his lap.

"You're too sweet to me," he said. "This is never gonna work."

Though he seemed to be talking about their fledgling relationship, Caroline replied, "Sure it will. When you sit down, we're about mouth-to-mouth, see? Because your legs are longer than your torso, so —"

Trent stole a kiss from her, then gave back a lush and longer one heavy with tongue. "Why didn't you invite me to Purim dinner?"

Eyes wide, Caroline demanded, "How did you —"

"Minerva."

She did her angry bumblebee imitation. "Um, I didn't — I was going to invite you to Easter dinner instead."

"You lying to me?"

"Maybe."

His eyes were a deeper blue than she'd ever seen, deeper even than they'd been when he'd confessed. "If you came to my sister's graduation, you'd have to meet Ginny and my Mama. And Shane, unfortunately."

"If you came to Easter dinner, you'd have to meet my U.S. Marshal brother, Hector, my lawyer brother, Phil, my crazy brother, Dizzy, and Julianna, who can be scarier than all of them."

"You really asking me or ain't you?"

"Are you asking me?"

"Maybe," Trent whispered against her lips.

While they were kissing, trading *maybe* merely seemed like a game they enjoyed playing, for she didn't feel anything uncertain in Trent's deep, slick rhythm. The force of his mouth bent her back while his hands pulled her hips closer, all as though he meant to bury himself so deep inside of Caroline that there would be no getting free of him.

A slightly frightened thrill shocked her when Trent dragged his knuckles across her jaw and down her throat. He seemed to be saying that he would never hurt her that way; the message was as obvious as him rigid and thick against the crotch of her panties.

"We gotta stop going at it in semi-public places," Trent rasped.

"Does that mean we'll be going at it in very public places?"

His laugh was half whimper, while his palm pushed down her strapless bra. "You don't want to make an offer like that to a man like—" He tore her dress strap. "Whoopsy daisy."

Trent looked apologetic and rocked her on his lap, but lust pooled between Caroline's thighs. The ruthless way that he wanted her felt so good. She hooked her thumb under her other strap and held it out to him.

"Might as well make me a halter."

By the time they made it back into the hall, Caroline's dress was strapless and her formerly sleek hair a reckless ponytail. Hands stuck in Trent's rear pockets, she let him drag her back to the recording studio, near which he turned to her and kissed her.

"Straighten up. You look like you just got fucked."

"Hee!" Her giggle was loud and blissful.

"Quiet, half-pint." Grinning, Trent pressed a finger to her lips. "Your boyfriend's gonna get pissed and fire me."

"He's not my boyfriend, and if you say that again, I'll fire you because I'm your boss."

"I love it when you talk mean to me." Trent kissed her again. "Now stop getting me worked up in public. We've already been gone fifteen minutes."

"Yes. Please do stop," Reyes interrupted.

Back to the wall with Trent pressed against her, Caroline had to resist snapping to attention at the sound of Reyes's voice.

Trent didn't back off of her an inch, nor did he look at Reyes.

Caroline tried for something similarly nonchalant. "Fifteen minutes? That's all?"

Trent snickered.

Reyes was not as amused. "May I speak with you, Caroline?"

"Later, sweet cheeks." Looking reluctant, Trent winked at her, then shouldered past Reyes and swaggered down the hall to the recording booth.

Caroline brushed her bangs out of her eyes and tried, as he had instructed her, to straighten up. "Yes?"

Reyes's gaze moved from her ravaged dress bodice to her hair, tied up with the dress straps, and then back down to her bright eyes and flushed lips and cheeks. "Haute couture? You're looking very sexy."

"Don't. I'm with Trent now."

"So I see. Apparently he enjoys dragging you down with his bad reputation. Do be careful. I would hate for your escapades to get caught for posterity."

"Excuse me?" Caroline thought he was talking about the tapes, but Reyes's face at first gave nothing away.

"Last fall, Jacks mentioned that you saw something you didn't want to see. With Milan's reputation preceding her, I assumed." He shrugged carelessly. "I suspected that you had something I could use against him. I started looking into it, and you and I happened along the way."

"There is no 'you and I.' Especially since you didn't really care about me this whole time."

"I cared enough to try and win your confidence, which is more than I can say for *him.*" Reyes nodded toward the studio door into which Trent had gone. "I hoped that you would turn to me for help. I started keeping tabs on Nez, and so I know that he had nothing to do with you being followed the other day."

Caroline's mouth fell open. "You've been spying on me!"

Reyes gave her a patronizing look. "Think bigger, please. You aren't the only client that he defrauded of thousands, *querida*. On my roster alone, there are several artists who would love to see him in jail. We can do it together, and you'll be rid of him."

Abruptly aware that she'd never thought of anyone but herself, Caroline couldn't deny she'd been extorting Nez for satisfaction, not justice. "No. Find another way to get their money. I'm giving the tapes back."

"Fine. I'll arrange a meeting with him, and we can trade the tapes for some kind of restitution."

Guilt sickened her stomach. "Extortion. Of course."

"Surely you wouldn't deny my artists the same chance that you've had to recover. Haven't you already obstructed justice enough?"

"Are you threatening to turn me in?"

"Do I need to?" He blinked rapidly, seeming to regret the words, but they couldn't be taken back.

"I'll arrange a meeting with him. I want this over with." Caroline flashed a glare at Reyes. "Now I have to go. My head hurts."

"You're famished, I'm sure, from your escapade. Let's continue this over lunch."

Caroline looked at him like he was crazy, but Reyes didn't react. He was too suave to let her hurt feelings muddy the conversation, too spotless to pause before he sent a man to prison.

"No, thank you," she spat and turned heel.

"Trent is a criminal, Caroline."

He spoke with a hint of real concern for her, but it was only a hint that tapped her backbone and rolled right off. Though the warning stirred up Caroline's as yet unconquered trepidation, she lifted her chin before she turned back to Reyes.

"Well, that's a relief, since I am too."

"He's *dangerous.*"

"Is that all? I thought you were going to say that he was an overbearing asshole, since it takes one to know one." She bristled when he rolled his eyes. "How dare you! You manipulated me for months, but you're rolling your eyes like I'm childish?"

"Manipulated? You ate right out of my hand and loved it." Reyes seemed to regret his words when her face fell. *"Querida,* I'm sorry. Truly. Please believe that I didn't set out to —"

"Use me to make Jackie jealous?" Caroline folded her arms, daring him to deny it.

Reyes sighed. "I wanted to tell you. After you saw Nez on television, I thought you would understand how I felt when I got those pictures *three days* after Jackie and I were together for the first time." He held up three fingers and looked miserable. "Three days. I don't even know what I did wrong."

"Last fall, I would have felt sorry for you. Now everything you say seems calculated to make me feel sympathetic, even scared, or else why did you wait for a big reveal to tell me it wasn't Nez who followed me home from the grocery store? You should have called the moment you found out! How many days ago was that exactly?" Caroline shook her head at his stricken expression. "I can't tell you what happened with Jackie, but I do know that no woman likes being controlled. So maybe you need to think bigger."

She straightened up her newly recovered backbone and marched off with every intention of going to the bank, getting those damn tapes, and giving them back before any other man presumed to tell her what to fear or how to feel.

Chapter Twelve

At a small tapas restaurant near the studio, Caroline took a siesta from the men in her life, but her anxious thoughts did not dissipate. Growing a backbone didn't make her a badass. She felt fragile climbing the height of the giant tires on Trent's truck, but once in the cab, she buckled the seat belt and patted the Chevy's steering wheel. She was safe inside of Trent's big green monster and tried to force that feeling into the little mental crevices that still feared Trent's fists.

In the nearly three months that she'd known him, Trent had used his hands mostly to play for her, to fix whatever was broken in her house, to bring her sex drive out of retirement, and lately, to pull her into impromptu slow dances that made up in kisses what they lacked in music. She couldn't even really find fault with the couple of times that he'd grabbed her by the arm and hauled her off. Most men were good for pulling the occasional caveman, and Caroline had let herself be hauled off, be pulled this way, and be pushed that. If there was anything to fear, it was the part of her that had so easily wilted before Trent's mind-blowing banging had taught her to bang back. Sex memories squeezed a smirk from her lips, and she emitted a giddy and high-pitched zing through her teeth while she pulled the truck into the downtown traffic between her and Regions Bank.

The contents of Caroline's stomach shot up into her throat when she saw what looked like a dark-tinted GMC Jimmy in the traffic behind her. Just a little way from the bank, she was stuck in a strict array of one-way streets that afforded no opportunity to make a U-turn back toward the studio. Terror crawled up the back of her neck too fast to resist, and Caroline's eyes watered from darting back and forth between tracking the GMC and dialing Trent. Praying for him to pick up, she turned right around Regions Bank and its attached parking structure. The small side street was nearly empty, so she gunned the engine, but the GMC was on her ass before Caroline could escape around the next corner.

"Please, please," she begged of her phone, of God, and of Trent, but he neither picked up nor called before she was forced back into traffic on the main drag. By the time she remembered that cell phones had to be turned off inside of the studio, Caroline had clipped a curb and come uncomfortably close to a bicyclist.

"Oh my God! Sorry!"

Not seeing the GMC, Caroline made a reckless right turn into the parking garage. The Chevy submerged under the street level and barreled over speed bumps that jostled her knotted stomach, but the GMC did not appear in the rearview mirror.

Caroline squealed around a concrete wall and into a parking spot as close to the elevator as possible. Her shaking fingers tried twice to release the seatbelt, and by then the knot in her stomach had turned into actual nausea. Still buckled in, Caroline threw her shoulder into the heavy driver's side door and just managed to retch onto the concrete. Sour-mouthed and dizzy, she scrambled out of the truck and across the parking level toward the elevator. She jammed the Up button, but took the stairs after cranking her neck toward the sound of an approaching car almost gave her whiplash. Adrenaline built in her veins with every step that she hammered up to the first floor, and when finally she burst into the hall directly across from the bank, Caroline wasn't surprised to find the security guard's eyes on her.

"You all right, ma'am?"

"Fine." She slipped past him toward an account manager's desk. Just a few minutes later, she was alone in a cold metal room with her safe deposit box, in which she wished she could lock herself up until Trent got there. She shoved three sticks of gum into her mouth to wet her throat and clean the bile from her tongue.

"You're fine. You're in a bank. You're safe. Just get it over with."

Caroline pulled out her cell phone to call Nez, but her hands shook terribly. She didn't need her nerves rattled by the sound of his voice, so she sent a text message requesting that he call "to resolve the matter that evening." Unfortunately, she could only hang around a bank for so long without arousing suspicion. Caroline jammed the tapes into her purse and closed the deposit box. She dialed Trent, but he didn't answer. She called Reyes next, and he picked up right away.

"Um, please, are you at the studio still? C-can you go get Trent? I'm in the bank, and—" She cut herself off until she passed the nosy security guard out in the hall. "I think I was followed again."

"What? *Tonta!*" Reyes seemed to cover the handset, but Caroline heard him yell at his assistant and then slam a door. "Stay where you are. I'm coming. Regions, right?"

"No." Her voice echoed through the stairwell, as weak as her knees. "Please go get Trent—"

Reyes interrupted with some really foul-sounding Spanish, and then she heard the sound of him running downstairs. "He is why you are being followed! He nearly killed someone, Caroline!"

"I know!"

"Then why did he put you in his truck and send you off alone? *Malparido!*"

His voice boomed on Caroline's eardrum, and she winced away from the phone.

"I wanted to leave. I was only going up the street." She had felt brave at the time, but now she felt foolish.

"If any harm comes to you, I'll have that redneck impaled in front of the CNN Center!"

Terror seemed to break out in thick hives in her throat. She couldn't speak. She could barely swallow.

"Caroline? *Querida*, answer me, please!"

"Don't!" She was desperate to make him stop saying exactly those things that he knew would scare her. "He's not a redneck. He didn't mean to. I know he didn't."

"The list of things that he didn't do is called neglecting you! Wait right where you are. I'm coming to get you."

"No, I'm just going to get in the truck and go. I'm being paranoid."

"No!"

"It's right there." Caroline stood inside of the bottom stairwell door and looked at Trent's truck through a small glass square. Fifteen feet more and surely she would be safe inside the Chevy's thick metal frame; surely she would feel safe the way she had before. The nearest car was ten slots away. "It's right *there.*"

Reyes seemed to acquiesce with, "Stay on the phone with me, please," but she knew that he was relentless and no doubt running red lights to get to her.

Caroline licked her lips. "I'm going." She shouldered open the metal stairwell door and sprinted across the concrete. Beneath the thin leather of her ballet flats, the soles of her feet stung when she stopped at the door of the truck and frantically mashed the Unlock button. It didn't work, and she dropped the keys. Caroline tried to calm down when she bent to scoop them up. She looked over her shoulder, right, left, took a deep breath, then jerked her gaze left again toward a hiss from a gash in the front tire.

Caroline's enormous eyes cut to the rear tire, which also had been slashed. She fell on her ass and the palms of her hands, scrambling away from those signs of violence. Her phone skid a foot across the concrete; grabbing it and sprinting forward in the same movement cost her a skinned knee and a scraped knuckle.

Just when her fingers touched the stairwell door, the elevator pinged, and Caroline's heart nearly popped. She tore up the stairs, dropping her purse and catching it as she stumbled around the corner to the second flight, but the clear plastic bag of tapes tumbled down to the first flight. Caroline rolled over the rail and jumped down two steps trying to retrieve the tapes, and that mistake sent her head-first down the rest of the staircase. Her shoulder and cheek hit the concrete before the rest of her body crumpled in a heap on the stairwell floor. A hot, metallic taste made her raise her fingers to her mouth to check if she still had teeth. She did, but she was bleeding from a busted lip that split further when a big pair of hands grabbed her.

She screamed.

"Shh, *m'ija*, it's—*Dios mio!*" Reyes blanched, having rolled her over and gotten a look at her face. He dropped to his knees and cradled her head on his leg. "Who did this? Did you see his face?" He pulled out his phone.

"I fell," Caroline protested, but not loud enough to stop Reyes from dialing every branch of Atlanta emergency services. He looked up, and she did too, when a door opened overhead and footsteps thudded down the stairs.

Reyes looked murderous. "Who's there?" He stripped off his navy blue suit jacket, exchanged it for his knee beneath Caroline's head, and stood up looking ready to rumble.

"Security! Upstairs just caught you on camera, said she fell down the stairs? She all right?"

The guard's voice grew louder as he came closer, and Caroline grasped Reyes's pant leg. "I'm fine." She tried to hoist herself up.

"Don't." He crouched and laid one hand on her ribcage. "Don't move."

"I'm fine. I want to get up. I don't need an ambulance, or any cops."

"You're protecting that *malparido?* You're going straight to the hospital to have your head examined."

The security guard rounded the elbow of the stairs and caught sight of them. "She all right?"

"Fine!" Caroline winced at the way her head rattled, but she propped up anyway on the tender palms of her hands.

"*Querida*—"

"No need to call an ambulance! I just took a little spill." Caroline brushed back her bangs, and her eyes crossed of their own accord. She swiveled her faulty vision to the security guard, and Caroline could tell from his wide eyes how badly she looked. "It looks worse than it feels." The soft fabric of Reyes's jacket seemed to have tunneled through her ears, into her skull, and turned into cotton, fluffy-puffy cotton, that expanded when she tried to stand up.

"*Querida*, please!"

"I'm f-fi—" Her eyes crossed again without request or warning, and Caroline stumbled trying to rise from her shaky knees. She managed to stand up and glance triumphantly at Reyes, who glowered in return and grabbed her arm. "I'm fine!" She yanked free of his grasp, and was just about to tell him what to do with his caveman behavior when that expanding cotton cracked her head wide open. The iron grip of Reyes's arms was the last thing Caroline felt before she floated away on a fluffy-puffy cloud.

When seven o'clock came and went without a word from Caroline, Trent worried that she'd changed her mind about being afraid of him. He'd left the studio to find four missed calls back-to-back without a message, as was her usual style. After waiting around Island Records for an hour, he'd called Jackie hoping that Caroline had returned to the office for a girlfriend therapy session about him. Sixty thirty found him back at Emory University Hospital trying to turn out any kind of penance that might impress her, but once again, he hovered outside of the room. In fact, he was angrier than ever that Courtney Vickers was fucking up yet another thing Trent loved.

A short, helmet-haired hospice nurse passed by and mistook his pacing for adjusting his stomach to suffering.

"Haven't I seen you here before?"

Trent's gaze snapped to hers.

"Poor thing, you look green!" She pulled out a packet of antacids and popped one tablet onto her palm. "Here, hon. Try not to let it upset ya, all right? He ain't in any pain anymore." She cracked open the door for Trent. "See how peaceful he looks? Best thing you can do right now is say a few kind words to keep him easing along toward a happy place, whether that's with us or on the other side." She glanced from the antacid on her palm to his face, and whatever she saw in Trent's eyes drew back her hand. "Um, well, whenever you're ready."

"Thanks." Trent reached for the tablet. He needed something in his mouth to keep from hollering that a drunk-driving, hit-and-run motherfucker like Courtney didn't deserve her goddamn sympathy. The nurse skittered away, and Trent chomped on the chalky tablet, but the hollering wouldn't go down his throat. He was hot with it, pissed beyond reason. He couldn't let go; he couldn't, as Caroline had once said, stop being mad.

Trent shoved open the door to Courtney's room, and there the fucker was laid out in a white gown with his dark hair neatly groomed as though he were a sleeping choirboy. Twenty different tubes were stuck in every orifice and vein that Courtney had, and if he was aware of anything, he had to feel miserable on top of being on his deathbed. Trent couldn't do anything to make Courtney hurt more, but the weight of still wanting to damage the dude sent Trent staggering to a plastic chair and wondering what it was going to take for him to stop hating.

A seething surge of spit flooded his chalky tongue. He yanked a small blue garbage bucket from beside the bed and spat onto his own face, featured on that copy of *Paste* magazine that had been in the waiting the room the last time he'd visited.

His brain connected the dots between Courtney's hospital visitors, the band's list of gigs in *Paste,* and Caroline being followed from Smith's Olde Bar. She was in his truck and hours late for their dinner date. Fear and guilt overwhelmed him, and he prayed that he was just being paranoid as Caroline had accused before he'd let her leave the studio.

Trent ran from the room to the elevator. He bashed the button while he pulled out his phone. An image of some bastard's lurid gaze and vile Wild Turkey breath on Caroline's face turned his stomach, and he bolted into the stairwell.

"Caroline, darlin', please pick up the phone. I need you to call me right this second so I know you're all right." He called Jackie, and when she didn't answer, Trent bit the bullet and called Reyes, but even Tex didn't pick up. Trent burst out of the stairwell and tried the nearest exit door, but it was locked. "Fuck. *Fuck.*"

Heedless of the frequent reprimands to slow down, he darted in and out of the traffic in the hospital halls. Trying to find a door to a parking lot, Trent waited for his phone to ring. He would be late for the gig if he drove to Caroline's house and back, but Trent didn't give a shit. Instead, he prayed to God that she would answer her door to yell at him about the speeding tickets that he planned to amass on the way.

When finally he found an open set of double doors, Trent ran outside to face a small medical plaza that hadn't been there when he'd parked. A brightly lit red sign on his left led to the emergency room. Wanting to kick his own ass for being on the wrong side of the hospital, he jogged toward emergency, and his phone rang. He saw Caroline's number in the display and nearly fell on his face from relief.

"Where the hell have you been? Where are you *right now?* Jesus Christ, Caroline, you scared the life out of me!"

"Then why aren't you dead?"

Trent bristled at the sound of Reyes's voice. "Put Caroline on the phone."

"That'll be difficult to do since she's having a CAT scan right now."

Trent stopped dead in his tracks; his breath stopped beneath the clinging cotton of his sweaty T-shirt.

"Rest assured that if she revives, I will inform her that you called to yell at her for not being readily available to you. Of course, if she doesn't revive, I'll be coming with your last rites. In fact, you should probably start running now, you miserable ill-born excuse for a man."

Trent felt as scared and shamed as Reyes had intended. "What happened?"

"Guess, redneck! And after that, why don't you mosey your worthless ass over to Regions Bank and replace all of the slashed tires on your monster truck!" Reyes hung up.

"Fuck!"

Trent called Caroline's phone back as well as Reyes's, but Tex didn't answer either one. Palms in his eye sockets and sick to his stomach, Trent heaved for breath trying not to cry or black out, avoiding it further by taking off full-speed on his feet across the parking lot toward the other end of the hospital where he'd parked. Halfway past the emergency room, he slowed down and called Jackie again.

Caroline was safe with Reyes, and that was most important. Planning out his apology was a distant second that made him call the city hospitals after Jackie didn't pick up. Trent had just backtracked to Emory's emergency room to find the quickest way across the hospital when his eyes did a double-take at a Shelby Mustang. There were plenty of bigwigs in Atlanta, but that car at that moment in that emergency room parking lot didn't even register as having odds; it seemed more like a sign from God.

Instead of getting in line at the reception desk, Trent followed the first body that was allowed behind the emergency room's trauma doors. He peeked into triage booths, behind curtains, and around all of the nurses that were suspicious of him until he found one of the few private rooms in the twenty-bed emergency department.

Peering into the dimly lit room, Trent saw Reyes yank up the sleeves of his white dress shirt spotted with bloodstains and pace back and forth as he spoke terse, authoritative Spanish into his phone. When he caught Reyes's eye, the Texan crossed past the empty bed and tried to shut the door.

"Hey—HEY! You want a piece of me; we'll arrange a time and place. This ain't it." Trent muscled into the room. "I'm here for Caroline. Where the hell is she?"

Reyes didn't say anything.

"Don't make me beat it out of you, Tex."

"Malparido del orto! Estás corriendo en la ching—"

"Stop!" Caroline came out of the bathroom clutching her skull. "No yelling! Stop before my head explodes or one of the nurses tells the cops!"

Sympathetic to her aversion to law enforcement, Trent was quick to step back and click the door shut.

"They're already on the way," Reyes growled. "I called them while you were unconscious in my car."

Caroline flopped on the bed, pressed a pillow to her face, and groaned. "I saw them in the hall on the way back from the CAT scan. I gave them my statement about the slashed tires for Trent's insurance, and that's all, so would you please *shut up*, Reyes? Everybody needs to stop talking so fucking loud until my drugs kick in!"

Her profanity startled both men into silence and brought a little levity to Trent's gloomy mood. "You must not be feeling too bad if you're cussing."

Caroline squeezed the pillow against her forehead. "I feel miserable."

Next to where she was sprawled on her back, wrapped back and front in hospital gowns, Trent gingerly sat down on the bed. He turned up the switch on the dim lamp and pried away the pillow.

Caroline kept her eyes shaded with one hand, but she tilted her face, giving him an eyeful. "It's not as bad as it looks."

His fingers shook where they touched the parts of her face that weren't swollen, bruised, or busted. Warbling like an old woman, Trent asked, "What happened, darlin'?"

"Are you crying?"

"Fuck no."

Caroline pulled his shaky hand away from scrubbing his eyes. "Your eyes are too blue. Yeah, you're crying. Don't. I fell down some stairs, trying to be all big and strong at the wrong damn time when I should have stayed in the bank. Don't fret over this." She squeezed Trent's hand. "I knew you were going to blame yourself when you got here, and—why did it take you so long to get here?"

He emptied his expression and tried not to think about Reyes, but she had apparently figured out how to read him.

Caroline glared at Reyes. "Didn't I tell you to call him?"

Reyes scowled.

"Get out. I'm serious! Get out! Ow!" Her palms clamped over her eye sockets until the door shut behind Reyes. "I might have a contusion, or a concussion, or something," she told Trent. "They'll say so in a minute, and then when we go home, you might have to wake me up every couple of hours."

Trent felt miserable to hear her say *we* in combination with *home*, two things that he didn't really deserve. "You won't be going home. I'm sorry, but I know how these boys drink. They know where you live, so you can't go home until I take care of this. Until I make sure that this never happens again."

"Don't!" Caroline sat straight up, though her eyes widened against her pain. "It doesn't need 'taking care of!'"

He shook his head and eased away from her clutch on his arm.

"Trent, it'll never end like that!"

"This has to end." He borrowed her gesture and circled five fingers around her face. "I have to end it. I felt like throwing myself in front of a car when I heard what happened. *Again.*" The word was as broken as his slumped shoulders and down-turned mouth. "All my ladies."

"It's not your fault."

"It is. My ladies. My fault."

"Stop trying to be a tough guy!"

"I didn't put my fists in my problems because I'm tough—"

"I didn't mean—"

"I used my fists 'cause *that's all I got,*" Trent said dismally. "I was a world away from here, and then I had to quit my job and come back under the worst circumstances. My sister's car accident? The guy, Courtney, was drunk, and it was a hit-and-run, and I let that be my excuse to beat him so bad. I'd been telling myself that I would pay him back for Gin, but when I got a hold of Courtney, it was like I was making him pay for everything I ever gave up. You don't how *mean* I got!"

His confession ran together hot and anxious like his blood pressure. "I barely had a second to myself between working and seeing about Ginny and Mama. I got so goddamn tired of giving stuff up; I had to stop wanting anything!" Anguish left his voice hoarse. "I'm sorry I'm hollering at you."

"Don't be. Let it out." Caroline took his hand. "I can take it."

"You shouldn't have to." He licked his lips. "You deserve better than this, better than somebody like me who almost killed a man and didn't feel anything."

Caroline bit her lip, but he could see it tremble.

He sighed. "Darlin', don't cry."

"I'm not crying. You don't need me to cry." She swiped at her eyes. "Maybe you're just too good at pretending like you didn't feel anything. You've been telling yourself that you're a stone-cold killer, but don't you see what you've been like with me? You're so nice—okay, not. I've already hit my lame platitude limit for the day." She took his hand and squeezed. "More than nice, like…"

Loving. Trent felt the word in the air, and saw it in her eyes, but she didn't say it.

"You take care of me like your mother and your sister. A man without feelings wouldn't bother."

"Maybe you're right. God, I hope you're right." Trent was relieved for a moment, and then fear for his family knotted his stomach. "Did you see who followed you tonight?"

"Trent, no!"

"I'm coming back to you, but I can't let my ladies be sitting ducks at home. Tell me everything you remember so I can find these fuckers, Caroline. Please."

"It was that black GMC Jimmy again. An '80-something model with tinted windows. I couldn't see who—Oh! But there was a vanity tag on the front. Eyes, like tiger eyes."

"It was orange and blue? The tag?"

"Yes!"

"Goddamn Auburn football fans." Bibb City had plenty of them, being so close to West Alabama. Trent sighed. "Promise me that you won't move a muscle until I give you the all-clear."

Caroline pursed her lips. "I promise that I won't move a muscle unattended."

"Reyes don't count as an attendant. He's got your cell phone."

"He does?" Caroline tipped over the edge of the bed, reaching for her purse on the floor. Blood must've rushed to her head, because she clutched her eyes and started crying. She fell back on the pillows.

"Quit before you make it worse," Trent whispered. He kissed the backs of her hands, then her eyelids after he pulled her hands away. Trent kissed her nose, her forehead next to the gash in her hairline, her one good cheek, and he brushed his lips achingly gently over the Frankenstein stitches in her lip. "Just call in and check your messages, all right?"

"Okay."

"All right, darlin'. I…" *Love you.* Trent swallowed that. He wasn't one to merely feel love; he did love, and he wouldn't make her a promise that he couldn't keep. "I think you ought to try and get some sleep."

The lamp abruptly dimmed, and in the near dark, Trent pressed his warm weight against her side. His hand drifted to her head and tugged gently on her hair over and over again. He wished that his touch would soothe her and shake loose her tight nerves. Maybe it worked because even after Reyes and a nurse came in with voices that darted back like stinging insects, Caroline didn't wake from a healing sleep. His wishes seemed to work, if they weren't for himself. Trent supposed that was no more than he deserved, and he wondered if that meant he couldn't have her.

He couldn't stop touching Caroline and didn't leave her side until Jackie arrived. He heard the attorney yelling at Tex even before the door opened. The overhead light came on, and Trent shielded Caroline's eyes.

Jackie burst in wearing jeans and a T-shirt that would have made her look ten years younger had not her face been cragged with worry. "Shut up," Jackie snapped over her shoulder at Reyes. "Why are you still here? Interfering, no doubt. And you." She scathingly looked Trent up and down. *"Move."*

Trent did as he was bidden.

Looking horrified with one slender hand over her mouth, Jackie eased down next to Caroline.

Reyes approached the bed where Trent stood. "I've arranged a suite for them both at the Four Seasons. They shouldn't be alone at Jackie's under the circumstances."

Jackie's neck wrenched around. "We won't be alone. I have a Sig Sauer P226, a pistol license, and a bad attitude."

Reyes rolled his eyes to Trent. "Who knows what your boys have learned about both of the girls in the time that they've had to trail your truck all over the city? They could be waiting in the parking lot right now."

Trent blanched.

"I'll drive them to the hotel."

"The hell you will!"

"Shut up!" Jackie stood and stalked toward them. "Are you fools going to make me call Hector?"

Reyes inched back toward the door, and Trent thought it prudent to follow his lead.

"Are you going to make me raise up Julianna's whole tribe? Because if I do, both of y'all are going to catch a beating." Jackie backed them out of the door with the force of her voice. "If you survive Minerva after she gets a hold of this."

The door closed in both of their faces.

Trent grabbed Reyes's jacket from the single chair nearby, threw it at Tex, and sat down.

"Don't you have a gig tonight?" Reyes asked.

Incredulous, Trent glared at him.

"Caroline has worked very hard to book the band. If you cancel tonight, the single release party at The Earl will be canceled as well."

"I know you think I'm dumber than a bag of rocks, but I ain't falling for that. And you should know that I'm in the exact right emotional place to rearrange your perfect face if you keep fucking with me, Tex."

"Leave, *malparido*. Leave her alone."

Trent stood up. "Listen here, you cocksure son of a bitch—"

"Make some excuse to get out of her life, or your family will suffer. I swear it on my name." Malice narrowed Reyes's dark eyes. "I will make you regret every day that you so much as touched her."

Balked, Trent's stomach bottomed out. He turned away from Reyes's look of smug satisfaction; the man had discovered the one thing that would make Trent back down. He didn't have any pride left. Caroline had plugged his hole, and he was full of a love that he could only hold onto by jettisoning every heavy thing that he didn't really need, starting with being a bigger badass than Reyes.

Trent knew he had to force his feet to move toward the car, the highway, and then home where he'd started the shit and intended to end it, but first, he turned back to Reyes. "If she'd ever so much as touched you, you'd know that a man could *never* regret it."

Chapter Thirteen

Two hours into the three-hour ride back to Bibb City, Trent finally got the best of the urge to turn around and beat Reyes into an early grave. Anger made him veer out of his lane more than once, and the sickening sensation of tires skidding on the road's shoulder reminded him that he was supposed to be getting out of the mayhem business for Caroline. Crashing her car and dying, therefore, was not how he wanted to retire.

It was near midnight when Trent turned into Shane's gravel-encrusted dirt driveway. He pulled Caroline's car to a stop between Shane's ancient Dodge and a newer blue truck.

Shane stepped up with a cold beer in his hand that he held out to Trent. "I didn't make two calls before somebody seen that Jimmy going down Old Creek Road toward Broke Down Bridge."

Trent raised an eyebrow and declined the beer. "Thought they closed off the last part of that road."

"Didn't stop us from getting in when we were kids." Shane drained half the beer while they circled around the Jetta. "Ya know, if you'd lost your leg on the bridge that time, you wouldn't be knee-deep in shit right now. Shoot yourself in the foot and see if these boys don't feel sorry for you."

Trent had to laugh at Shane's morbid brand of optimism.

"So what are we doing?"

"You ain't doing anything except letting me borrow your truck." Trent leaned into the window of the ancient Dodge to check for keys that were in the ignition as usual. "I don't want Caroline's car involved in this. Matter of fact, pull it around behind the house." He tossed the Jetta's keys over the Dodge's rusted roof.

Shane caught the keys, yanked open the truck's creaky door, and climbed into the passenger seat. Trent cussed him under his breath while he got behind the wheel.

"Don't worry about me," Shane said. "You're the one who looks like you need a drink."

Only a best friend could make Trent admit that he was scared shitless. He snatched Shane's beer. A long, cold swig numbed the anxious path down to his stomach. "Get out of the truck, Shane."

"You can't tell me to vacate my own vehicle."

In a strained attempt at joking, Trent said, "I need someone I trust to keep an eye on my ladies afterward. I guess you'll do."

"After what?"

Silence stuffed the truck cab while they stared each other down.

"Get out of the truck," Trent repeated softly.

"*Shit.*" Shane took back his beer and emptied the bottle. Then he threw it out the window. "Let's go."

Little was said on the way to Broke Down Bridge. When the asphalt road gave way to threaded concrete, gravel, and tire-jarring clumps of clay, Trent knew to turn off the radio and cut the truck's headlights. Beneath the nearly full moon, the Dodge crept toward the tree line that ran up and down Muscogee Creek. He could hear the hiss of the dam from miles upstream and the retreating whistle of a train, the only transportation that had a decent reason to be in that part of the woods. Trent came as close to the woods as he could before tall pines blocked out the moonlight, and he put the truck in park.

"Stay here, Shane. If I'm not back in ten minutes, call the sheriff's department."

Shane gaped at him. "You tell on them and they'll tell on you."

A distantly familiar, inappropriate laugh jostled Trent's stomach. Equating tire-slashing with manslaughter was a crazy kind of funny. "Can't make a deal without a bargaining chip."

"Prison ain't something to joke about, hoss. Hey!" Shane grabbed his arm after Trent cracked the driver's side door. "They'll beat the shit out of you long before the sheriff gets here."

"Then let's hope Deputy Do-Right has a first aid kit in his cruiser." He lurched away from Shane's protest and shut the truck door. "This time is for Gin, and this time I'm ending it. Whatever it takes. Call the sheriff."

Pine needles cut across Trent's bare arms and face before his eyes adjusted to the thick midnight between the trees. He followed the creek's deceptively innocent trickle to a haggard clearing that had been a lookout point back when the bridge was whole and part of a scenic route. A loud voice cracked from across the creek; he looked upstream near what remained of the ancient iron bridge, and his mouth fell open.

A GMC sat in the half dried-out creek bed. It was hard enough getting a four-wheeler down there, so Courtney's crew obviously had plenty of evil plotting time on their hands. Trent scrambled and fell down the steep embankment from the lookout point to the creek bed, and then he sucked a breath and walked calmly toward the water.

Courtney's crew fell quiet as soon as they saw him. They stood up from five-gallon paint buckets behind the GMC's open back gate.

Trent crossed shallow water and dense sand, leaving footprints as heavy as his heart. Moonlight glinted off of small glass bottles strewn around the GMC. A large bottle, half emptied of Wild Turkey, passed between two hands before Trent got close enough to see the boys' faces, which were obscured by hats and hoodies.

Jesus God, they really were *boys*, young'uns no more than twenty years old with nothing to do but share a six-pack and a bottle of cheap bourbon probably pilfered from one of their daddies. Two of them were sandy-haired and skinny, possibly brothers. A taller and older-looking one with mousy brown hair and a square, acne-scarred jaw hulked protectively near the GMC, indicating his ownership. The fourth was a thick-framed brunette with the same round, brown eyes as Courtney Vickers.

Trent stared at them until the liquor in their gazes seemed to give way to an understanding of who he was and what he was doing there. The two brothers sobered up the quickest and turned sickly pale. The GMC Hulker tried too hard to show no reaction except for squaring up his shoulders. Vickers was the only one to betray even a hint of outrage, but he looked scared instead of pissed as soon as Trent stepped within three feet of him.

Slashed tires and warning bottles thrown across the yard made sense all of a sudden; they were the passive-aggressive gestures of kids. For Trent, on the other hand, it had only been a matter of not knowing who or where Courtney was that kept him from immediately fucking the guy up. Trent was a man, after all, and the shadow that he cast across the boys carried a threat of death. Though it sickened his stomach to play into the legend of what he'd done, Trent summoned Stiff Lips McStonyface hopefully for the last time.

"One way or another, this ends tonight. You want justice? The sheriff's on the way, and I'll spill my guts. You want revenge? Here I am. Have at it." He spread his arms, making an appealing target of his clean white T-shirt as compared to the menacing dark colors they all wore. "But I'm warning you now not to even think about going near my ladies again, or my house, or Atlanta. Otherwise, you'd better go on and kill me while you have the chance."

Heads jerked and eyes widened at Trent's words, which were so strong despite their soft utterance and lack of profanity. One of the sandy-haired brothers tried to mutiny with a mumbled, "Fuck this!"

The GMC Hulker shoved the Wild Turkey bottle into Mutiny's slender chest, and then he shoved Vickers forward, hard.

"Man-up," Hulk said. "Ain't this what you've been waiting on?"

A tense, few-seconds' wait actually relieved Trent. The boys would've pulled a pistol if they'd had one, and Vickers, though physically big enough, obviously didn't have the necessary desperation to try something.

Courtney's little brother waited entirely too long to spit in Trent's general direction. "You can't come to our spot giving orders."

Trent laughed, a terrifying sound coming from a man who looked like a sociopath. "Your spot? They call this place Broke Down Bridge because I broke it." He took off his shirt, and the moonlight illuminated a ghostly white scar that cut in the shape of a scythe across his lower back and around into his deeply indented hip. "Me and my friend, trying to be tough guys just like y'all, trying to cross the bridge and not fall through the broken slats. 'Course we did, me first. Damn near cut off my leg and then ended up with a two-by-four splintered in my kidney."

"I came down on top of him." Shane appeared behind the boys seemingly from thin air. "Broke my arm, right over there." He swept one beefy hand across the creek like a goddamn tour guide. "Never did find those teeth I lost in the sand, and the fuckin' tooth fairy don't take IOUs, let me tell ya."

Though Trent would have bet money there wasn't a high IQ in the lot, the boys seemed to realize that four against two crazy man-slaughtering motherfuckers did not add up to good odds. Headlights and sirens carried from clear across the creek, and the sandy-haired brothers were the first to beg Hulk to retreat. They all scrambled to the GMC, except Vickers who had enough guts to stand his ground and wait for the sheriff to come.

Shane's urgent gaze shifted from Trent to the kid and back. "Let's go!"

Trent shook his head. "You get out of here. I made a deal." He looked Vickers right in the eyes and took the full red blare of the boy's belligerence. He hoped that the kid was doing it for his brother and not for pride, which was never satisfied.

"Justice it is then."

Dawn came before Trent and little Ned Vickers saw any sign of being sprung out of the Muscogee County jail. Their holding cell had been full of the previous night's drunk drivers, a fact that might've affected Ned if he hadn't fallen asleep on Trent's shoulder. Stripped of his watch and lacking a clock in the cell, Trent only realized that it was morning when a fresh-faced jailer came around to check on him, Ned, and Stan the Frat Boy who was having a colorful conversation about crystal meth with the toilet in the corner.

Deputy Fresh Face came right up to the bars and gave Trent the stink eye. "Wake him up." He nodded at Ned. "He's got a visitor."

"What time is it?" Trent asked.

"Time for him to go home."

A heavy metal door burst open and Courtney Vickers's mother charged in with her husband in her wake.

"Ned!" Mrs. Vickers's scream echoed off of the concrete walls. She wasn't wearing a bra beneath a rayon dress, and her breasts shook with every coarse word. "What the hell you doin' in here, boy? And drunk? I ought to skin you alive!"

Ned scowled in a way that suggested he was used to getting in trouble. He scrubbed his sleepy eyes and crusty mouth. He pointed at Trent. "You're hollering at me when he's the one who put Courtney in the hospital?"

They all looked at Trent, especially Deputy Fresh Face who straightened up from his spectator's slump against the far wall nearest the door.

Since nodding a confession on the creek bed, Trent hadn't said a word about what he'd done to Courtney Vickers, and all of the deputies had been waiting to break him ever since. He swallowed hard.

Mrs. Vickers shouted, "You're on the same path, Ned!"

The door to the holding cell jutted open again, and with a big grin on his face, Shane came in just far enough to wink at Trent. He held the door for Hank and Ginny, who made an entrance with her voice cranked up as loud as Margie used to get back in the day.

"Tell me where I can't go and see how fast I get the ADA in here, OSHA, anybody about those sorry-ass wheelchair ramps outside!" As soon as Hank pushed her past the door, Ginny grabbed her wheels and high-tailed to Trent.

He motioned her to the corner of the cell away from Ned's argument with his mother. Ginny's stricken expression bruised Trent's heart.

"Tell me you didn't. Not that Ned ain't a highly deserving punk, but I don't want you in here. You shouldn't be in here." She grabbed the bars with both hands.

Trent squeezed his sister's fierce little fists. "I didn't." The relief in her eyes choked him up.

"Margie's across the street at Cheryl's. She actually noticed where I was going for a change, asked me what was wrong. 'Course I didn't say, seeing as Cheryl's nosier than a bloodhound. Like some other people I might mention." Ginny cut her eyes to Mrs. Vickers who'd been staring since Ginny had wheeled into the room. "What are you looking at, lady?"

"Gin," Trent reprimanded.

Mrs. Vickers ran her eyes over Ginny's useless denim-clad legs. "What happened?"

Ginny glanced at the deputy and then at Trent, and he could see the thought of lambasting Courtney cross her face. Instead, she said, "Car accident."

Mrs. Vickers's face went beet red. "H-he told me it was a deer. He drove that wreck into the yard and lied right to my face about —"

"Shut up, Selma." Mr. Vickers glanced at the deputy too.

Mrs. Vickers whirled to her husband. "No! You never told them no. You let them drink and carry on like it was a *game*. Now look at our boys!" Her gaze cut back and forth between Ned behind bars and Ginny, from whom she recoiled as though Ginny was a Wheelchair Woman of the Apocalypse. "When we got to the emergency room, h-he was in and out," Mrs. Vickers stammered. "When he could speak, he kept saying, 'Sorry. Tell them I'm sorry.'"

Ginny blanched and looked at Trent; her knuckles tightened white and bloodless around the bars.

"Get her out of here," Trent ordered Shane. "She doesn't have to hear this."

Mrs. Vickers looked shamed, and she took it out on her son. "You know how many times I had to bail your brother out of this same cell? You know how many times Courtney almost killed himself before he got this girl instead? Well, I've had enough! This is the end of the line, and that train gets off at this station," she told her son and husband both. "Cross your heart and hope to die, or I swear, Ned, I'll leave you here to rot. And don't even open your mouth," she threatened her husband, "unless you want to spend the rest of your life on the couch!"

Shane giggled.

Mrs. Vickers turned to Deputy Fresh Face. "Can you put my son in a real cell overnight?"

"Ma!" Ned's belligerence vanished pretty damn quickly, and he suddenly looked every bit of his seventeen years.

"It's for your own good. Another night with him ought to set you right." She glanced at sick and stinking Stan. Mrs. Vickers's gaze wandered to Ginny again, and the woman obviously had to overcome a lot of apprehension just to touch Ginny's shoulder. "I'm so sorry. Please forgive my boy before he passes so God will forgive him."

Trent watched his sister, who did a scarily good impression of his impassive face while she watched the Vickerses leave. When the deputy held the door and stepped across the threshold for a private word with them, Ginny turned to Trent and pulled a folded envelope from under her thigh. She dropped it through the bars into her brother's hand. "I called Caroline."

Trent scowled. "I told you not to—"

"Yeah, well, I wouldn't have if I'd known she was hurt and knocked out on drugs. You should've said. Her lawyer answered the phone, and then he showed up this morning and told me to give that to you." Ginny looked over her shoulder, but the deputy wasn't looking.

Trent glanced at Ned who was too busy trying to overhear his parents to pay attention. He tore open the envelope to find a photocopied blank check bearing Reyes's signature. The memo line read, "Trent's defense fund/ Cancelled contract." Beneath the check, Trent read, "For you and yours, provided that you don't say another word to me and mine." Furious, Trent crumpled up the paper and shoved it in his pocket.

Worried, Ginny glanced from him to the deputy and back. "What?"

Trent shook his head and jammed his palms into his eye sockets, trying to push back the indigo blue. In a few days, he would be arraigned on an aggravated assault charge, but he knew the state would take their time going to trial in hopes that Courtney would die and the charge could be bumped up to manslaughter. Perhaps because he'd given up thinking of his life as his own, he couldn't summon any emotion for the prospect of ten years or so in prison. His head hurt at the idea of Ginny giving up college to take care of Margie. He ached to know that he would never get to make love to Caroline in that tender way that would have made her body his own special possession. His heart broke.

"Trent?" Ginny reached for her brother through the bars. "We're gonna get you out of here. Shane *said* he could get bail money."

Shane came from across the room. "I just need a couple more hours."

Trent cleared a lump from his throat. "Don't worry about it. That lawyer's gonna take care of it. He gave you his number?"

Ginny nodded.

"Call him back and tell him that he has my word." His voice cracked.

"What about Caroline?"

"Don't tell her nothing." Being in jail would help him do the same. "Don't call her again, Ginny. I mean it. She's been hurt and doesn't need to be bothered with my mess. Now you go home and get ready for class. I don't want to see you back here during school hours."

Ginny gaped at him. "What?"

"Shane, take her home. You shouldn't have brought her in the first place."

Trent's broken tone seemed to weigh down all of their expressions. Shane simply nodded.

"Everything's gonna be all right." Trent's promise sounded so hollow that he didn't blame his sister for looking skeptical. "That worried look on your face is killing me, sweetheart. I'm expecting a big check from singing, and that's gonna take care of you and Mama no matter what happens to me, all right?"

Ginny's eyes widened. He'd wanted her to get out of there before her young brain registered the prison time that he might be facing, but it was too late. Her amber eyes filled with tears.

Trent turned his back to his sister and swiped at his eyes. "Shane, for chrissake, take her home."

Chapter Fourteen

Sleeping on and off through heavy medication made Caroline's accident seem like a dream. Her heart rewrote the story as a fairy tale in which she ran from a bad guy, and Trent saved her before she fell and hurt herself. She remembered him lying in the hospital bed beside her, but in dreams, they had made love on sheets as soft as his touch had been in her hair.

When she woke up from her prescription drug dose, Caroline was lying in her own bed at home, clutching a pillow between her thighs instead of Trent. She reached for her phone to call him. Instead of her old cell, she found a gift bag and a new phone charging on her nightstand. Confused, Caroline pushed the bag aside and looked at the bedside clock. She was surprised to find that the digital date displayed showed that two days had passed, and the band would release their single at The Earl that night.

In a letter taped to the new phone, Jackie explained that she'd gone to run errands but that she would be back to stay over as she had the past few days. The rest of the letter was filled with messages that Caroline needed to return, and her head ached to think of all the last-minute work that she needed to do for the band. She fired up the new phone and called Trent, but he didn't answer. She called Marlon next.

His tone was loud with happiness to hear from her. "Dang, boss lady! You all right?"

Caroline rubbed her temple and held the phone a little away from her ear. "Fine." She licked the dry stitches in her lip. "Have you seen Trent?"

"I was just about to ask you that. He ain't been showing up for rehearsals. Next thing I know, Tex tells me our boy might get replaced."

"*What?*"

"Who's singing tonight? We had to put Kyle on the mic at rehearsal this morning."

Shaken, Caroline hung up on him and called Trent again. She called his home when he didn't answer his cell phone, and then she called her voicemail to check for messages. There were several, but not from him. Caroline buzzed with frustration and staggered to the bathroom. Reyes also didn't answer her call, but she forgot to leave a voicemail after she saw her face in the bathroom mirror. Inappropriately, Caroline laughed.

She looked as battered and bruised as her heart had felt before Trent, but she felt fine on the inside. She was shaken, achy, and hungry, but she didn't feel a weakness in her middle threatening to cave her in. Longing for Trent, she called him again, and then she tried Jackie.

"C.C.? Are you okay?"

"Actually, yeah. I'm fine. But Trent…" Caroline wasn't sure if his business was hers to tell, particularly to her lawyer best friend. "Uh, he isn't picking up, and neither is Reyes. Have you seen them?"

Jackie snorted. "The jig is up, girl. I know way more than I want to about that hillbilly putting you in harm's way."

"It's not his fault, Jacks."

"Bullshit! If either of you had thought this mess through—" Jackie blew out a breath. "Look, we'll be back in fifteen minutes, and we'll talk then."

"We?"

Jackie hung up.

Caroline was left to assume that "we" included Reyes, whose deceptions and rescue attempts pursed her lips. She was too lightheaded to think clearly. Instead of showering, she went for a snack and clamped a hand to her nose as she approached the kitchen. The sickly sweet aroma of decaying flowers turned her stomach. She found several mangled bouquets on the island. Nauseated, she fled to the bathroom.

By the time Caroline showered and changed, Jackie and Reyes had returned and started a late breakfast in the kitchen. They both looked strangely relaxed in casual clothes, considering the circumstances and the fact that it was a workday. Caroline frowned. "Hi. What's going on?"

"Hey, C.C. Sorry about the flowers." Jackie crossed the room and tilted Caroline's face toward an open window. "Reyes tried to make up for this with remorse bouquets, but I wasn't having it. I made my usual castration threat, if he crosses you again. I think it sunk in this time."

She cut her eyes to Reyes who looked appropriately chastened.

Jackie again studied Caroline's injured face and then sucked her teeth. "I'm going to make you an appointment with a plastic surgeon, or else you'll scar."

"Plastic surgeon?" Caroline pulled away from Jackie's grasp. "I couldn't care less! Would you mind telling me what's going on with Trent?"

"There's good news and bad news. Rey-Rey?"

He came from the stove with a spoonful of scrambled eggs that he held out to Jackie. "Blow. It's hot." To Caroline, he said, "The good news is that I was able to bail him out in time enough for the show tonight."

Fear widened Caroline's eyes. "He was arrested? Oh God, is he hurt?"

"No, he's in much better shape than you are, unfortunately. He turned himself in." Though he spoke to Caroline, his eyes watched Jackie approve of his eggs.

Caroline folded her arms. It was cold on the careless side of Reyes's affection.

"But I've taken care of everything. You don't even have to go tonight if you don't feel up to it." Reyes brushed her bangs back from her scabbed forehead. "The bad news is that Nez won't finalize the agreement until he speaks with you. He doesn't trust me; can you believe it?"

Jackie snorted.

"What the hell does that have to do with Trent?"

Caroline's ungracious response raised Reyes's brow. *"Querida,* I recovered your copyrights from Nez."

The girls gaped at him.

"I traded the tapes for a good bit of his catalogue. He has made enemies beyond you and me, and I want him out. I want him *finished.* Before I move my artists to another publishing company, I thought you might want to discuss starting one of your own. I'm buying Trent out of your new song. If it's a hit, that'll be great buzz for your business."

Jackie beamed at him. "Oh my God, C.C., that would be perfect for you! And talk about revenge. Twenty bucks says Milan drops Nez as soon as he's useless to her."

"Poetic justice." Reyes laughed warmly, but Caroline was left cold.

"What is wrong with you?" She glared at them both. "Trent's facing charges, and you're talking about it like it's a business opportunity?"

Jackie squeezed Caroline's shoulder. "The charges probably won't stick. The State's already buying time to dig up evidence, but it could all get thrown out in the preliminary hearing. There isn't much of a case, based on what Trent told Reyes."

Caroline's mouth fell open. "You talked to him?"

Jackie smiled proudly. "I made Rey-Rey go to Podunk and fix it."

"You call this fixing it?"

Reyes put up his hands against Caroline's angry expression. "There was only so much I could do. At the arraignment, Trent declined the attorney that I brought in favor of the public defender." He shrugged. "Maybe he's going to take the money and make a run for it. I'm sure he'll fit right in down in Juarez."

"What money?"

"We have to buy him out of the band, *querida*. He didn't disclose this incident when he signed the contract for the single. If legal finds out about this, they'll pull the plug on the band, the record deal, everything. He won't get a dime, and he'll go to jail with half the rights to your song. I've arranged for him to sell them back to you."

Caroline shook her head.

"I'm writing him a check against the rights and the projected royalties. After he launches the single tonight, we'll replace him."

"No!" Caroline whirled away from them. "I'm not writing him off like a liability. He wouldn't do that to me."

"Really?"

She turned around and saw him open a briefcase on the counter.

Reyes pulled out a document that he handed to Caroline. "He already signed it. I wonder whether he would be coming tonight if he didn't have a check to pick up."

Caroline tried to read the papers, but her head shook and her eyes crossed. She crushed them in her fist. "No, I don't believe this. You're not telling me something! He wouldn't just drop me." She ran to her room for her cell phone.

Jackie followed. "Girl, put down the phone."

"Don't tell me what to do, Jacks!" Yelling rattled Caroline's light head and empty stomach. She pressed a hand to her temple and pointed the papers like a baton. "You and Reyes apparently ran my whole life behind my back while I was hopped up on drugs, and I do *not* appreciate it!" She dialed Trent.

"Can we talk about this before your head explodes?"

Trent didn't answer.

"Ugh!" Caroline grabbed her purse and shoved the phone and the papers in it. "I'm going down there, to Bibb City."

"Hold your horses." Jackie folded her arms and blocked the doorway. "Trent's predicament is certainly unfortunate, but that doesn't mean that you need to bounce your soft behind down there and...well, and what exactly, Caroline? This man let you get hurt, and now he's putting a hole in your life. It'll turn into another crater if you let yourself get carried away."

"Another crater? Don't compare this to what happened with Nez."

"Didn't I tell you not to fall for this guy?"

"I tried!"

"Try again. Or else what are you going to do, knit him sweaters and wait around until he gets out of prison?"

"I thought you said the state doesn't have a case!"

Both women shifted their gaze to Reyes, who had appeared to investigate the yelling.

"Caroline, I don't know for sure. I'm not his lawyer. He settled for a public defender." Jackie rolled her eyes. "Whatever that's about, it doesn't change the fact that he hasn't called you. I know because I was waiting for him to call so I could cuss him out." She reached into her pocket and pulled out Caroline's old cell phone. "Reyes said he lost it, but I knew he was lying." She elbowed him in the ribs. "Then I kinda cracked the screen on the back of his head."

Caroline bit her lip. Neither Jackie nor Reyes had her voicemail password to delete any messages from Trent. He simply hadn't called.

"I'm not saying you shouldn't talk to him at all. I'm just asking you, for once, to worry about you first. You need rest and food. Let him come to you and explain himself. If he doesn't, at least you won't have driven to his house and put your heart on a dirt road to get stomped on. Don't be stupid, sweetie."

"I'm not stupid! But I'm not going to sit around here like you, acting like you're not in love because you're too scared to get hurt."

Their jaws dropped, and putting that truth on the table made Caroline feel strong for the first time that day. She raised a brow, daring either of them to deny it.

Eventually, Reyes cleared his throat. "She's talking to you."

"She's talking to you, motherfucker!" Jackie socked his shoulder. "You are *terrified* of my beautiful bisexual ass!" Jackie flipped up her skirt and slapped one bare butt cheek. "You can't believe that worshiping your dick didn't change my religion."

"You called me a god. More than once as I recall."

"That was just the tequila talking."

Caroline let out a loud sigh. "Give me a break. As badly as she treats you, Reyes, I think you like it, or else why do you keep going back for more? Bite the bullet and admit that you want her to dominate you."

Reyes turned bright red. He turned his back to both of them, but not before Caroline saw what her suggestion had aroused beneath the loose fabric of his pants.

Jackie peered at him and grabbed his shoulder, but he shrugged her off and left the bedroom. "No way. He's got too much pride for that."

"The proof is in his pants, Jacks." Caroline shoved her feet into a pair of mules and slung her purse on her shoulder. She moved past her friend toward the front door. "Trust me; he's never been that happy to see me."

With a gray newsboy cap pulled down over the scabs and bruising on her face, Caroline spent most of the day sitting through matinees in the back row of a movie theater. She wasn't sure if her trumped-up courage had fled with falling down the stairs or if she was just too woozy to drive all the way to Bibb City. Either way, the occasional sting of popcorn salt between the stitches in her lip felt better than possibly walking into the icy arms of being dumped again.

Caroline lingered in the comforting dark right up until The Earl opened for the night, and then she took her time driving into town. She found a good parking spot on the street, but didn't go into the club until shortly before the band's eight o'clock start time. They were only opening for Keb' Mo', and she wanted to enjoy the hour-long show in case it was the last.

Easily jostled as usual, Caroline strained through the upstairs restaurant crowd and went downstairs to the concert room. Her black maxi dress was lost in the swirl of trendy spring fashions. She hunkered down on a high-legged chair on the dark side of a circular bar where lovers usually corralled. She ordered a Coke and pulled down her cap after Leslie, the gorgeous gay bartender, was appalled by her split lip. With a big tip, Caroline thanked Leslie for not inquiring.

Kyle appeared at Caroline's elbow and clapped her across the shoulders while he ordered a round for the band. "The free stuff they gave us in the back tastes like piss." He made a kissy face at Leslie who in turn gave him the middle finger. "Keep making obscene gestures and I might have to ask you to turn me."

"Into what? A gentleman?" Leslie stuck out his tongue.

Kyle didn't say anything about Caroline's face, probably because he stood on her right while the stitches were on her left. Still, she kept her Coke glass close to her mouth. "Have you seen Trent?"

"Minute ago, yeah." Kyle squeezed her shoulders. "Minerva yelled at him about you sitting in a corner. *Dirty Dancing* and all that."

Caroline's face fell. "Okay. Thanks."

Her wounded expression seemed to make Kyle wary. "Yeah, uh, sorry. I shouldn't have…I'm just gonna…" Kyle slapped down a twenty for Leslie, snatched three beer bottles, and then shucked his thumb toward the door next to the stage that led to the artist green rooms.

Caroline tapped her forehead and tried to get a grip. She winced when she thumped her injured eyebrow. When she turned back to her soda, she found a full shot glass next to it.

Leslie's chin tipped at Caroline's split lip. "You don't have to wait for three strikes to dump him, hon'."

"You know what's funny? I can't dump him because we're not even official. Apparently if I weren't so stupid, I would have drawn up a contract and made him sign, 'Boyfriend.'" She sniffed and picked up the shot glass. "On the plus side, that means I can't get dumped, right?" Caroline sat up straight and smoothed down the front of her dress. "Bottoms up." She faked a laugh, but only managed to let half the cognac burn a searing path down to her ice-cold stomach.

Behind her back, the crowd exploded in whistles and cheers, but Caroline didn't bother trying to catch a glimpse of Trent over all of the tall patrons closely packed around the stage. She ordered another shot and dragged her chair into an obscured corner by the sound booth where no one would find her, even if Kyle told.

On stage in the heat and glare of the blinding lights, Trent felt like he was back in court at his arraignment. The band didn't know of his criminal activities nor did the strangers before him, but he was painfully aware that Caroline was hurting because of him. Reyes had forbidden him from calling her, and Trent had decided that to be for the best. She would let go faster if she hated him.

"Evening, everyone." Trent tried to clear a dull tone from his throat and adjusted the microphone. "I'm Trent, and this is the Trent Michaels Band."

Rowdy applause cut his introduction of the band members into short, strained bursts that bent Trent's wire-thin nerves to the snapping point.

"We'd like to thank Keb' Mo' for — " While the crowd exploded with enthusiastic anticipation, Trent thought about his truck, parked in the rear lot. Reyes had arranged everything so that Trent only needed to walk off stage and leave right after the show. That truck, cleaned up and with new tires, was a reminder Trent had sworn not to say a word to Caroline that night.

Suddenly thick of throat, he took a sip of water, then nodded to Marlon to start their duet of Jonny Lang and Michael McDonald's "Thankful," one of several songs Trent had added to their set list so he could sing to Caroline all of the things he wasn't allowed to say.

He couldn't see very far beyond the bright lights and didn't know where she was. Fear that she wasn't there at all added a piercing desperation to the almost gospel duet that he and Marlon rendered in their respective baritone and tenor. Usually it took two songs for Trent to warm up, but in the very first words of his verse about a prisoner, his heart cracked and his feelings oozed dumb and ugly and aching into the microphone.

Marlon moved downstage and grinned. He signaled the keyboardist to go to church with the organ melody, for Trent was indeed giving testimony and giving up his ghosts.

Though she'd turned her back and pressed her head and shoulder into a wall much colder than her insides, Caroline couldn't stop Trent's torrid voice from curling in a thick ring of smoke surrounding her. Especially after he let Kyle set the tone for The Black Keys' "Lies" and Trent devoted himself solely to breaking hearts with his tender take on the haunting, swampy lyrics, Caroline felt like he had curled up in her ear. His voice thrilled the back of her neck and made her brain feel like a sheet of cellophane that was one jarring note away from ripping, but Trent's crooning reassured her with every lap of his tongue that he wouldn't intentionally tear her asunder.

He carried the same raw undercurrent of intensity through a mostly new set list, whether he was belting out the blues or wrapping sultry suggestions around rock and roll. Three months ago, Caroline would have been able to tell the difference between a siren and a torch song, but by the time Trent ended the set with "The Way that You Play It," she knew only that his voice owned her.

> Quiet girl, sitting over there,
> Won't you let down your hair on my shoulder?
> Tell me why, somewhere behind your eyes,
> I can see the flames, but I don't feel the fire?

> Who told you them two legs wasn't good enough to dance,
> Told you not to take a chance on a man like me?
> Luscious, lovely girl, I like everything I see
> If you'd only look at me and smile…'cause
>
> It ain't the hand that you're dealt; it's the way that you play it
> It ain't the size or the cost, but the way that you rate it
> I know you got a love game that you say is your favorite
> So c'mon, play it with me.

Caroline couldn't help getting up and glancing around the corner of the sound booth, but she couldn't see Trent over the crowd that had converged on the very last of the standing room around the stage. She dragged her chair along the wall and stood on it near one of the support pillars dotting the intimate, basement-like venue. Over rows of bobbing heads and arms flailing along to the song's Delta thump, Caroline watched Trent's hands cradle the mic and his lips coax a climax out of a piece of equipment as though he were its lover.

> Chubby Cheeks, and your sister Big Bone too
> I love what you do with the things you got on you
> And oh, Shorty, my little Half Pint darlin' baby
> You're more than a lady; don't let 'em look down on you
>
> Stop stretching tapes and shame across all your pretty parts
> If you show me your heart, everything else is art
> I can't stand to hear you crying to be what you're not
> Just turn this way, lady, and let me love what you got
>
> It ain't the hand that you're dealt; it's the way that you play it
> It ain't the size or the cost, but the way that you rate it
> I know you got a love game that you say is your favorite
> So c'mon, lay it on me.

Marlon, Kyle, and the keyboardist fell off of the melody, leaving Minerva and Trent to carry the song across its bridge. The fans' clapping hands and stomping feet gave heart to the beat. Caroline thought she could feel Trent stretching every vowel to the breaking point of yearning while he made her believe her flaws were her outstanding features.

> Lay it on me
> Baby
> Look this way
> And show it to me

Say it to me
Lady
Try me on
And play it with me

When I get you alone
Down to that sweet skin
I'll take it all in
And we gon' have us a ball *playin'* all night long.

Over the final chorus, the crowd exploded in applause, and its catcalls became deafening when Keb' Mo' joined the band on stage. He exchanged a back-clapping hug with Trent that ended in an impromptu jam session through Keb' Mo's rousing "Am I Wrong." Then the fans begged for an encore.

She watched his squinted eyes jump over the crowd, as though he was asking the fans if they really wanted him. However, when he began to sing, Caroline knew that he was asking her.

"I know, I know, I know, I know," Trent ad-libbed an aching intro. "Darlin', I know. You and I know I got a bad reputation."

He cut his mouth away from the mic more than one time, as though the upcoming words were too much to take.

Women screamed and went weak in the knees. Caroline almost fell off her chair.

The first verse of Freedy Johnston's "Bad Reputation" clawed out of Trent's throat one confessional line at a time and played tag with the rest of the band, which came to life in reverent spurts that echoed Trent's broken tone. When finally the melody got rolling, his voice sounded hoarse with emotion, especially when he asked through the simple bridge, again and then again, if Caroline still wanted him despite his flaws.

She had an answer before he finished the chorus. She tried pushing through the crowd, but the set ended, and those wanting a drink before the next show herded her back toward the bar. Caroline made it to the support pillar nearest the green room door before her still aching head reeled. She backed against the pillar and tried to ignore the passing bumps to her bare shoulders.

One particular nudge turned into an arm snaking around her waist.

She knew the hardness of Trent's forearm and the sweaty sex-charged tang of his scent, but he didn't say anything while he slipped behind her. Bracing her against the pillar with his arms around her waist, his body shielded her from the traffic of people darting left and right.

Caroline twined her fingers with his; she couldn't help it. But then she straightened up her shoulders and put a little space between their bodies. "I signed those papers. They're in my purse, if that's what you want."

Even if he'd been allowed to speak, Trent had nothing to say that didn't start with, "I love you, but…" His kiss sent that message better than words could.

Holding her as though she were his to keep, he kissed her neck and rubbed his nose into the tiny curls at her nape that stayed spiraled no matter how she straightened the rest. He ran his hand down her hip and squeezed, urging her to turn around. Eventually she stopped resisting, and when she faced him, Trent immediately pecked her on the lips.

Caroline frowned until he licked the stitches in her lip.

With both hands, Trent held her face very still and coaxed her lips open enough to play inside them. His kiss was like licking an ice cream cone when he really wanted a bite. Every little wet brush of her tongue made his mouth water, and soon his hands were playing percussion on her ass.

Passersby leered and whistled, arousing a possessiveness that Trent had to resist for fear of kissing her too hard. His frustratingly gentle kiss moved to her neck and throat, but his hands gripped her tighter. He felt her yield in his arms, but then she stiffened.

"I planned all these badass things to say to you, and now I can't remember any of them. You make me stupid."

Trent saw conflict in her eyes, and he tipped the scales in his favor by sucking her neck.

"We need to talk."

He nodded and tilted her head with his hands. Sucking on her tongue wasn't talking, but she seemed too delirious to care when he stopped.

Trent kissed her forehead, and his lips gauged the elevated temperature of her skin. He pushed back her cap and then her bangs from a fine layer of sweat on her forehead.

She tugged on his shirt. "Can we just go home and start over?"

Trent's eyes smarted. He drew a haggard breath to say the necessary words, and then he remembered that Reyes was watching. Keeping Caroline captive as long as he had was probably going to cost Trent five grand, since a final figure hadn't yet been put on the check. He took Caroline's hand and kissed it.

She linked their fingers. "Please let's go home to bed. I want to. You, I mean. I still want *you.*"

Trent grabbed her hand, then bit a welt into his lip after he turned to pull her toward the green room door. Away from the safety of the support pillar, the crowd surged upon him in particular. Other women's bodies came closer than their slurred compliments. Trent felt Caroline's little fingers slip from his more than once before he realized how easy it would be to lose her in the crowd if he just let go of her hand.

Twenty feet from the stage, he saw Reyes's raven head. He thought of the check and of Ginny and Margie, who were waiting at home for Trent to take better care of them than his father had. All he had to do to spare all three of his ladies unnecessary pain was to let go of what he wanted.

Twenty feet shortened to fifteen, and he couldn't see through the blue in his vision or feel anything but the sudden empty chill in his palm after he let Caroline's fingers slip from his. She called his name, but Trent didn't turn around. He didn't want her to see how dumb and ugly he looked while his heart was breaking.

Chapter Fifteen

From the club, it took about an hour and a half for Trent to get back to Bibb City. He stopped at the Hold-Up Saloon and left his ridiculously large check on the floorboard of his truck. It was only partial payment against the royalties. He wouldn't get the rest until Caroline signed for the rights, but what he had was enough to start preparing for the inevitable. Trent looked at the dashboard clock. It was eleven o'clock on a Saturday night, and he was at the local bar like the past three months hadn't even happened.

He tried not to cry.

Inside the Hold-Up, Trent went to the back and dressed in black to continue his bartender training. Though being there felt surreal since he was wrecked on the inside, the alternative to work was going home and being dangerously alone with his feelings. His criminal act had finally gotten him entry into Chris's heart. The bar owner had offered Trent unlimited hours and set up a donation program to raise money for the Buckney family. Of course, the program mostly involved leaving coffee cans bearing a hideous picture of Trent's face all over the bar and around town, but it was the gesture that counted.

Shane wandered in with the hard-drinking single crowd just as couples and a bowling club were going home for the night. He put a five-dollar bill in the coffee can on the bar along with a toothpick and a chewing gum wrapper.

Trent poured his friend the usual cheapest house draft.

"How's it going, hoss?"

"Great." He handed over Shane's beer, tipped the coffee can, and squinted into it. "I'm about eleven dollars and twenty cents closer to freedom. I feel a miracle coming on."

"A miracle, huh? Have you perhaps been praying for sweet Caroline to waltz in here and vow to stand by her man?"

With a threatening glare, Trent ignored him.

"No? Because I just saw her in Chris's office asking about you, and he looked like he would be happy to take her off of your hands."

"What?"

Shane smirked and put one hand to his ear. "Sorry, what? I could've sworn you were ignoring me."

Trent's eyes skidded toward the door, but he snatched his gaze away. He yanked a dish towel from the shoulder of his black T-shirt, snapped it for no particular reason, then tucked it into the back pocket of his black work pants. Nerves in overdrive, he pulled the towel from his back pocket and tossed it on the bar. "You're lying."

"Why would I lie when the truth is so much more interesting? And why didn't you tell me she was Black?"

"Because you would've asked me what the sex was like, and then I would've had to start adding up how much of a racist you are."

"I ain't a racist! I'm a pervert. Big difference."

Trent didn't laugh; he could barely hear over his heart hammering. He managed not to watch the door while he filled several drink orders with beer and then cheaper beer, but every cell in his body was tuned in its direction. He knew when Caroline came in because a short burst of silence started on that side of the bar and did the wave all the way back to the restrooms. There were other Blacks in town, but folks in Bibb City weren't colors so much as they were numbers, too old, too young, and mostly too poor. She was exactly the kind of well-to-do demographic that Bibb City lacked.

Carrying an expensive gadget in one hand and her purse in the other, Caroline crossed the bar in the same black dress and cap that she'd had on at the club. Trent shook his head and laughed like feeling nauseated was any kind of funny. She looked way too good to be there for his busted butt.

When their eyes met, Caroline slipped between two empty pool tables and quickly moved to a stool in front of him. She looked scared when Shane wiped his hand on his paint-splattered coveralls to offer her a handshake.

"Shane." His accent was as sloppy as a swamp compared to Trent's buttered grits and biscuits drawl, so Trent was pleased with how graciously Caroline took Shane's leathery hand.

"Caroline Curran. Pleased to meet you. I've heard, uh, things."

Shane winked at her. "They're all true." He got in one good ogle before Trent slammed a full beer mug on the bar in front of him. Shane lapped up the sloshed foam. "Looking is free."

Trent scoffed, and then put on his mask as he looked at Caroline.

"Hi," she said.

He only blinked, though it hurt him when she started to wilt under his gaze.

"Um…" She sat on the stool and set the radio on the bar. "I was going to come in all Lloyd Dobler from *Say Anything*, but I didn't know if you'd get the reference."

Without a doubt, Trent was the Dobler in that situation, but he kept his mouth shut.

"I'll take that as a no." Caroline cut the radio on at low volume. "Your song's coming on for the first time in a minute. I thought you'd want to hear it."

Trent didn't say anything to her, but he did make a warning growl at Shane, who then got up and moved a few seats down the bar.

Caroline leaned in and whispered, "You know, I'm trying not to fight with you in a bar in front of people, but are you really not going to talk to me? Because that's mean."

"What can I get you to drink?"

"I think I need a shot. In fact, I've become kind of partial to cognac."

"I'm partial to you making it back to Atlanta safely, so it'll be sweet tea or Coke for you."

Her eyes seemed to plead with him. "I wasn't planning on going back home this evening."

Trent shook his head, giving away the fact that she was getting to him, but he managed to keep his mouth shut while he filled a glass for her. He stuck a straw in Caroline's drink and pushed it across the bar. "Sweet tea it is then."

"I want to talk to you!"

"Talk."

"Why didn't you call me?"

"It was kinda hard to get phone calls out from the county jail."

Caroline's eyes widened. "You spent all this time in jail? I thought Reyes came down and bailed you out right away."

Trent shook his head against the sympathy in her eyes. He cut away from her to fill an order for a couple bourbons, and then he returned with his resolve restored. "Yeah, Caroline. I'm a criminal. That ain't exactly news, so what'd you drive two hours down here for?"

"I want to know why you won't talk to me, Trent. I want to know why you just *left.*"

He almost blamed Reyes, but the bastard could be counted on to take care of Caroline, and she wouldn't let him if she was pissed at him too. Trent didn't say anything. He was sure that one more minute of the silent treatment would make her quit.

Instead, he was gutted when the radio blasted "The Way That You Play It," dedicated "to Trent from Caroline, your number one fan." His tender singing voice made a big fat lie of the way he was pushing Caroline away. Groaning, Trent went to fill another drink order.

Caroline had readied another line of attack by the time he came back. "Marlon said that he won't sign the record deal without you."

Trent laughed even though he felt tortured. He pulled out his cell phone and tried to stop stealing glances at Caroline while he waited for Marlon to pick up. The call went to voicemail. "Only an idiot would pass up this opportunity. While I'm sure that Minerva has a habit of blowing your mind in the sack, I didn't think that she'd actually screwed you stupid. Sign the goddamn contract."

Trent hung up and glared at Caroline. "Anything else?"

Her pretty mouth fell open.

He worked hard not to jump over the bar, grab her around the ankles, and cry like a baby that he didn't mean it. "That's settled then. Now get your sweet ass on the road to Atlanta and don't come back."

Caroline's eyes clouded. She scrambled off of the bar stool and hurried toward the door.

As soon as she hit the ground running, Shane glared at Trent. "What are you doing, asshole?"

"What's best for her, and if you know what's good for you, you'll keep your fuckin' mouth shut."

Caroline lingered just inside of the bar's front door for five minutes. She scrubbed off her mascara with the back of her hand, and tried to get her quaking chest under control so that she could drive. By the time she calmed down, her brain registered what her heart already knew about Trent's repertoire of ways to be a jerk. He'd just put a lot of work into his Stiff Lips McStonyface schtick.

She dug in her purse for a compact mirror that only confirmed how tearful and childish she looked beneath the brim of her cap. She was no Jackie and never would be, but maybe that was a good thing. Jackie had never had her heart broken because she'd been too scared to open it to Reyes for almost twenty years. "I can take a lick and bounce back," she said of her face.

Caroline put away her compact, pulled out her copy of the papers, and retraced her steps to the bar. She slumped a little beneath Trent's arctic glare, but hurt feelings didn't keep her from shoving the papers across the bar. "Why did you go with the public defender, since you have plenty of money to afford another attorney?"

Trent's very blue eyes jerked away from hers. "None of your goddamn business."

"You're saving it, aren't you? For your sister. You're convinced that you're going to prison, so you don't want to waste the money on a lawyer." She held up the "In Trent's Defense" coffee can.

He looked away.

"And you don't want me wasting my time visiting you in the prison or waiting for you to get out, right? By the way, assuming that I would be that nice to you is *really* arrogant — like Reyes arrogant."

Trent scowled like he was about to protest, but then in the funny way that he'd done in the past, he looked almost proud of her.

"Stop looking at me like that! I'm not a young'un. I'm thirty-fucking-one, and I can handle it. I'm resilient, as it turns out." She pointed to her face. "Do I fall hard? Yes. Does it take me a while to bounce back? Yes. But when I do, I can love someone new with everything. That could be you."

Caroline tried to put her fists on her hips, but her hands shook and slipped down her slick dress. She cast a cautious glance over her shoulder, but no one was eavesdropping except Shane.

Apparently hanging on her every word, Shane gave her a thumbs-up.

Trent looked stunned.

Caroline sat down and flattened her shaking hands on the bar. "Now before I lose my confidence and throw up, pour me a goddamn shot and tell me you love me!" Nervous, frustrated tears sleeted down her cheeks. "Even if you only like me a lot, I'm sure I'll grow on you while you're locked up."

Trent wanted to laugh. He wanted to jump over the bar, grab her, kiss her, and carry her out, end scene, cue credits. However, the happy ending that Caroline deserved wasn't waiting in his truck with a diamond ring and a bouquet of fucking flowers. "Go home, Caroline. This ain't a movie where everything turns out okay because you say so, and I ain't a hero. You'll get over it—"

"I don't want to!"

"But you will. Go."

He turned his back, staggered to the supply room, and hid. When he came out, Caroline had left. Shane had waited only to give Trent an especially disgusted glance before he paid his tab and left as well.

Those who said that doing the right thing felt good were either saints or liars. Trent spent every second of the rest of his miserably slow shift trying not to call Caroline. The hurt was the only way he knew that his heart was broken and not dead yet.

Eventually and with cantankerous complaints about Trent's surly mug, Chris took over the bar and sent him home. Both hands fisted in his hair, Trent walked through the bar's front door and then around to the back of the building where the staff parked. He probably would have retched if there'd been anything in his stomach to throw up, but there was nothing there at all. He had reverted to being nothing at all.

He got in his truck and turned on the stereo. The Black Keys' "The Lengths" amplified the ache of all that he had sacrificed to love his ladies. He might as well go back inside and have a drink or five. Prison would sober him up, unless he was lucky enough to drive into a tree trunk before then. Imagining what Ginny would say to that, Trent reached to cut on the ignition.

He brooded during the short drive around Bibb City's town square full of closed and boarded-up businesses, then along a quiet country road to his place. New brick houses with neat yards gave way to old wooden slat houses that needed to be demolished. He turned onto a gravel road and into a little community of modular homes. Eight of them sat in a cluster much like the cul-de-sacs in Caroline's gated community. A larger but older trailer with a freshly built wheelchair ramp sat off to the side closest to the road. Trent pulled up behind it and cut the truck engine.

He scowled at Hank's suv, which had been there when he'd left for Atlanta earlier that day. Then his face fell at the sight of Caroline's Jetta.

The truck bed jostled, and Trent jumped out to investigate.

Nestled into an enormous paint-splattered canvas tarp she'd gotten from Shane, Caroline rubbed make-up from her eyes that had also made a mess on her cheeks.

"Oh my God!" Her cap fell from her head when she sat up. "What time is it?"

"Late." Trent braced his elbows on the truck's tailgate. "What the hell are you doing back here?"

"Shane drove my car to your house so that you wouldn't have any excuse not to take me home. In case you discovered me."

Trent's eyes narrowed.

"His idea."

He blew out a breath. "Why are you still here?"

"I thought of something else that I needed to say."

Caroline then challenged his insolence with her silence.

"Well?" He didn't sound harsh enough to convince either of them that he really wanted her gone. Something hungry in his eyes made Caroline shift toward him, but he backed up from the truck.

"You're not fooling me. I'm not stupid," she said. "But you are if you let being bull-headed send you to prison! Jackie's a lawyer, and so is my brother Phil, and we can all put together some kind of rescue. You don't have to be the hero, and I'm not promising you everything will be okay. I'm saying that I want to stay and play out the hand that I've been dealt."

"Geez Louise. How long did it take you to spread all that cheese on a cracker?"

She glared at him. "A minute. I was working on a speech when I feel asleep. Now that it's out there, I might as well add that just because I could get over you, I don't have to start doing it right now unless you're just going to punk out!"

"I'm trying to protect you!"

"Punk! You're overwhelmed and scared, and you're wilting. I know because I do it all the time."

"Shit." Trent buried his face in his hands for a long time. "If you don't say goodbye now, it'll only hurt more later. Especially after I tell you that I'm crazy about you. I'm *gone* over you, Caroline Curran."

He didn't use the word *love*, but Caroline didn't care. She was strong enough to carry their love down to the last drop; that was her talent, and perhaps that made her exactly the right kind of woman for a man like Trent.

She lunged across the truck bed and grabbed him. Trent didn't resist, but he didn't return her kiss. Caroline moved to his tense neck and pressed her lips to his pulsing jugular. His heartbeat was raging, and his skin burned her lips.

"I'm rescuing you because I know you'll do it for me when you can. You've already done as much as you could, Trent. You played a good hand."

He shook his head.

Caroline grasped his knuckles and rubbed them with her thumbs. "These are good hands."

His eyes were a miserable blue like the sky before a storm. "How can I believe that when they only do good for you?"

"I believe it. I'll believe it for you, so stop trying to get rid of me." When he spat a laugh, she couldn't believe it. "You're laughing?"

"My other option is crying. God damn it!" He jammed his palms in his eyes.

Caroline touched his shoulder. "Trent."

"I don't know what to say to you! *I'm sorry? Please forgive me?* Even *I love you* ain't magic words for this one."

He snapped down the tailgate and sat in a slumped heap. "This don't feel like being a man, putting you through this."

Caroline scooted to sit beside him. The awkwardness of their role reversal was as thick as grease in the air between them, but she could think of no way around him surrendering all of his pride. She pulled his hand onto her lap and held it.

Trent exhaled like his lungs were about to give out. He looked up at the sky instead of at her, but his grip tightened around her hand.

"Jackie sent me an email earlier. She's looking into your case—"

"Didn't think she cared that much about me."

"Well, she doesn't," Caroline joked, but he remained stiff. "I'm mad at her and Reyes, and Jacks is trying to get out of the dog house. She said we can argue that the deputy who arrested you didn't have probable cause. The whole thing might get thrown out in the preliminary hearing—"

"Or it might not."

Caroline smacked the pessimism from the back of his hand. "Even if it goes all the way to trial, they can't prove that you laid a hand on Courtney. A motive isn't enough to convict you, and you don't have to take the stand."

"They'll see it on my face."

"You're thinking about this like a decent man." He glanced at her, and Caroline tried not to let his scowl dissuade her. "This isn't about truth and justice anymore. The only thing on the line here is a punishment, and I think you've already sentenced yourself to enough."

"Are you talking about my mama and Ginny?"

"I'm talking about the way that you keep taking responsibility for everything that goes wrong and refusing help. You say you're not sorry, but I think if you had it to do over again, you wouldn't have. Maybe not for Courtney's sake. Maybe just because you don't like the kind of man that you had to become, and isn't living with that punishment enough?"

Tongue-tied and reluctant to take her into his glorified trailer, Trent studied her earnest expression for a long time before looking up again at the night sky. He didn't offer or ask for forgiveness exactly, but he did sincerely sign his name to God's will being done, and a whole ton of pressure lifted off of his heart.

Beneath hers, Trent's hand shook. He forced a little sugar into his voice. "I know it's late, but maybe you ought to go on home, get some rest, and we can talk in the morning."

Caroline looked stung. "I understand." Then she kissed him on the cheek, jumped down from the truck, and hustled toward the kitchen door.

Trent was fast, but she managed to knock before he caught up to her. She smirked at him until towering Hank opened the door. Wide-eyed, Caroline backed away from the door and into Trent.

"Miss Caroline?" Hank's baritone was booming and cheerful. "I'm Hank." He held up one beefy hand in a shy wave.

"Move it, beanstalk! I can't see," Ginny hollered from behind him.

Hank shifted to the side, and Ginny appeared in her lime green wheelchair. Trent hadn't seen his sister smile widely in a while, and he'd forgotten how much they looked alike when she did.

"Well, don't just stand there! Come on in. The neighbors have been watching our house all night trying to figure out whose fancy car that is in the yard, and now here you are. And you are fancy!" She winked at her brother. "Oh, I'm Ginny." She giggled and stuck out her hand.

Caroline stepped into the tiny kitchen and shook hands with both teens. They stared at her as though she were a celebrity. Trent laughed.

"I see you've met my brother," Ginny said. "Please excuse his total lack of manners and have a seat. Me and Hank made lemonade."

"From real lemons." Hank flexed a little muscle. "I squeezed all of them myself."

Caroline giggled, but Trent was not amused by the idea of Hank squeezing anything in the vicinity of his sister. "It's late, boy. Shouldn't you be at home?"

"Shane asked him to stay," Ginny answered for Hank, "and anyway, we were doing homework."

Trent sidestepped to the pile of magazines, comic books, and notebooks on the kitchen table. He held up one of Ginny's favorite tabloids. "You're going to college to major in gossip, is that it?"

Hank laughed and Ginny rolled her eyes, but Caroline only took the magazine from Trent's hand.

"Actually," Ginny replied, "I was reading in that *Paste* magazine about your band and all the songs that Miss Caroline wrote. And me and Hank were wondering, since we're on prom committee and everything, if there was any way that you could get Milan Taylor to come to our prom. Even for just one song? We have—"

"Ginny." Trent looked at Caroline, who didn't say anything. She was so intent upon the magazine that he thought she was hiding behind it, and his hand protectively went to her waist.

Ginny and Hank exchanged a glance, and Trent knew when his sister was about to push her luck. She took a deep breath. "I was thinking maybe I could make a wish or something, and then it'd be like celebrity charity."

Trent scowled at her. "Genevieve Buckney!"

"What? If I gotta be in a wheelchair, can't I make the most of it?"

Hank guffawed.

"We'll talk about this later. It's time for your company to go home and for you to go on to bed." Trent took Caroline's hand.

She looked up from the magazine and replied to Ginny and Hank's chastened goodnights. "Oh! Uh, yeah we'll talk. It's okay. It's really okay."

Trent pulled her through a small den and into a closet-sized area that faced a bathroom. A door on the right was closed and another on the left opened into his bedroom. Trent nudged Caroline toward his room, and then he went to the other door, knocked softly, and peeked inside to check on his mother.

When he joined Caroline, Trent turned on the light and thanked God that he'd made the bed the last time he was home. "That's Mama across the hall. Sometimes she doesn't sleep too good," he euphemized his mother's midnight rages. "I gave Gin the big bedroom on the other side of the kitchen so she can get her sleep for school and have her space, so this is all I got to offer right now."

He stretched an arm toward his bed and the Crimson Tide comforter set that Ginny had bought him last Christmas.

"It's fine, and I'm fine about Milan. Really." She held the magazine up for him to see.

Trent squinted at the tabloid under the ceiling fan's dull single bulb. Under the title "Dumped!" were several photos of popular celebrity couples, including one of Milan Taylor holding hands with some basketball player. Under Milan's foot in a tiny thought-bubble was a photo of a scowling man with the caption, "Nez Peterson, music executive."

Though he should have rejoiced that good old Nez had received a dose of his own medicine, Trent commented from pure male possessiveness. "He ain't all that great-looking. You could do better than him on a bad hair day." She laughed, and Trent did, too, when he looked into her eyes and saw that she really was all right.

"Publicly dumped!" Caroline touched a hand to her grinning lips. "I'm being petty, huh?"

Trent shrugged. "Petty is as petty does. He started it."

"And I finished it." She squared her shoulders and grasped his hands. "That's all over. There's nothing standing in the way of the band or our album now."

"*Your* album."

"A pending trial doesn't mean that you can't work; don't believe Reyes. It'll probably make you famous in *this* industry. Then you'll have royalties —"

"That's great." Trent pulled free of her hold on his hands. "I appreciate it, darlin'. I really do. I want my ladies taken care of, no matter what."

"You don't have to worry about that. In fact, I'll take care of them myself."

"No. Listen to me." Trent licked his lips. "I thought about this in the truck out there. I know how you are, Caroline. You've got a soft heart and a hard head."

"Speak for yourself."

Trent ignored her. "Right now, you're feeling all this sympathy for me, and I appreciate it, but I don't want you confusing that with something else. So until this trial gets sorted out, I think there should be you and me, not *us.*"

Caroline's face fell. "How can you say that to me?"

"'Cause it's for your own good, and that's exactly why I'm sleeping on the couch tonight. Shush." He put a finger to her protesting lips. "I'm just asking you to sleep on it. That's reasonable. If you get up in the morning and realize you don't want any part of this, I'll understand."

Caroline smacked his chest. "I came here for you!"

"I know, sugar, but I come with them." Trent pointed toward the bedroom door on the other side of which Margie and Ginny were sleeping peacefully. "It might seem like a prison sentence to you, but it's a responsibility to me."

"I didn't mean it like that!"

"Well, sleep on it, and maybe in the morning, you'll start saying exactly what you mean."

While she crossed her eyes and did her frustrated bumblebee bit, Trent left her to go take a shower, but she followed right behind him and barged into the bathroom.

"I'm going to take a shower," she said.

"Ladies first." He began to put his shirt back on, but then Caroline stripped off her dress, and his mouth fell open. He could see through her panties.

"You like that, huh?" She walked past him to the shower and bent over right in front of him to slip off her panties. Back turned to him, Caroline threw them over her shoulder. "Could you help me with the bra strap?"

Trent had to laugh. "Don't think I don't know what you're doing."

"Is it working?"

Instead of speaking, he pushed his pants down and pulled her back against him. Her purr hinted at pleasure when he took off her bra. She curved one hand around his neck to hold his hot mouth to her earlobe while his hands made cookie dough of her breasts.

Thighs pushing hers, Trent walked them to the shower and turned it on. He stuck one hand in the water and waited for it to heat up. Grinning, he tucked the other hand between Caroline's thighs and made her squeal.

"Wait. Wait!" Flushed, she pulled away from him. "I called Julianna and told her that I was bringing three guests to Labor Day dinner. That would be you, Ginny, and your mother, so mark it on your calendar."

Maybe because he'd forgotten to be unhappy for a moment, the hope in her eyes flooded his heart. The longer he stared at her, the less he could think of to say. Eventually, he kissed her.

"Now that I've told her, if you don't show, my brothers will come after you."

Trent put a stool in the shower, got in, and pulled Caroline with him. He sat so that, with her on his lap, his back took the brunt of the water.

Caroline frowned. "You haven't said that you're coming."

"I was hoping to make you come."

"Trent—"

"I'm not saying no. That's all I got right now. Except this." He pushed into her, and she hissed. He was happy he had something to give her.

Between gentle kisses, Trent watched her greedily. "Did you miss me?"

"Yes."

Trent was too grateful to smile. Her stare seemed full of feeling, and fear of breaking that contact kept him staring right back at her instead of kissing her.

She held his gaze for a long time, which only convinced Trent that he wasn't giving her enough. He put his hips into it, and Caroline's eyelids drooped as the pleasure mounted. He matched his pace to the way her thighs strained closer to him, and her nails dug into his back. She seemed hungry for intensity, and the falling water disguised the squeak of the stool's rubber feet while he fucked her toward the shower wall. Soon her ass was sliding on and off a handrail with every thrust. Caroline cooed, and Trent replied with a moan because raw sex was exactly the kind of gruff catharsis that he needed. He watched her lean back against the wet tile and breathe in the steam. It was as deep and heady and wet as Trent and her orgasm, which quickly hit.

He kissed her then, all over her sweet face and lips. She wilted in his lap for all the right reasons, and he leaned back and pulled her into the spray.

"Uh-oh. Your hair's getting wet."

"I don't care."

"This from the woman who threatened my life the last time." He took that as an invitation to wash her hair.

Caroline seemed to fall asleep beneath his massaging hands and the hot water in her hair. Suddenly, she roused. "You're still hard. You didn't…?"

"I want you to get all you want out of me tonight." He kissed her. "And since I can't kiss you the way I want to, I figured we'd go in the room, and I'd slip you some tongue somewhere else." He waggled his brows.

Trent soaped up a bath sponge and started washing her back. Her smile was dazzling while she played in his hair and rolled her hips for his pleasure.

"You know what?" she said. "This is amazing."

He snorted.

"Really! You and I in a handicapped shower in a trailer on the trashy side of Bibb City is pretty fuckin' amazing. This kind of magic doesn't happen every day."

Laughing, Trent tilted his head and studied her. "It's scary how good you're getting at knowing exactly what to say to me."

Caroline bounced in his lap and kissed him. "I'm just trying to lighten your load. Get it?"

"Geez Louise." He tried to laugh, but his throat was too thick with feeling. "Fuckin' amazing," Trent repeated her phrasing. "Looks like I'm rubbing off on you."

Caroline pushed his hair off of his forehead, and looked him right in the eyes. "I'd like you to, for a *long* time."

Trent took a deep breath. "I'll try," he promised, and she smiled and kissed him. Healed of that hole, his heart inflated in his chest like a big balloon, and Trent knew that he was very much in love. He hadn't known that love would lift him up to a strange and heady place called Hope, but it sounded like a great name for a baby girl.

Epilogue

The Friday of Labor Day weekend, Trent woke up at the crack of dawn as usual and rolled over to stare at Caroline. He'd gotten used to her snoring and wild kicks in the night, but he couldn't get enough of how peaceful she looked curled up in a ball on her side of their bed.

They were living out the lease on her rental house while their new five-bedroom place was built. Dreams of that house, and sometimes nightmares, woke Trent at odd hours every morning. He always turned to Caroline and prayed that one more day would come and go in peace and bring him closer to being free. The State of Georgia had given him a right to a speedy trial that his lawyers had demanded, after unsuccessfully attempting to get the charges dropped for lack of probable cause. A speedy trial meant that the State had two court terms to bring him to justice, and an overeager prosecutor at the preliminary hearing had made that unlikely by charging Trent with a higher crime than could be proven. Delaying the case in the hope of gathering non-existent evidence was working against the State. Courtney Vickers had died, his family had moved on, and there was no evidence and nobody to say who had thrown punches that night or who had driven Trent's ladies off the road.

It wasn't right, but it was fair, and Trent was on day 157 of the 180-day wait to get the case dismissed. He had trouble believing it was as simple as that, but as much as he was paying in legal fees, he didn't really care if his lawyers were doing voodoo behind the scenes as long as he went free.

Trent brushed back Caroline's bangs and kissed her forehead. From the headboard, he untied a pair of her knee-high socks that had made very handy restraints the night before. Grinning, he quietly climbed out of bed, pulled on a discarded T-shirt and boxers, and went to the bathroom to get cleaned up for the day. While brushing his teeth, nostalgia carried him to the second bedroom, which had served as a storeroom, a studio, and Margie's bedroom in the past six months. It had been hard for Trent to put his mother in assisted living, but fancy rehab and a social life had made Margie capable of calling just to talk to him and coming home on weekends without raising hell. Margie had been there to congratulate Gin on getting into the University of Georgia and was aware enough to share Trent's disapproval of Ginny and Hank sharing a house with two other young'uns. Abruptly aware that he hadn't made his weekly threat to Hank Bassett's life, Trent finished brushing his teeth and called the boy.

Ginny answered on the second ring. "Hello?"

Trent bit back a complaint about his sister answering a man's phone so early in the morning. "Do you screen all your boyfriend's calls, or only if it's me?"

She laughed. "I only screen when I know you're in a mood. Caroline tipped me off by text message last night."

"Yeah, yeah. About what time are you gonna be ready today? We need to get on the move by noon."

"Say what?"

"It's meet-the-parents day," Trent said of his six-month-old obligation to meet Caroline's entire family all at once. He shuddered. "Gin, I know I told you about this, as much as I complain about it."

"Didn't Caroline tell you?"

"What?"

"I'm already on the way to Tennessee with Hank. Caroline said I could—"

"Caroline ain't your mama."

"You ain't either! Need I remind you that I'm a legal adult?"

Scowling, Trent stomped to the kitchen to keep his raised voice from waking Caroline. "Genevieve Buckney, don't take that tone with me."

"Caroline said it was fine by her. Sorry, hoss."

"Fine." In the kitchen, he yanked a frying pan from the dish rack. "Fine! Abandon me in my hour of need." Ginny's laughter collided with the clatter of the pan against the stove, and Trent was glad. He didn't like it one bit, but that didn't mean he wanted his little sister to feel guilty all weekend. "Do me a favor and call twice a day even if you just leave a message? And you tell Hank—"

"'The bigger they come, the harder they fall.' He already knows, as much as you threaten him. You do realize that he's my boyfriend and that he ain't gonna do nothing to me that I don't want him to do?"

Trent didn't like the sound of that. "Just call in. Twice a day."

"Once, and I will, now goodbye. Have fun!" She hung up on him.

Though Trent liked his sister feisty, he was still adjusting to not being needed or living in a constant state of crisis. Feeling surly, he made a lot of noise putting the coffee on, and then he gleefully began to make his morning round of phone calls to people that he didn't mind yelling at. Most of them didn't pick up, due to the hour and due to the fact that Trent Buckney had a reputation for leaving ornery messages. It had only taken a few run-ins with reporters for him to completely quit giving a shit about being politically correct.

He called Jackie first. "These doggone lawyers sent me another stack of papers that I can't understand. They said something about how they have to prove prejudice to file this speedy trial dismissal? Much as I would love to get credit for all the folks that I ain't lit into for giving me and Caroline the stink eye, I don't think that's the kind of prejudice they're talking about. Call me back, please, ma'am, 'cause I need this translated into English."

He called Marlon to complain about Minerva, since Trent was a little afraid of calling her directly. "For the last time, tell your woman that the lyrics I wrote for track four are not country. Even if they were, they're a darn sight better put together than that sassy-ass booty music she wants to do. I ain't shaking my groove thing on stage, and that's that."

By the time coffee was done, he'd weeded through his emails and found a ridiculous estimate from the homebuilders. "Who do y'all think you're talking to? CPVC don't cost this damn much. I used to work construction, and I'm pretty sure I said that I want PEX for my pipes. Let's try this again, fellas. I ain't made of money."

That last wasn't exactly true. Between songwriting royalties, performances, music publishing, and the notoriety of being a drunk-driver slayer, Trent had been cleaning up in the past six months, and Caroline was making even more money than him. It was almost too good to be true except, "Twenty-three more days. Please, God, let me make it down the home stretch."

Across the house and in the bathroom, Caroline sank to her knees in front of the toilet and twisted a big burgundy T-shirt into a knot over her upset stomach. She'd gotten used to nausea in the past few months, but it was growing worse as Trent's trial deadline drew nearer. At first, she'd spent a fortune on home pregnancy tests, and then a hopeful trip to the doctor had ended with an ulcer diagnosis. She hadn't told Trent because she didn't want him to worry, but the fear of losing him was never far from her thoughts.

After washing up, she carried a brave face to the kitchen, where she found him watching the news and making bacon. Though it was her rental house, Trent had been doing most of the chores since he'd moved in. He seemed to love being domestic and taking care of her, and it seemed to make him feel safe from the uncertainty that lurked right outside the front door.

He smiled as soon as he saw her. "Hey, darlin'."

Caroline yawned. "Hi."

"You sleep all right?"

"Fine." She shuffled across the kitchen to him.

"Then what are you doing up so early?"

Caroline dropped her head against his chest. "Big day. Long drive."

He trapped her in his arms. "Speaking of long drives, you let Ginny out of meeting the parents to go to Tennessee with a boy?"

Caroline's eyes widened, but instead of answering, she kissed him on the mouth.

"Sugar, I know y'all are close, and I'm real glad of that, but don't leave me out of the loop when it comes to my sister, all right?"

"I didn't *let* her do anything. I said that I wouldn't be upset if she made other plans. She doesn't need my permission — or yours, for that matter. She's a legal adult."

"Legal adult, huh? I knew I'd heard that phrase way too many times in one morning. I know a carefully disguised lecture when I hear one." His brows knotted. "Both of y'all can kiss my old-fashioned grits, all right? Being a legal adult ain't the same thing as being grown."

Caroline kissed him again.

"I'm dead serious right now. I'm not having any more of this behind-the-scenes tag-teaming."

"I understand."

"Don't think I don't know that that's code for 'I'm ignoring you, Trent.'"

She laughed at him. When he sulkily disentangled her arms from around his neck, Caroline sat down on a nearby stool, grabbed him by the shirt, and pulled him between her thighs.

"I'm not ignoring you. I'm just not arguing with you."

"Feels like the same thing to me."

"I'm sorry," Caroline said very sweetly.

"No, you're not!"

By the neck of his shirt, she pulled him down to her mouth and laid one on him. The bacon on the stove crackled in the background while his hot hands crept up her thighs under one of his Roll Tide T-shirts. Caroline was giddily waiting for him to discover that she wasn't wearing any panties when the phone rang.

Trent mounted a wet assault on the side of her neck. "Don't answer it."

Caroline squinted at the handset that lay at the far end of the counter. "It's Jackie!" She lunged for the phone.

He didn't protest as much as he could have, probably because Caroline sat back down straddling the stool and made sure his shirt rode up over her bare butt.

"Hey, girl!" Caroline inched away from Trent's hands on her ass. "How's it going?"

"Miserably," Jackie said of the Bardem family wedding that Reyes had talked her into attending with him. "I'm stuck in the middle of Nowhere, Texas, in a mansion full of Reyes's snooty-ass family. Half of them are White and half of them are Mexican. It's like the Alamo in here."

"That sucks." Caroline clamped her hand over the handset. *"Stop."*

Trent was trying really hard to get his hand between her thighs. He grinned fiendishly.

"Get a hotel room. You don't have to stay right in the middle of the family drama."

Jackie sighed. "I can't. I promised Reyes I wouldn't abandon him, mostly because he locked my wallet in a safe and won't give it back until the end of the weekend."

"Do you want me to — stop! — book you a room?"

"'Stop?' Who are you talking to, Trent?"

"Who else?"

"Put me on speaker, please." After Caroline pressed the necessary buttons, Jackie crowed, "Boy, if you don't stop calling me at six o'clock in the goddamn morning, I'm going to hurt you."

"Hey, Jacks." Trent snickered. "Miss you."

"Don't play with me! Stop calling at —"

"You don't pick up any other time of day."

"That's because I don't like you. Take the hint." After Caroline and Trent laughed, Jackie sucked her teeth. "What is so fucking funny?"

Caroline wiped her eyes. "I thought you were going to talk to Reyes about your feelings. Obviously, you haven't because you're —"

"Acting like a bitch," Trent supplied.

"I'm not acting! This is natural."

She went off on a rant that made Trent lean on Caroline's shoulder and crack up.

Grinning ear to ear, Caroline grasped his forearm and pulled his hand across her heart. All she wanted in life was more of the same moments with him, and that didn't seem like much to ask.

After Jackie was done kvetching and they finished breakfast, Trent and Caroline showered together and got dressed. The process took longer than usual, and not because Trent tried to take off everything that she put on like he usually did. For a change, he was deeply concerned about how he looked.

"What do you think of this?"

Caroline turned from the bathroom vanity mirror to the doorway, in which Trent stood in a three-piece navy blue suit. She tried not to make a face. "You know I love that suit, but you aren't going to court, babe. Could you go for something more like, uh, shorts?"

"I want to make a good impression."

"That gives off the impression that you're trying too hard."

He left and then came back in starched beige pants and a white shirt buttoned up to his neck and down to his wrists.

Caroline grimaced. "You don't even look good in that."

"This is a church shirt!"

"We're not going to church."

"Yeah, well, we are going to meet your brother Hector, who carries a gun. I would like to look innocent."

Caroline laughed. "He's not going to have a gun at a family party."

"A marshal always has a weapon nearby. I looked it up." Trent yanked loose the collar of his shirt. From the bedroom, he called out to Caroline, "His wife's name is Linh, right?"

"Right. She's Vietnamese."

"Okay, and Phil and his wife are White. He's Julianna's son from her first husband?"

Caroline poked her head into the bedroom and grinned at him. "You've really been paying attention!"

"All I do is pay attention to you, Caroline Curran." He winked at her. "What about Dizzy? He's half Julianna and half your daddy, right? What's his wife, Black or White or other?"

"He doesn't have a wife. He has a husband named William." Caroline smirked while Trent seemed to try really hard not to react at all. "We're very happy for him."

"So am I," Trent said right on time.

Caroline eyeballed him, and though he looked a little thrown, Trent didn't get his back up. He was more conservative than she was, but he tended not to judge. "Thanks." She beamed at him and then returned to the bathroom to finish her make-up.

"A family that welcomes criminals is all right by me. I wouldn't care if they were all Williams. I wouldn't care if your name was William so long as you still had that soft ass and sweet smile."

Caroline laughed. "That's sweet, kind of."

He appeared in the bathroom doorway in a Bob Marley T-shirt and jeans. She he approved his ensemble with a kiss on the mouth.

"You look great. Go get the camera."

Trent grimaced. "Don't you have fifty thousand pictures of me by now? You take one every time my foot so much as twitches."

"Doesn't hurt to have one more"

They stared at each other for a moment, and the past and the uncertain future filled up the space between them. They'd agreed months ago not to belabor the facts. Instead of talking, they loved harder. Instead of fretting, they cherished each moment. Everyone had a deadline on the horizon, and much higher prices than an ulcer and insomnia had been paid for love. Caroline touched his face, Trent kissed the palm of her hand, and there really wasn't anything more to say after that.

ACKNOWLEDGMENTS

Beej would like to thank the following for their contributions to this novel:

The Big G for being with us, for holding me to the things that I've prayed for, and for limitless tough love.

My Dad and my Shiva for loving who I am not who I'm expected to be and for always putting in more than you take out. Special thanks to my R.O.D. chick for her detailed feedback.

Omnific for the opportunity, the editing, and everything else.

Rafik for being my first fan and oldest friend.

The Writer's Block crew because my niche started with you, and Nuri in particular for being my biggest fan, my friend, and my graphic artist.

All the women of my tribe that I've met through the website. It's raining, ladies.

The red dirt side of the South because you're in my blood, for better and for worse.

ABOUT THE AUTHOR

Though raised in California, BJ Thornton digs the Dirty South where she was born and currently resides. She enjoys ink, kink, comedy, introspection, evocative experiences, and writing. Above all, she believes in God, in being authentic, in going with gusto, and in treading as lightly as possible on others' lives.